GET YOUR KIT OFF

NIKKI ASHTON

Copyright 2013 by Nikki Ashton
All Rights Reserved ©

ISBN-13: 978-1502334466
ISBN-10: 1502334461

Get Your Kit Off
Published by Bubble Books Ltd

The rights of Nikki Ashton as the Author of the work has been asserted by her in accordance with the Copyright and Related Rights Act 2000 All rights reserved. No part of this publication may be reproduced, stored in a retrieval system, or transmitted, in any form or by any means without prior written permission of the publisher, nor be otherwise circulated in any form or binding or cover that in which it is published and without a similar condition being imposed on the subsequent purchaser. A reviewer may quote brief passages for review purposes only

This book may not be resold or given away to other people for resale. Please purchase this book from a recognised retailer. Thank you for respecting the hard work of this author.

Get Your Kit Off
First published May 2014
All Rights Reserved ©

Cover design – ebook-designs.co.uk

This book is a work of fiction. Any references to historical event, real people or real places are used fictitiously. Other names, unless used with specific permission, characters, places and events are products of the author's imagination. Any resemblance to actual events, places or persons living or dead, are entirely coincidental.

ACKNOWLEDGMENTS

Thank you to everyone who has ever read one of my books and enjoyed it. You and your reviews have given me confidence in what I do and encouraged me to keep writing. For those of you that haven't enjoyed my books and are reading this dedication, then thanks for giving me another go, I appreciate it.

Thanks to my family, friends, work colleagues and anyone else who has given me support – you will never know how much it means to me.

Finally, thank you to the Diet Coke Man, Andrew Cooper, for giving me the inspiration for Joe. Check him out ladies, I don't think you'll be disappointed.

CHAPTER 1

♥

"No, his name is Jimmy Cavanagh, that's K-VA-NER...no, not CAV-A-NAR like the 90's pop star, no!" Molly Pearson sounded the name out, knowing how much the aforementioned Mr Cavanagh hated it being mispronounced. "Yes, that's right, the City midfielder, yes he's supposed to be having his car delivered to the training ground this afternoon." Molly sighed and shook her head. "Sorry, yes that's right, the Audi R8 Spyder in Samoan Orange. At three, okay, I'll let him know – you know the address do you? Okay repeat it to me...right that's fine, thank you." Molly replaced the receiver and sighed again.

As the Player Liaison Manager for a Premiership football club, she spent her life sorting out the lives of dozens of footballers, but due to her organisational skills, she did an excellent job, and had done so for the last five years, running her department with military precision. She was so good that the club relied on her to do a lot more than most clubs' Player Liaison Managers. Never once had a player missed a flight, been late for training or a team meeting, or been photographed anywhere they shouldn't have, in fact, their whole lives were organised by Molly and her team. All in all, Molly loved her job, despite players who couldn't arrange their own car delivery or, stupid managers who locked their families inside the house!

"Do you need a cuppa?" asked Katie, one of Molly's assistants.

"No thanks Katie, I need to get over to the manager's house with some spare keys, he's locked his wife and kids in, and flown out to Spain for two days this morning." Molly gave a wry smile as she imagined the profanities that would be coming from the foul mouth of the manager's ex-supermodel, Italian wife.

"I have no idea how they manage to get through a day sometimes, do you?" Katie giggled as she continued with the passport application of one of the reserve team.

"Nope, although some are more stupid than others, like Fernando who forgot to pick his son up from nursery last week. Anyway, I'd better get going otherwise I might have a divorce on my hands. Marcus is down at the training ground getting some rental forms signed if you need him, and I think Rosetta is translating for Luis and his family at the dentist. I'll probably go straight home once I've dropped these keys off, so don't stay late."

"Okay, no worries, I'll go as soon as I've finished this. Night Molly."

With that Molly left the office and made her way out to the car park.

***

Just as she got inside her car, Molly's mobile started to ring. She glanced at the screen and sighed.

"Hi, what can I do for you?"

"Ooh now there's a thought."

It was her fiancé, Rob, on the other end. They'd met two years ago, when Molly had gone out clubbing with her friend Becky, one of her first nights out after a self-imposed, two year ban on fun, laughter and men. Rob had spotted Molly in a bar and that night made it his mission to get her to agree to a date. A year later Rob proposed in front of everyone at a family party, and Molly, highly embarrassed, said yes, and in a few months they were to be married.

"Seriously, what do you want me to do?" Molly drummed her fingers on the steering wheel impatiently. Living with Rob was pretty much like being at work as he was hopeless without her organising him.

"You know me too well don't you?" he laughed. "Well, I was wondering if you could call and get me an evening paper. I want to see what the gossip is regarding transfers; the transfer window shuts in a couple of days." Rob, was a City fan, but he knew that it was pointless asking Molly what the rumour and gossip was; she never talked about football to the players, or listened if they were talking about it.

Molly groaned inwardly; it was a nightmare trying to get a parking spot outside the newsagents on a Wednesday night as it was packed with people buying lottery tickets for the midweek draw, but trying to find a parking space was preferable to Rob sulking all night because he didn't have a newspaper.

"Okay," she sighed. "As long as you start dinner." That was one thing Rob was adept at - cooking.

"It's a deal. How long will you be, do you think?"

"Oh erm, about an hour. I've got to nip over to the Manager's house first."

"Okay, I'll have something delicious waiting for you."

"Sounds promising. See you then."

***

After listening to Mrs Ribero call her husband a whole host of names for a full five minutes, Molly was able to escape and make her way back towards home and to the newsagent to pick up Rob's newspaper. Luckily she'd been able to pull up outside, so had been in and out within a couple of minutes. She threw the paper onto the passenger seat next to her and then leaned over to put her handbag into the foot-well. Suddenly she noticed the headline on the back page. Molly felt the breath rush from her lungs as what felt like a brick dropped to the pit of her stomach. She gasped and with shaking hands pulled her mobile from her bag, and after three attempts managed to dial a number.

"Hi Moll," the voice on the other end answered.

"Becky, you'll never believe this," Molly replied, her voice cracking with emotion.

"Molly, what's wrong?" Becky asked. "Has something bad

happened?"

"Shit, shit, shit, oh Becky I don't believe it." Molly dragged a shaking hand through her hair as her stomach turned over like a washing machine on a spin cycle. "Molly, bloody well tell me what the matter is, please!"

"It's Joe; he's coming back to the club Becky." Molly paused to take a breath. "That's where Franco Ribero has been today. He's gone to Spain to get the contracts signed."

"Oh fuck. Are you sure? It's not just paper talk is it?"

Molly shook her head. "No, it's in the Evening News and there's a picture of them together, shaking hands."

Becky sighed and was silent for a moment.

"I don't know what to say except I'm sorry." Becky truly was sorry. She'd been there when Joe Bennett had broken Molly's heart, she'd been one of the people who'd had to pick up the pieces and help put her back together.

Molly thought for a moment, and then exhaled. "It doesn't matter, it's not a problem. I can be professional about this can't I?"

"Of course you can," Becky agreed. "He's just another player that you'll have to deal with. It's just a shock that's all."

"Yes you're right; it'll be fine I know it will." Molly gave a weak smile to herself, unsure of who she was trying to convince.

**

Molly had met Joe Bennett six years earlier, when she and Becky first started working at the club; Molly in Marketing and Becky in the store. They were often given free tickets to club events, and in return for being chatted up by spotty teenagers from the youth squad, they got to eat lots of lovely food, drink delicious wine and more often than not drool over the first team into the bargain. It was at such an event that Molly met Joe.

**

Slightly late, due to almost three hours preparation, Molly and Becky were stepping out of Molly's elder sister's car.

"Cheers Sophie you're a star," yelled Molly over the howling wind and rain. "And don't tell Mum and Dad where we are, they'll go mad if they think I'm mixing with footballers." Molly's parents hated the idea that Molly had chosen to work over going to University, especially working at a football club.

"I won't don't worry, now get inside we don't want all that effort ruined do we?" Sophie grinned at her younger sister. "Have a great time and don't get so drunk that you forget which famous footballer you've snogged."

"Don't worry," shouted Becky, "I will make sure we have photographic evidence." She held up her mobile phone to Sophie.

"Okay, but let me see before you sell it to Hello magazine." And with a short burst of her horn she drove away.

"Come on Becky, quick before my hair starts to frizz up," Molly grimaced as she tried to protect her hair with her handbag.

The girls ran into the reception area of the boutique hotel where the party was being held, desperate to get out of the rain, their high heels clicking on the black and white tiled floor.

"Urgh it's awful out there" exclaimed Becky, bending forward to brush rain off her skirt. "Have I got splashes up the back of my legs?"

"No, but I can see your knickers," someone replied behind her to a chorus of giggles.

Molly and Becky turned around to see members of the youth team standing around, trying to look suave and sophisticated in much cheaper versions of the outfits usually worn by their first team counterparts. Becky and Molly staring started them all bouncing around like hyper-active thirteen year olds.

"Well that's about as close as you are going to get to my knickers little boy so store the image in your memory." Becky scowled at the young wit that had cracked the joke. She recognised him as the star striker who had recently scored a hat trick in a youth cup semi-final.

The rest of the team all laughed and started to push Becky's admirer, some jumping on his back and pummelling him playfully. Molly shook her head at their childish antics and pulled Becky towards the door into the large, fairy lit room holding the event.

"Come on, leave the boys to play, let's go and get a drink." They both sashayed across to the bar, totally unaware of the glances that they were already getting from men and women seated around the edge of the room. "Vodka and coke?" she asked. Becky nodded. "Two vodka and diet coke please, actually make them doubles."

***

Two hours later and there were no signs of the first team arriving, which resulted in quite a few nubile young ladies from a local teenage soap opera disappearing, hoping to catch some major talent in one of the clubs in town instead. Their disappearance, in turn, had been followed by the exit of a quite a few young men, leaving only about fifty people. The reserves had turned up, but none of the big stars had, but Molly and Becky weren't too disappointed because they had a great time anyway, dancing and drinking.

"Do you want another drink?" Molly shouted above the sounds of the Grease medley.

Becky nodded. "Okay, but just get me a coke would you I don't want any more."

"Okay," Molly sauntered off having no intention of omitting the vodka. "Two vodka and Diet Coke please," she called to the barman.

"I'll get those." Someone appeared at the side of Molly. "If that's okay with you?"

Molly turned to see where the voice was coming from, and almost passed out on the spot. In front of her was the most gorgeous face she had ever seen, and as she stared at him, taking in every bit of his profile, she swore she could hear the Diet Coke Ad' music tinkling in her ear. His tall, slim figure was the perfect clothes horse for his black suit, and he had a strong jaw line, close cropped dirty, blonde hair and a long, but not too large nose, all finished off with a gleaming white smile that crinkled his blue eyes. As she stared, open mouthed someone behind Molly jostled her and pushed her towards him, God and his smell, Calvin Klein had never smelled so delicious!

"Th-th-thanks" she stuttered holding in a moan of appreciation. "But you don't have to." Molly shivered as the stranger smiled at her.

"I know, but I would like to. I've tried to pluck up the courage all night but just haven't had the nerve. Can I have an orange juice as well please?" He was now turned to the barman, who was leaning across the bar so that he could hear above the music.

Having got their drinks he turned back to Molly, who convinced she had been drooling, wiped the corner of her mouth.

"Sorry, I suppose I should introduce myself; Joe Bennett." He held out his hand.

Molly took it and shook it gently. "Molly Pearson. Thanks again for the drinks, that's really nice of you."

"No problem, like I said it's taken me all night to pluck up the courage. Would you like to sit down?" Joe nodded towards a table that had suddenly been vacated by a group of local radio stars.

Molly nodded, trying not to do it too enthusiastically. "Yes, great. I just need to give my friend her drink."

Joe laughed and pointed towards the dance floor. "I wouldn't bother I think she's a little occupied."

Molly looked over to see Becky with her tongue down the throat of the star striker from earlier. She too laughed.

"Okay, maybe I'll leave it. Thanks," she said as Joe held out a chair for her. "Manners and generous, there aren't many like you about, not that I've been around of course." She dropped her head and groaned inwardly.

Joe smiled. "Well my mum has always taught me to treat a lady properly."

They both sat down, each taking a sip of their drink.

"So Molly," Joe finally said, "at the risk of sounding corny, what are you doing in a place like this?"

"Oh Becky, that's my friend, and I work for City, so we get free tickets to a lot of these events. What about you, oh I know," Molly suddenly realised that she recognised the name, and he certainly fitted the criteria for a cast member "you're a soap star aren't you?"

Joe laughed and shook his head. "God no, no I play for City. I've just signed from Preston."

Molly suddenly froze. He certainly wasn't a first team member, so was her golden rule being broken - never swap the same air space with a member of the youth squad. "Are you in the youth squad, you're not sixteen are you?" She plonked her glass on the table and pushed her chair back, ready to make a getaway. He certainly didn't look sixteen, but you couldn't be too sure.

Joe laughed again and rested his hand lightly on her knee resulting in Molly's heart drumming a samba beat inside her chest. "No, I'm twenty-two. I haven't played for a couple of months because I've had an injury, so the boss wanted me to get a few reserve games under my belt, obviously then I hope to play for the first team as soon as possible."

Molly sighed with relief, he certainly was too gorgeous to let go.

"That's great," she said. "That you think you'll be in the first team I mean, not that you've had an injury. Oh and it's great that you're not sixteen." That was one rule that she couldn't break, no matter how gorgeous he was. "I have a cousin who is sixteen and he's vile; so I would have to get up and leave I'm afraid." Molly screwed her nose up at the thought of her disgusting cousin, Adrian.

Joe threw his head back and laughed. "Well I promise I'm not sixteen, and I don't think I'm vile. Although, I do have a confession to make."

"What?" Molly asked. "Please don't tell me that you're seventeen."

"No, I really am twenty-two. No, I lied when I asked you what you were doing here, I already know."

Molly moved her seat back and tipped her head on one side. "You haven't been chatting to me for a bet have you?" She put her glass down, once again getting ready to leave. "Is it anything to do with Lee Taylor, the little scrotum, just because I tipped a pint over him at the Christmas party? He's sent you over here to get one over on me, hasn't he?"

"No, honestly he hasn't," Joe pulled his chair closer to Molly's and leaned towards her. "He is a little scrotum though as you put it. No, I know you work for City because I saw you there last week. I was at the training ground when you came over to put the posters up for tonight. I asked the scrotum about you, but he told me to steer clear because you were frigid."

They both laughed and now a little more relaxed Molly sighed and sat back in her chair. "So did you bother to get anyone else's opinion then, or just Lee's?"

"Let's just say you are quite a pin up for a couple of lads in that squad and to be honest I can see why." Joe gazed into Molly's large brown eyes as he reached across and gently pulled a strand of her long, chestnut coloured hair between his fingers.

Molly, unaware of how attractive she was blushed in the darkness. "Well I wouldn't take much notice of them, the only women that most of them have had any physical contact with is Pam and her five lovely sisters." Molly waved her hand about, making Joe smile

"Maybe, but they still know a sexy woman when they see one." Joe dropped his head and coughed nervously. "Anyway, they said that you'd probably be coming here tonight, so I decided that I would come too and try and get to talk to you – once I had the nerve." He shifted awkwardly in his seat and stared at the glass in his hand.

"Well you don't seem the nervous type. You seem like most footballers - balls of steel when it comes to chatting women up?"

"Oh so you have a certain impression of footballers, and by the sounds of it not a very good one." Joe took a sip of his orange juice, staring intently over his glass at Molly all the time.

She stared back, unable to take her eyes off him. God he was truly gorgeous and the thought of what it would be like to kiss those perfect lips of his was creating a knot in the pit of her stomach.

"Maybe I've seen too many of them working their magic on the ladies. What makes you so different, how do I know that you're not just like them?"

"I suppose that you'll just have to get to know me so that I can show you that I'm really not like them." After a slight pause, Joe leaned closer still to Molly. "So," he whispered shyly, "will you come out for a drink with me?"

Molly smiled, he didn't seem like the others, and she could tell that it had taken a lot of nerve for him to speak to her – he appeared confident, but she didn't think that he was. Maybe it was the way his glass trembled as he drank from it, or the way he kept wiping his hands on his trousers, or the occasional nervous cough that he gave. "Yes, I'd love to," she replied.

Joe blew out his cheeks and sighed. "Phew, that's great, and I promise that I'll take you somewhere nice." He clutched her hand. "I also promise that I will not work any magic on you." His mouth was close to Molly's now, and she was beginning to lose herself in his smell again.

"Oh," she breathed heavily, "that's a shame because I think that you would be quite good at it; magic I mean." Her breath quickened, and Molly knew, after only fifteen minutes of knowing him, she had to have Joe Bennett.

Joe broke her thoughts. "Look Molly I have to say this." He was still holding tightly to her hand as he moved his head closer. "You have got to have the sexiest mouth that I have ever seen." He rubbed a thumb across her full lips, sending a shiver down Molly's spine.

"Well I don't really know what to say to that." Molly licked her lips instinctively as she too moved closer.

At that moment, Joe took his opportunity and kissed her as she had never been kissed before. Joe's tongue probed at Molly's lips as he gently stroked her cheek. Molly responded, pushing herself towards him, breathing heavily as their kissing became intense. Molly ran her fingers through his short hair with one hand, the other clutching his knee. Joe held Molly's face in both his hands, while his lips turned the knot in the pit of her stomach into a fire.

Eventually, they pulled apart, both breathing heavily at the passion of the kiss "Blimey," gasped Molly. "Now that's magic." They both began roaring with laughter at her poor attempt at a Paul Daniels impression.

After a few minutes, they stopped laughing, and Joe stroked her hair. "Do you know how gorgeous and sexy you are?" he asked, gazing at Molly's bright, smiling face.

"Well maybe you can show me again," she said, this time taking the initiative and leaning in for her lips to meet Joe's.

As Molly lost herself in Joe's gentle kisses, everything around her ceased to exist until suddenly she was brought back to earth by Becky tapping her hard on the shoulder.

"So, who's your friend then?" asked Becky, a mile wide grin on her face.

"I could ask you the same thing." Molly nodded toward the star striker who was nuzzling Becky's neck.

"I know I broke the rule, but he's twenty-one and reckons he's on the verge of breaking into the first team plus…well it's been a while, a girl has needs!" Becky, irritated, turned to her companion. "Will you stop chewing my bloody neck; what are you an extra in that new Twilight film?" Becky's eyes lit up. "Ooh now if you looked like that Robert Pattinson guy, well I'd tell you to chew for your life."

Molly and Joe, still holding hands, smiled up at Becky as she pushed the star striker away.

"What's his name anyway?" Molly arched an eyebrow, knowing full well that Becky would have no idea.

"Erm, it's err…oh I don't bloody know" she cried, laughing at herself.

"It's Robin Patterson," muttered the star striker slightly embarrassed that the beautiful Becky had no idea of his name.

Molly and Becky screamed with laughter. "No, really what is it?" asked Becky, nudging him.

"It really is Robin Patterson," Joe chimed in, a huge smile breaking out over his face. "It's close enough, so his nickname is Twilight!"

"No way, is it really?" Becky let go of Twilight's hand, turning to face him. "No you don't look anything like him, but beggars can't be choosers I guess."

"Oh cheers," muttered Twilight.

"Hey don't worry that's a massive compliment coming from Becky." Molly smiled sweetly at Becky. "I suppose you came to tell me that I need to get my own taxi home then?"

Becky nodded. "Is that okay, if you hadn't been with handsome here I would have come with you, but I guessed that you wouldn't mind." She leaned closer to Molly's ear. "I mean he's pretty damned hot Moll I wouldn't want anyone around either if I had him for company."

"I'll make sure she gets home okay, I promise," Joe said leaning forward and squeezing Molly's hand.

"Hmm, I do believe you will" giggled Becky. "You don't look like trouble so make sure you don't prove me wrong because I have a big brother who will hunt you down if you hurt my friend."

Molly nodded earnestly. "She's right, she does."

"Well I promise I will be the perfect gentleman." Joe turned to Molly and gave her an incredible smile.

As the butterflies in her stomach did a synchronised fly past, Molly knew that she was a goner as far as Joe Bennett was concerned.

For the next six months, Joe and Molly enjoyed an intense, happy, loving relationship. They adored each other, and Joe treated Molly like a princess, treasuring every moment that they spent together. Then disaster struck, the club hit hard times and unless they made a substantial amount of money pretty quickly, they would be faced with administration. So they started to sell off their assets and after having enjoyed a remarkable rise to the first team, scoring eleven goals in his first season, Joe had become a significant asset and was sold to Galatasaray. Molly and Joe made plans for them to go out to Turkey together, but Molly's Dad forbade it. As he saw it, they'd only known each other a short time, so it was far too soon to be making such a commitment. Molly argued that she was twenty-one and could do what she liked, but her Dad was adamant, he was worried about Molly being alone in a foreign country as Joe would be away a lot, and worried about how she would cope without her family for support when she couldn't speak the language. Reluctantly Joe agreed that Mr Pearson was right, so after many hours of arguing and crying, Molly and her parents compromised and agreed that Molly could join Joe in a year's time if they were still as serious about each other.

They made it work for a while, with Molly flying out most weekends, but after a couple of months of Joe being there Molly's world collapsed. Joe had been pictured in the early hours of the morning, leaving the hotel room of one of Britain's top glamour models who was doing a photo-shoot in Istanbul. During a tearful telephone conversation with Molly, Joe vehemently denied anything had happened, but the model had said otherwise, selling her story to two or three magazines and newspapers – Joe was a fast rising star, having played a couple of games for the full England squad, and she was paid handsomely for her story. After that, Molly refused to answer any of his calls; he'd broken her heart, and she'd never forgive him. She was distraught and spent every night crying for Joe, closing her eyes to picture his face, reliving everything they'd said to each other, every moment of passion that they'd shared; she knew that if someone had actually punched her in the stomach, it couldn't possibly have hurt as much as this did now. Molly's parents and sister, Sophie, were worried about her as she wasn't eating either, but her Grandma told them just to ride it out as Molly would get over it in her own time and in her own way.

After a while, Molly proved her Grandma right, and decided to get on with her life, immersing herself in her work. So, even though she liked working in the marketing department, Molly decided to try for a position in the player liaison department. She'd had the strange idea that she might get over Joe if she surrounded herself with footballers – her own form of reverse psychology. Bizarrely it worked - Molly got the job, and she was good at it. She wasn't star struck by any of the players, in fact, was quite indifferent to them, and so took no nonsense from them, which they all respected her for. Plus, if truth be known one or two of them had a little crush on her. Molly also had a strong relationship with their wives and girlfriends, they all knew that she was on their side and wasn't going to try and steal their partner from them. They also liked that she treated the players as normal people and didn't pander to them, thus making life at home a little easier for them as they didn't have a massive ego to deal with. Molly was so successful at what she did, when her boss eventually left Molly was promoted.

More responsibility meant longer hours and more work for Molly, but she didn't care, it meant that she was too busy to watch T.V., or read magazines, and so had no idea whatsoever what Joe Bennett was doing with his life; just as she liked it. All she knew, from hearing the players talk, was that he was a massive star now, and one of the best strikers in the world, but as for anything else she didn't know or care – or so she kept telling herself.

CHAPTER 2

♥

Molly let herself into the house in a daze, and leaned back against the front door as it closed behind her. She took a deep breath and tried to pull herself together and stop her hands from shaking. Rob couldn't know that there was anything wrong; it wasn't fair for him to see her so het up about an ex-boyfriend. Plus, they hadn't been getting along too well recently so she didn't want there to be another row, as only this morning they had both agreed to try and make more of an effort with each other. Molly glanced at her reflection in the hall mirror; she didn't look too awful, a little wide-eyed maybe but nothing too obvious. She ran a hand through her hair and plastered on a smile before moving towards the kitchen, where Rob would be making dinner.

"Hi," she called as she opened the door.

Suddenly Molly stopped in her tracks. Lying on the breakfast bar, naked, except for an apron, was Rob, with a huge smile beaming at her.

Molly sighed and shook her head, a smile touching her lips. This was typical of him – if anything needed to be discussed or sorted out between them, then his plan of action usually involved sex.

"I told you I'd have something delicious waiting for you."

"You certainly did." Molly smiled, moving toward him she

kissed him tentatively, hoping her kiss didn't betray that she had been thinking about Joe.

After a few minutes, Rob pulled away. "Much as I'm enjoying this can I get down, this granite is a bit cold on my arse."

Molly started to laugh and pulled Rob down from the worktop.

"Come on then Chef, why don't you show me what you've prepared for starters."

"Oh you'll like it," Rob replied as he kissed her neck. "It's French." He then took hold of Molly's hand and dragged her up the stairs.

***

A couple of hours later, with dinner finished and everything tidied away, Rob suddenly remembered the newspaper he'd asked Molly to buy.

"Hey Moll, did you get me the 'Evening News'?" he called from his chair in the lounge.

Molly, who was in the kitchen making a cup of tea, froze. She'd not thought about Joe for the last two hours, now it struck her again, he was coming back, and she'd probably have to work with him in some capacity.

"Molly, did you get me the paper?" Rob was now at the kitchen door, looking her up and down.

"Oh erm, yes sorry it's in my bag on the breakfast bar." She turned and nodded to her handbag.

Rob took the paper that was sticking out of Molly's bag, as he walked past he slapped her on the bottom with it.

"I'll go and see what the transfer rumours are, oh and those jogging trousers do you no favours by the way."

"Thanks for that," Molly sighed and stared at Rob through narrowed eyes. "I'll bring your tea through in a minute, Prince Charming."

She leaned against the work surface and looking up to the ceiling; she wondered why on earth Joe coming back should have affected her so badly. It was over between them six years ago, and they'd only been together a relatively short time, plus she was with Rob. But, maybe that was the problem, yes she loved him, but if she were honest she hadn't really wanted to get married, but saying yes seemed preferable at the time to embarrassing him in front of fifty members of her family by saying no. He should have been everything she wanted in a man, the epitome of 'Mr Tall, Dark and Handsome', but just lately it didn't seem to be enough. He was disorganised, and extremely moody, and although he had a decent job as the Manager of a betting office, he constantly toyed with disaster. He appeared to be the model employee, his bosses and staff liked him, as did his customers, but Molly had a hunch that some of the things he did at work weren't totally ethical. She didn't have proof, but had an inkling from an overheard telephone conversation that he was putting bets through for people, after races had already started, as well as selling dodgy DVDs to his customers for one of his friends – both of which he'd vehemently denied when she had tackled him about them. Rob had been a little bit wayward as a teenager and into his early twenties and still associated with some of his less honourable contacts from that time, and it worried Molly. In fact, that was generally what they argued about – his lacklustre approach to work and the people he mixed with. Despite all of this, Molly still felt an immense wave of guilt to her reaction at Joe coming back to the club. How could she feel like this about him? But this was Joe she was talking about – the man she had never really got over losing.

After taking Rob his drink, Molly decided to call Becky. She closed the kitchen door gently and settled down in the armchair by the window overlooking the garden. After three rings, Becky answered.

"Oh Moll I was going to ring you and see how you are – so, how are you?"

Molly blew out a long breath. "A bit shell shocked to be honest, and feeling guilty that it's affected me so much"

"Hey don't feel guilty, he was your first love, you're bound to feel strange. Have you said anything to Rob about it?" Becky was Molly's best friend and confidante, so knew exactly how Molly was feeling about her life with Rob

"No, he knows I went out with Joe, but he doesn't know how serious it was. He just thinks it's great his fiancée went out with one of the best footballers in the world a couple of times. Plus, you know how jealous he gets; it's not worth another row."

Becky sighed on the other end of the line. "Hmm, I suppose, just play it cool for now, and try and forget about it until you actually have to meet him. You might feel differently about him once you meet him again, and if you don't then you ask Marcus to deal with him. Be careful though, you know he may not be interested in starting anything up again, you don't want to embarrass yourself."

Molly gasped. "Things may not be great with Rob, but that doesn't mean I'm not going to jump on Joe the moment I see him. Apart from anything else, he broke my heart don't forget."

"I know that, but let's face it, he's pretty hot." Becky started to sing her, slightly out of tune, version of "I Just Wanna Make Love to You."

"Very funny, Becky trust you to remember."

"Every time I drink Diet Coke I have a hot flush." Becky laughed loudly.

"Well, whatever Marcus will have to deal with him."

"You'll be fine, you're a professional."

Suddenly the door burst open, and Rob came bounding in clutching the newspaper, a huge smile on his face.

"Bloody hell Moll you'll never guess who we've signed, only Joe bloody Bennett, how cool is that?"

"Oh really, great, that's brilliant," Molly replied, plastering the smile on her face once more.

***

The news spread like wild-fire amongst Molly's family, her parents and sister ringing to find out how Molly was feeling. By the end of a half hour conversation with her mother, Molly had convinced herself there was nothing to worry about seeing Joe again. Sophie, her sister, on the other hand, made things worse by going on about how gorgeous Joe was, and how beautiful their children would have been and as good looking as Rob was, he was no Joe Bennett.

CHAPTER 3

Three days later, Molly took a deep breath before opening her office door. Today was the day she would come face to face with Joe again as today was the day he arrived at the club for his official press conference and photo shoot with his club shirt. It was on days like this that Molly was at her busiest. She usually spent most of the day with the player and his agent, showing them around the club, going through all the training timetables, finding out theirs and their family's requirements regarding schools and housing, and generally helping them to settle into the hotel that they usually stayed at for the first couple of weeks.

Molly knew that she could ask Marcus, her second in command, to deal with Joe, but he'd wonder why as Molly always insisted on doing the "Welcome Committee". Anyway, Molly reflected, she was a professional and could handle it, plus she'd quite like to see the look on Joe's face when he saw she was still at the club.

"Ooh Molly, are you excited?" Marcus asked as soon as Molly walked through the door.

"Not particularly, why?" She knew exactly what he was getting at, but she put on her best poker face.

"Joe Bennett of course, one of the biggest signings we've ever had and you can't be arsed." Marcus laughed and poured her a cup of coffee from the pot bubbling away near his desk. "He's been here before, about six years ago according to my Dad. You were here then weren't you, do you remember him?" Marcus asked, turning to his computer.

"Vaguely, I was in marketing then and didn't have many dealings with the team." Molly lowered her head and pretended to sort through some papers.

"My sister drove me crazy last night, going on and on and on about him. You know he did an advert for energy drinks, and he was only wearing his underwear in the picture? Well she had it made into this giant poster that's she's got above her bed. She kisses it every night." Marcus shook his head and laughed.

"Really," Molly muttered, wondering how she'd missed a picture of Joe in just boxer shorts, but then she'd made it her mission for the last six years to avoid knowing anything about him.

Suddenly the phone on Molly's desk buzzed, the flashing light told her it was the Chief Executive's PA. Molly groaned inwardly; she knew what this meant.

"Hi Karen," Molly answered, trying to put a smile in her voice.

"Hi Molly, just to let you know Joe Bennett and his agent have arrived, so Mr Grahame said to let you know he'll meet you in the main reception. You lucky bugger," said Karen sighing.

"Why am I a lucky bugger?"

"Oh come on Molly, he's one of the most fancied men on the planet, and you're going to be spending most of the day with him."

"I suppose so," Molly laughed. "I obviously need glasses."

"Well you are getting married in a few months, so I suppose you should only have eyes for Rob. Anyway," Karen's laugh tinkled, "just make sure you have a close look and report back how gorgeous he actually is."

"Okay, will do."

"He's arrived then?" Marcus smiled broadly at Molly as she put the phone down.

She nodded and sighed. Why was everyone so excited about

the arrival of one man? Molly knew exactly why; he was one of City's biggest signings and most expensive. Not only was Joe, at twenty-eight, at the top of his game, but he'd just been made England Captain, and come second in World Player of the year. He was an enormous deal for the club – a statement of intent of how influential they wanted to become.

"Right I'd better be off, Marcus. You can get me on my mobile if you need me." Molly smoothed down her skirt and buttoned up her club jacket.

"Okay, good luck, and get as much gossip as you can for my sister, she'll love you forever."

"Alright, leave it with me. See you later."

As Molly reached reception, her heart started to hammer in her chest, in fact, it felt as though it was working its way up her throat, and out of her mouth, and her legs were shaking as though she had just climbed a steep mountain. After three or four trembling steps, she spotted him.

Taking a sharp intake of breath, Molly took a moment to look at Joe who was standing at an angle to her, talking with Mr Grahame and another man she assumed to be his agent.

She gasped as she stared at the man who had broken her heart – he was even more handsome than she remembered. She could see that he'd filled out and was broader now, but his hips were still narrow, his hair was different, no longer close cropped, but short at the sides and longer on top, and his slim-fit navy blue suit and leather shoes were undoubtedly more expensive than those he used to wear, but he filled them perfectly, in fact he *was* perfection.

"Ah Molly, here you are," said Mr Grahame as he looked around. "Please, meet Joe Bennett, and his agent Tony Atkins. Gentlemen, this is Molly our Player Liaison Manager, and believe me she's worth every penny we pay her. I tell you something Joe, anything you need, day or night, Molly is your woman. Our players wouldn't cope without her."

"I don't know about that Mr Grahame. Anyway, lovely to

meet you gentlemen." Molly looked Joe directly in the eye as she held out her hand, willing it not to shake. Any shock at seeing Molly certainly didn't show in his face.

"Great to meet you Molly, although I think we met before, when I was a player here previously. You worked in marketing then."

"Really?" said Mr Grahame. "That's before my time, but do you remember meeting Joe then Molly, you obviously made an impression?"

"Hmm vaguely, I think I do," Molly replied before turning to Joe's agent. "And lovely to meet you too Mr Atkins. Shall we get down to the press room? I believe the press will be here in about half an hour."

"Come on then Joe," said his agent. "Let's go and sign your life away."

***

Throughout the press conference and the photo-shoot, Molly watched Joe as he worked the press. He was charming, polite and modest, playing down his ranking amongst the world's best players and his giant money move three seasons ago to Real Madrid, stating that he'd had a lucky break being part of some good Galatasary team performances in the Champions League – games that Real Madrid had seen him play in. At no point did he drop his guard and give any hint at how well he knew Molly, staying professional at all times. So much so, that Molly was beginning to think that he'd actually forgotten that they'd had a serious relationship and honestly thought that they'd only met briefly before.

Finally, when all the press had gone, it was Molly's turn to spend some time with him. They were about to sit down with some coffee and sandwiches, in one of the executive boxes, when Mr Grahame suggested he take Joe's agent for some lunch. Molly felt her face redden at the thought of being alone with Joe, but she couldn't protest as this was the normal thing for Mr Grahame to do.

Molly and Joe watched the two men leave for lunch, and then

stared at the door in silence for a few minutes.

Eventually, Joe gave a nervous cough.

"So, how have you been Moll?" he asked, reaching his hands across the table towards her, before quickly pulling them back.

"What since you cheated on me?" As soon as the words left Molly's mouth she wished she could take them back. "Sorry, that wasn't very professional of me."

"I swore to you then, and I swear to you now – I never cheated on you, she lied for the money."

"So you say Joe, but three magazines and two newspapers believed her. Anyway, we've got a lot we need to get through, and that's all water under the bridge, so let's just forget about it." Molly started to tap away at her iPad.

"Okay, but you need to know I'm telling the truth, and that one of the main reasons I've come back is because of you."

Molly gasped, her finger poised in mid-air above her iPad. "You came back because of me? What a ridiculous thing to say, you couldn't know that I still worked here, and anyway, why would you even think about coming back here for me?"

"Football is a small world Moll, when I knew the club was interested in signing me I just asked some of the England boys a few questions. Charlie Gates and Brad Nixon were both extremely complimentary about the 'hottie' who looks after the lads."

"You've no right to talk to Charlie or Brad about me, I don't want them knowing my business," Molly blasted, slamming her hand down on the table, as colour rose up her neck and to her face.

"Come on Moll you know what we footballers are like, a little bit stupid at times. If I'd hit them around the face with a wet fish and then told them it was a new moisturiser, they'd have believed me, so there was no way they'd guess why I was asking."

Joe flashed a smile that Molly felt hit her, with a thud, to the chest. She bit on the side of her mouth and gripped the arms of the chair to stop herself from reacting - he'd always had an innate ability to turn Molly into a quivering ball of longing for him with just one grin.

Molly looked at Joe impassively, without responding to his comment.

"Mum and Dad send their love by the way, my Mum still talks about you." Joe shifted uncomfortably in his chair.

"I heard they moved out to Spain, will they be moving back now?"

Joe shook his head. "No, not a chance. They love it there and have a brilliant life."

"I'm glad that they're okay, but, you still haven't answered why you would think of coming back here for me?" she asked, turning to stare out of the window, at the lush green pitch below. "And please, don't bullshit me Joe, because I'm guessing your decision has more to do with the two hundred grand a week wages you'll be getting, not me."

"If that's what you think, but I could have gotten more money at Real if I'd wanted to stay."

Molly sighed, she actually hadn't wanted to get into conversation with Joe about the past, because that's what it was – the past.

"Look Joe, can we please just forget about what happened. I have a job to do, and, unfortunately, for the next few days we're probably going to be spending a lot of time together, so we need to be professional about it."

Joe nodded and smiled that beautiful smile *again*.

"Okay, we can be professional, but I *did* come back for you. I've never forgotten you or stopped loving you and I will make it my mission to get you to believe me and hopefully take me back."

Molly's heart started to beat faster and faster as she looked at Joe. She felt a pricking feeling at the back of her eyes and she breathed in – she *would not* cry.

"It's not going to happen Joe; I'm getting married in just over five months."

Joe gasped and flopped back in his chair.

"You're joking, right?" he asked, rubbing a hand through his hair.

Molly shook her head and bit her bottom lip.

"No, it's not a joke. What did you expect, Joe? Did you think I'd wait for you?" Molly's eyes narrowed as she looked at Joe. "You did, didn't you?"

"No way, of course I didn't. I just *hoped* you'd be single." He got up from his chair and started pacing the room, his hands deep inside his trouser pockets. "How long have you been together?"

"Not really any of your business, now if you don't mind I've got a lot to get through."

"Sorry, I know it isn't, but it's just floored me. I knew I should have come back sooner." He returned to his seat and dropped his head to his hands.

"Unfortunately Joe your timing wouldn't matter one bit, because you hurt me and I can never forgive you for that, so let's just try and be professional about this and let me do my job."

As Joe sighed and nodded, Molly wondered whether it would be possible to stay professional with him, because even though he'd broken her heart, he was her first love and once upon a time he'd been the one she wanted to spend the rest of her life with, plus if her racing heart was anything to go by, he still had a devastating effect on her.

CHAPTER 4

♥

"But Molly, Cara mia, ees no right, I can not?" Faustino Grimaldi the Italian Left Back was pleading with Molly, outside the dressing rooms at the training ground.

"I'm sorry Tino you have to take it back. It's not possible to have a Llama as a pet when you live in a penthouse suite, in the city centre; I don't understand what made you buy it in the first place"

"I love her at first sight"

"Well, Gerry isn't happy. He's been generous enough to let you leave it here for a couple of days, but it keeps shitting on the training pitch, that he works hard to keep in good condition. So, he doesn't want her here any longer." Molly had to bite the inside of her cheek to stop herself from laughing.

"Molly, Molly, Molly the sheeting as you say, it good for the grass, no?" Tino stroked Molly's cheek, hoping to charm her into letting the Llama stay.

"No, Tino, it's not good. Fernando and Ducky were covered in it yesterday, and it's not fair on Mrs Mac and the girls when they have to wash the kit." Molly now couldn't help but smile. The pictures of the two players, Fernando Ferrara and Kevin Mallard, covered in Llama shit had gone viral on Twitter and Facebook.

"Hah, fools, because of them I must lose my Donata," Faustino hissed and raised his hand to the heavens. "I will miss her."

"I know Tino, and I'm sorry, but wherever you got her from, she has to go back. Let me have the details, and I'll get someone to sort it out for you." Molly rubbed his arm gently.

"I have papers in my bag, I get for you Molly."

"Okay Tino, you do that, and I'll wait here."

Tino disappeared leaving Molly giggling to herself. Just then her phone rang; she looked at it and saw it was Becky. She almost didn't answer, knowing that Becky would want to know how things were going with Joe.

"Hi Becky," she answered brightly.

"Hiya, are you busy?"

"No, I'm just at the training ground waiting for Tino's paperwork for his Llama."

Becky started to giggle. "What?"

Molly explained everything. "I will be so glad when May gets here, and they all piss off home for the summer – just over four more months, then bliss."

"It's like having dozens of kids. Anyway, you probably know why I've called; what's happened with Joe?"

Molly sighed and rubbed her eyes. "Not much, it's all been extremely professional. We filled in all the necessary forms and I got all the details I needed from him, he knows where he needs to go and when. The only downside is I've got to go to view apartments with him tomorrow."

"Why do you have to, it's not like he doesn't know the area?" Becky asked.

"Because he's worth millions of pounds to the club, so he has to have the best attention at all time. God, I'll be alone with him again and I don't want to be." Molly kicked at a stone, imagining it to be Joe's head.

"If it's all professional, what's your problem? Don't you trust yourself?"

"God Becky, only you could get away with asking me that."

Becky laughed. "And your answer is…?"

"Of course, I trust myself, but he's my first love Becky and I…"

"And you keep wondering - what if? Christ Moll it's only

natural," Becky replied.

"Well, I'm not sure Rob would agree. Anyway, I'm going to have to go, Tino's back with his Llama paperwork."

"Okay darling, I'll speak to you soon. Maybe come round for cuppa tonight, Pete's on night's this week so we can have a good old gossip."

"Okay, I'll text you later and let you know what time." She said goodbye to Becky, and then turned to a dejected looking Faustino. "Right Tino, is that everything I need?"

"Ees all there Molly, but I think you must come inside, it Charlie, he been how you say?... 'Vomitty', and he loose his teeth. He no find them in vomitty, so you must come."

Molly sighed and looked up to the sky. "Lord help me survive just a few more months, please."

***

Later that evening, having visited Becky for a couple of hours, Molly was back home, relaxing on the sofa with Rob, watching a DVD.

"Are you actually watching this?" Rob asked with an edge to his voice as he paused the film.

Molly turned to look at him. "Yes. Why?"

"Because you're doing that thing you do when you're worried about something."

"What thing?" Molly sat up.

"Grinding your teeth."

"Get lost, no I don't!" She glanced at the thumbnail on her right hand; it *was* much shorter than the rest of her nails – *that* was what she did when she was stressed, chewed her thumbnail. It had been a habit since childhood, chewing at it when she was stressed or frightened.

"I wasn't having a go; I'm trying to make and effort and show you some concern. I know you too well, biting your thumb and the fact you didn't moan when I just belched down your ear tells me something is wrong."

Molly sighed, how could she tell him what was wrong?

"I'm sorry," she whispered. "I'm just tired, and worried about how I'm going to get rid of Tino's Llama, that's all."

"Okay, I won't ask about the Llama, but I was wondering whether it was more to do with Joe being back?" Rob replied.

"What do you mean?" she asked, hoping her face wasn't as red as it felt.

"Come on Molly, he's a massive star and you've got to make sure he's happy and settled so that he can score plenty of goals. I know how seriously you take your work; it's bound to be worrying you."

Molly gave a quiet sigh of relief, glad to have dodged some difficult questioning; but then Rob turned the relief to worry again.

"Plus, I've kind of guessed it wasn't a casual thing between you two before, much as you like to play it down. Your silence on the subject says an awful lot." He glanced sideways at Molly.

"I don't get what you mean." She picked up a cushion and started to play with the zip.

"If you'd just had a quick fling with him I don't think you'd zone out every time I go on about what a brilliant player he is, and when he did that interview after the last England game you couldn't have sprinted any faster into the kitchen if you were Jessica Ennis – in fact you do that every time he's interviewed."

Molly shook her head vigorously. "I do not, no way," she cried.

"You do, believe me." Rob tutted and then sighed. "You've told me loads of stories about you and Becky and the scrapes with different guys and boyfriends that you got into throughout school and college. But, the stories stop when you started at City, when you met Joe. Plus, I can't believe that the two dates, which is all you say you had with him, would be so bad that you'd decide it would be best to become celibate for the next four years." He took hold of Molly's wrist, holding it a little too tightly. "What is it that you're not telling me?" he asked, his eyes narrowing.

Molly pulled away from his hold. "Rob, really you've got it all wrong," Molly insisted, still desperate to keep up the pretence that Joe Bennett never had, and never would mean anything to her.

Rob shook his head. "Seriously, I want the truth. I'm not as stupid as you seem to think. I know you say it wasn't serious, so why the hell is it so difficult seeing him again?"

Molly coughed nervously. "I never said it was difficult."

"He's back and you suddenly start brooding about work, I know it's the norm for you to think about it twenty-four seven, but this is different." Rob breathed in deeply through his nose. "Do you still have feelings for him?"

Molly looked at him and could see that there was a coldness in Rob's eyes. He'd always had problems with jealousy, but there had never been any reason for it previously, but this was different and she could understand why he might feel worried, but knowing how jealous he could be, would it be stupid to tell him how she was really feeling?

"No, I don't still have feelings for him, don't be silly. It's going to be a little weird, I can't deny that. But, my main worry is we do a good job Mr Grahame made it clear that he's our most valuable asset and has to be given the best treatment. All heads of departments have been told, whatever he wants or needs we have to do our best to provide it."

"I hope that doesn't include wanting or needing you," Rob said a hardness to his voice.

"No, it doesn't. But it does mean I have to spend all day tomorrow showing him around apartments." She felt Rob stiffen next to her.

"Why, he knows the area?"

Molly looked at him warily. "For the reason I've just told you, Mr Grahame has requested it."

"Okay, well you're a professional and you handle more difficult things than this every day; remember the incident with Aaron Dempsey's deodorant can? You dealt with that without anyone finding out."

Molly blushed as she recalled the incident. She didn't know who had been more embarrassed her or Aaron.

"You only know because you heard me on the phone to him,

when I thought you were out," she cried. "You promised never to speak of it again!"

Rob held his hands. "Okay, okay, it will never be mentioned again, but my point is you *can* deal with Joe, but just make sure it's totally professional and if he tries anything then I *have* to know, okay?"

"He won't."

"*Molly.*" Rob tilted his head and frowned.

"Okay, okay, I'll tell you, but it will be totally professional."

Molly looked at Rob and smiled weakly, hoping that it would be.

CHAPTER 5

♥

"Okay," Molly sighed, "where's the next one on the list?" She glanced quickly at Joe, before thrusting her car into gear. Today he was wearing loose fitting jeans, and a plain white t-shirt under a pale blue V-neck jumper, and *yet again* he looked sexy as hell, which was causing Molly no end of problems as far as concentrating on her driving was concerned.

"The old nightclub that's been converted into apartments…look Molly I'm sorry I know this is the last place you want to be, but come on, it is part of your job description to help me find a home." Joe frowned as he flicked through various Estate Agents' brochures.

"I'm fully aware of what my job description is Joe, but what I don't get is exactly what was wrong with the last three properties that we looked at. They were gorgeous, especially the second one."

Joe screwed his nose up. "Nah, not what I'm looking for. Listen, why don't we grab a bite to eat? There's no one waiting for us at the next place. I've just got to get the keys from reception."

"Erm no. If I don't want to be house hunting with you, I'm damn sure I don't want to break bread with you."

"Okay, but if this next one is rubbish, we definitely go for coffee, and a sandwich, I need to eat before travelling out to

Cheshire."

As Molly slammed the breaks on, Joe shot forward and almost hit his head on the dashboard.

"I'm not driving out to Cheshire; I certainly didn't include a property in Cheshire on the shortlist!" Molly glared at Joe, who was cowering back against the passenger door.

"Okay, calm down." He held his hands up in mock surrender. "Jeez, I'd forgotten how angry you can get. I need to go and see it because if I don't put in an offer it goes up for auction tomorrow."

"So, it'll have to go up for auction, no way am I driving you to Cheshire today or any other day, and if you don't like it go and tell Mr Grahame," Molly almost spat at him.

"Sorry Moll, but it's your job to help me find the property of my dreams, and if it's in Cheshire, then that's where we will go. Now, I don't want to tell Mr Grahame, but I do believe he won't be very happy if you don't take me. Imagine him finding out, the club's star striker, and record signing, has been driving aimlessly around Cheshire, not knowing where he's going and without a club representative?" Joe put the brochures in front of his mouth to hide his smile.

"Don't be so pathetic, that only would be a problem if you were a foreign player who had no idea where he was and couldn't speak the language. You know exactly where you are and how to get there, and how to ask for directions if you get lost," she blasted.

"Que?"

"God, *you* are an absolute idiot, and I wish you'd never come back."

"So you say, but I have noticed you're wearing red lipstick today, and you know what that used to mean." Joe started to chuckle, enjoying that he was making Molly slightly uncomfortable.

Molly, embarrassed by memories of their past passion, coloured up to match her lipstick. "Argh you, you...shit!"

Joe was beaming widely now. "I know I am. So, do we stop for something to eat now, or once we get to Cheshire?"

***

A little over two hours later and Joe had navigated Molly to a cobbled street in a Cheshire market town. She pulled up in a marked parking bay and peered out of the window.

"What are we doing here? It doesn't look like a place where you'd find a luxury apartment." She looked up at the row of black and white buildings, all of them different shapes and sizes.

"That's because it isn't," replied Joe, getting out of the car quickly before Molly could throw a punch at him. After what had happened at lunch, he figured that she was almost at breaking point.

After viewing the nightclub apartment, with much persuasion, Molly had agreed to get something to eat. Joe, thinking he was helping, popped into a sandwich shop and got them a tuna mayonnaise sandwich each, to eat on the way – which was fine, apart from the fact that he was almost mobbed by a group of teenagers who spotted him going back to the car. Then, when he finally made it back, he dropped half of his sandwich on the seat. After much rubbing with a tissue to remove the mark, Joe had actually succeeded in making a worse mess – a mixture of mayo' and tissue had left a large white streak across the seat. Also, he'd somehow managed to tread in dog poo on the way back from the sandwich shop, and didn't realise straight away that he'd trodden it into the car mat. The smell had got worse the higher the heating was despite scraping it off, thus, unable to stand it any longer, they'd travelled the last five miles in freezing conditions.

Molly definitely at the end of her tether sighed heavily as she slammed the car door with some force.

"Seriously Joe, what are we doing here if there isn't an apartment for sale?"

"We're here to view this place," he answered, gazing up at the double fronted, black and white building. "I'm going to open a restaurant." He turned to Molly, a triumphant smile spread across his face.

"What do you know about running a restaurant?" she asked incredulously.

"More than you think, Miss Pearson. Come on let's look inside." Joe nodded toward the door as he brandished a set of keys.

"I hate my job," Molly hissed following Joe, who'd now let himself in.

"Well, what do you think?" Joe turned to Molly as she stepped through the door.

Molly looked around, and was pleasantly surprised at how lovely it was. The floors were light oak, and the walls were a delicate duck egg blue, crystal chandeliers were hanging at irregular intervals, where, Molly guessed, the tables would be. A small bar ran along the right hand wall, and behind it were glass shelves in front of a mirrored section of the wall. At the far end of the room was a raised area that appeared to be for private dining, as teal coloured voile curtains were hung either side of it, but that too was lit by three more of the crystal chandeliers.

"Well, it's lovely," Molly finally replied. "But really Joe, what *do* you know about running a restaurant."

"I don't as such, but I was part owner of one in a little village about 30 kilometres from Madrid. My business partner Gabi ran it, and his wife Luna was the chef." Joe wasn't looking at Molly, but gazing around the room.

"Erm that's great Joe, but if they're in Spain, who's going to be running this one for you?"

"Gabi and Luna are, we sold the one in Spain, they're coming out here in a couple of weeks they're going to be renting a house down by the river in the short-term."

"Blimey that's quick work you've got it all worked out haven't you?" Molly was amazed; this wasn't the disorganised, laid-back Joe she used to know. The same Joe who would never talk about what he'd do after football in case it jinxed his career.

"I'd been thinking of coming back for a while, so put some feelers out and got a local agent and solicitor to work on my behalf; hence why I get to see this place before it goes on open sale."

"It's not going up for auction tomorrow then?" Molly asked as she shook her head.

"No, sorry a little white lie."

"So if you've been thinking of coming back for a while, you obviously had it all planned before the club approached you."

Joe turned to look at Molly now; his eyes were full of sadness. "I did, but it was always because of you Moll. I was going to come back and sweep you off your feet and prove to you that I never cheated on you, the restaurant was just a bonus. But, trust me to take too long planning it all."

Molly chose to ignore Joe's comment. "Well, it seems like a lovely town, and this place is great, so what are you going to call it?"

Joe grimaced. "Erm Bennett's...you think it's terrible don't you?"

Molly laughed. "No, as long as you don't put pictures of yourself behind the bar, or signed football shirts on the wall."

"Christ no, this is Cheshire, not Tenerife! No, I like the feel of the place as it is; I love the chandeliers and the décor. I may just spruce it up a little. What do you think?"

Molly thought for a few seconds as she looked around. Finally, she said.

"Hmm, I agree I think it has a warm feeling. I'd maybe have tall glass vases on each table with long stemmed flowers in them, all the same colour, probably purple and...Sorry, it's nothing to do with me; you should go for it and just do whatever you think."

Joe shook his head. "No, I value your opinion, I agree that sounds fantastic. I thought lots of candles around the place too."

"Yes that would work. But why is it closed down now, aren't you worried that it won't be successful if the previous owners had to close?" Molly was genuinely concerned; it was part of her job to worry about the player's welfare after all.

"I've seen the books, and it was doing quite well, the guy who owned it had a heart attack, and as he did all the cooking, and his wife was front of house, I couldn't buy it as a going concern. That's another reason why I want to get it open as soon as possible; I don't want the regular customers to start going elsewhere."

"You'd best get onto the estate agent then, hadn't you." Molly smiled and shook her head. "And then will you please put some effort into finding somewhere to live."

Joe nodded. "Okay, and I'll pay whatever it costs to valet your car – I'm not sure I could stand another afternoon looking at apartments with the smell of dog shit invading my nostrils."

CHAPTER 6

♥

The morning following Joe's house hunting expedition, Molly was working in the office when there was a brief knock at the door.

"You busy?" asked Rob, peering around the door, a wide smile on his face.

"Hiya, what are you doing here?" Molly beckoned him in. "Come in, there's only me here, everyone's out today."

Rob came in, leaned across Molly's desk and gave her a kiss.

"I was just wondering if you fancied lunch. I've sneaked off and thought I'd take you for lunch, you know 'make an effort'."

Molly sighed at his obvious dig, but didn't feel in the mood to bring it up and provoke a heated discussion about it. "Lunch sounds great, where do you fancy going to?"

"Italian, Gio's?"

"We may need to book; it gets quite busy in there." Molly replied as she started to clear her desk.

"I made a provisional one earlier. He said as long as we get there before half past one we should be okay."

"Okay, just let me finish this email and I'll be with you."

"So, how is lover boy anyway?" asked Rob. He picked up a match day programme from the desk and started flicking through it.

Molly felt herself become suddenly hot, and her heart started to pound – she felt uncomfortable, despite knowing that she hadn't done anything except spend the day with Joe in the capacity of Player Liaison Manager.

"What do you mean?" she asked, her eyes glued to her screen.

"Greg Pounder, there's a facts and stats section on him in the programme. I was just wondering how he's getting on now it's come out that he's got two women on the go." Rob shoved the page under Molly's nose.

"Oh," she said, breathing a quiet sigh of relief, "he's fine."

"Is that it?" Rob asked.

Molly finished her email and hit send. "Rob, don't even ask; you know I'm not allowed to tell you anything."

"I'll just have to ask him next time he comes in to put a bet on." He looked at Molly, a wry smile on his face.

"What, he comes in to your betting office and you didn't think to tell me? Rob, I should know if he's got a problem." This was exactly what infuriated her about him. As long as his business was benefiting what possible harm could there be in someone handing over thousands of pounds on the outcome of a race.

"It's not like he comes in every day. Christ Molly, it's once a month if that. Calm down." Rob shook his head and continued to read the programme.

Suddenly Molly had little appetite, for food or for Rob. All she wanted to do was tell him to get out so she could be alone with the cheese and beetroot sandwiches that she had brought in, but she knew if she did that another evening would be wasted being angry and silent.

"Come on then," she sighed. "Let's go."

Rob threw the programme back onto the desk, and moved to the door. Just as he was about to open it, Tino came rushing in, almost sending Rob flying.

"Watch it." Rob cried, as he stumbled backwards. "You want to watch where you're going, idiot."

"I sorry, I not know you have visitor, Molly. I come back," apologised Tino.

"No, no, it's fine," Molly said, arching her eyebrow at Rob.

"I'll wait outside." Rob muttered.

"Rob, be careful!" Molly cried as Tino lurched forward when Rob pushed past him, shoulder to shoulder.

"Sorry, Tino. What's wrong?" she said once the door had closed

"I have problem Molly. I help man in street yesterday, he cold and hungry, so I say to him come back to my house and my Mama she cook for you." Tino flopped into a chair opposite Molly and hung his head.

"Okay, so what happened?"

"He no go Molly, he still in my house. My Mama no stay with him, she scared, so she come with me today. Mr Ribero, he no happy that Mama is at training."

"Hang on a minute, so you've not only taken your Mother to training, but left a homeless man alone in your house. Is that right?"

Tino nodded. Molly dropped her head to the desk and screamed inwardly.

"Tino, what on earth were you thinking? No, I already know the answer, you weren't. Right okay, give me your keys to the house." Molly held out her hand as she started to dial the local Police liaison officer.

"Hi George, it's Molly Pearson from City. We may have a problem." She explained the situation to George, arranging for Tino's keys to be picked up from reception by an officer. She put the phone down and smiled at Tino. "The police will go and remove him. And next time just give him a couple of quid for a hot drink, okay?"

Tino nodded and got up from his seat. "Thank you Molly, I love you."

"I'm honoured," Molly gave him a tired smile. "Now get down to the viewing room, or you'll be late. Oh and where's your Mum now?"

"She go into town to shop, she get bored watching DVD of opposition and she no like it when Mr Ribero he shout."

"Okay, bye Tino." Molly waved him away, shaking her head

in despair.

Rob came back in moments after Tino had gone, but his eyes were narrow and his lips thin.

"Okay, I'm ready now. What's wrong with you?" she asked recognising the look of irritation on his face. "We've still got plenty of time"

Rob nodded his head towards the door. "Joe Bennett is here to see you *now*."

"Oh, right, I suppose he'd better come in. You can stay if you like. I doubt it's anything urgent."

"Are you sure you don't need to be alone with him?" Rob thrust his hands to his hips and sighed.

"Rob, please don't get sulky with me"

"I'm not getting sulky, I'm fine. I just get sick and tired of them taking up every minute of your time, even when we're at home."

Molly crossed her arms and shook her head, looking at him warily. "This is my job and I have to deal with him, you said you were okay with it."

"Oh, I'm peachy, honestly," he replied, sarcastically.

"Don't be so pathetic," she hissed. "Come in Joe" she called her eyes on Rob.

Joe came in and smiled at both Molly and Rob.

"Sorry," he said, looking from one to the other. "If you're busy I can come back."

"No, it's fine. Joe, this is my fiancé, Rob. Rob this is Joe Bennett."

As she bit her thumb nail Molly's eyes darted between each of the men in the room, wondering what their reactions to one another would be.

"Nice to meet you." Joe stuck out his hand toward Rob.

Rob took it and shook it firmly. "You too." A small smile crept onto his face. He couldn't help it; this was his hero. "Good goal on Saturday, by the way."

Molly felt relieved that there was to be no trouble, because despite what Rob had said about understanding her having to work with Joe, she sensed that he wasn't. But, it wasn't just Joe, he could be jealous and hot headed about any man who showed her attention – she'd once had to pull him off a drunk in a club who'd pinched her bottom. Waiting until Molly had gone to the ladies; Rob had repeatedly punched the guy in the stomach.

"So, what can I do for you Joe?" she asked, anxious that time was getting on.

"I just wanted to let you know that my offer has been accepted on the restaurant," Joe said. "So, just thought you should know in case there's anything I need to do from the club's point of view."

"Not at this stage, no. We may have to check your insurance out, but if you're not actually going to be working there, then it's not a problem. Erm I assume you're not going to be working there." Molly smiled inanely, inwardly praying that Joe wouldn't reveal that she already knew what the set up was.

"No, I have a business partner."

"Oh that's great; just keep me informed on how things go." With her heart beat increasing, Molly moved over to the door, gently pulling Joe with her by his elbow. For some reason, and she didn't know why, she hadn't told Rob about her outing to Cheshire to look at the restaurant.

"Oh are you buying a restaurant?" Rob asked, stopping Joe from leaving. "I hope that doesn't mean you'll be giving up football anytime soon."

"No, Joe sorted it all out before he came to the club, it's for his future. Sensible move I say, not many players think that far ahead. Well that's great news." Molly realised that she was rambling. "Sorry, Joe was there anything else."

Joe shook his head and gave Molly a strange look.

"Well, we'll have to pop in one night, won't we Moll?"

"Yes, you must," said Joe. "Although, I don't think we'll be doing cheese and onion pie."

"Cheese and onion pie?" repeated Rob.

Joe pointed at Molly. "Moll's favourite food," he explained.

"I didn't know that you liked cheese and onion pie." Rob turned to Molly, his arms now crossed firmly across his chest.

"I used to, I don't eat it so much now," she said quietly.

It used to be Molly's favourite food in the world and Joe's Mum would make her one every other week, but after their split even looking at one would send her into floods of tears.

Joe, realising he'd probably said something he shouldn't, decided he ought to leave.

"Well I'll be off, let you get back to whatever you were doing. Nice to meet you Rob." He laid a hand on Rob's shoulder and managed a smile.

Rob ignored Joe and turned to Molly. "Can we get off to Gio's now, get some of your favourite pasta Marinara for lunch."

"Hmm, yes, can't wait, I'm starving. Okay, thanks for letting me know Joe."

Joe simply nodded and slunk quietly away.

***

On the way to lunch, Rob was silent, and Molly didn't even try to engage him in conversation. The look on his face told her that there would be no point. By the time they were parking the car, Molly had resolved to have the least amount of contact with Joe as possible. Rob obviously didn't like it and she didn't want to make him feel uneasy thus making her own life difficult, so from now on Marcus could liaise with Joe. Unfortunately, Joe didn't appear to be reading from the same page as he was waiting outside her office when she returned to the club.

"Oh hi," Molly said, surprised to see him, but glad of an opportunity to talk to him. "Look Joe, about this morning, it was all a little bit awkward."

Joe frowned. "Yeah," he said. "Just a bit."

"I know. Which is why I think that you should deal with Marcus from now on." Molly lowered her eyes, unable to look at Joe in case he saw how sad she felt about everything. She was good at her job and was annoyed at herself for not being able to just deal with this man professionally. She didn't love him anymore, and she couldn't say she hated him anymore, but she certainly didn't like him – or was she kidding herself about all of the above? Because she certainly couldn't deny that she found him attractive.

"That's fine Molly, but why?" Joe sat opposite her and leaned on the desk. "And why did you feel you had to lie to Rob this morning?"

"I didn't lie." Molly was indignant.

"Splitting hairs, but never mind. Okay," he sighed, "Why was your use of the truth a little sparse?"

"Because whatever I do is supposed to be confidential."

Joe shook his head and gave Molly his most dazzling smile. "Ooh, crappy excuse Moll," he laughed. "Come on what's the real reason you didn't tell him about our trip yesterday?"

Molly felt a heat crawl up her neck and face. No matter what she told herself, that it was for confidentiality reasons, she knew exactly why she hadn't told Rob – because he wasn't stupid and would know what she'd actually enjoyed being with Joe. Plus life would be much easier at home if he didn't know

"I've just told you why." Annoyed with herself more than Joe, Molly threw her pen down onto the desk and watched it bounce before rolling onto the floor.

"Hmm, could it be you still fancy me?" Joe asked bending down to pick up the errant biro.

Molly shook her head. "Don't big yourself up Joe. I've told you why, but also I don't want him to feel uncomfortable about us spending the whole day together."

"He doesn't trust you then, is that it?" Joe sat back in his chair.

"Of course he trusts me. There's no reason *not* to trust me." Molly wondered whether she could actually trust herself. "Look at it from his point of view, his fiancée spending the whole day with her ex-boyfriend, who also happens to be a famous footballer. How would you like it?"

Joe thought for a few moments. "If it was you, well then I'd be jealous as hell, but if it was some other girlfriend, then I'd be okay if it was in a professional capacity."

"Bullshit Joe, you'd hate it, any man would."

"Like I said if it were you I'd hate it, I wouldn't want any man spending time alone with you. So, I understand what you're saying about keeping the information you give him to the minimum, but I don't think I understand why you don't want to do your job; why I make you feel uncomfortable. I'm pretty sure you don't hate me, much as you'd like to, so it can only mean one thing."

Molly didn't want to ask what that one thing was as she knew what he was going to say.

"Look Joe, I don't want to argue with you, so just go, please. I'll get Marcus up to speed with all your details so he can deal with you from now on."

"If you insist, but if you want my opinion you still love me, and no matter how much you try and fight you've got a little niggling feeling that I'm right. I love you, and I'll keep my distance out of respect for you and your relationship with Rob. He seems an okay bloke, but one day that little niggle is going hit you so hard you'll have to admit it." He got up to leave, and closed the door quietly behind him.

The second Joe left, Molly gasped for air as though she'd just run a marathon. Her hands shook and her eyes filled with tears as she realised with a deep gut wrenching fear that Joe might just be right.

CHAPTER 7

♥

"Oh Molly sweetheart, you look beautiful." Molly's mother, Wendy, sniffed into her handkerchief while beaming at her as she tried on her wedding dress.

Molly gazed at her reflection in the mirror. The corseted bodice was embellished with a delicate pattern of tiny glittering beads which carried on to the full tulle skirt and then on to a long flowing train at the back. It was exquisite and complimented her olive skin and dark hair and emphasised her curvaceous breasts and small waist. She hadn't wanted all of the fuss, she hadn't even wanted to get married yet, trying to persuade Rob that they should wait a little while longer, but like most things he'd steam rolled her into picking a venue, and a date. He was adept at persuading her that he knew what was best for them both. Molly had decided that if she had to get married then at least it would be in the dress of her dreams.

"What do you think Soph?" Molly asked her sister who was absently flicking through a magazine. Sophie looked up and nodded.

"Yeah, lovely," she replied, looking back down at her magazine.

"Don't be so gushing Sophie; you'll have me in tears with Mum." Molly tutted.

"What? What do you want me say? You know me, I can't lie."

"Do you think it looks awful then?" Molly looked down at the dress, wondering whether she should have chosen something simpler.

"Ignore her Molly; if it's not split to the thigh and down to her navel, she's not interested." Wendy threw a frosty glare at Sophie.

"What about the gown I wear in court, you couldn't get anything less sexy, unless it was something you wear, Mother."

Sophie happened to be a successful barrister within family law, but made it her mission in life not to look or act like one in her private life.

***

"Don't be so rude about my clothes, there's nothing wrong with what I wear. I'm not an exhibitionist like you, that's all."

"I like to show off what God gave me," Sophie cried. "What's wrong with showing a little bit of cleavage?"

"Nothing Sophie, but I'm afraid it's more nipple where your concerned."

"Mother!" Sophie and Molly chorused.

"Well, it is, and don't think I'm not aware that you go SAS half the time." Wendy wagged her finger at Sophie.

"Eh?" Sophie looked at her quizzically.

Molly started to giggle. "I think she means commando," she explained.

"Oh right." Sophie simply nodded and went back to her magazine.

"Anyway, at least you like the dress, Mum." Molly turned backwards and forwards.

"Beautiful, as I said, and Rob will love it too."

"Oh let's hope so," Sophie cried. "You know how difficult it is to please Captain Caveman."

Molly tutted at Sophie's nickname for Rob. "Please don't call him that."

"Sorry, but he is a caveman. What about Joe anyway sis, what does he think about you getting married?"

"Oh Sophie, if you can't say anything nice to your sister, don't say anything at all."

"What's wrong with that? It's a perfectly normal question. He was her first love, and now he's back, looking hotter than he did when she went out with him. He's earning megabucks and from what I can tell from the advert, where he's wearing his 'Tighty Whiteys', his deal with City isn't the only decent package he's got."

"What exactly is your problem Sophie?" Molly refused to bite her tongue any longer. "You've been an absolute bitch ever since we got here"

Sophie shook her head. "No, I haven't. I said you looked lovely, and all I asked was what Joe thinks about you getting married."

"I'm sure he's not interested. He made it clear six years ago what he thinks of your sister. He couldn't wait to cut her loose and hook up with a big bosomed bimbo." Wendy scowled.

Molly gave a thin lipped smile. "Not comforting, if I'm honest, Mum."

"Yeah Mum, that's a mean thing to say to Molly," Sophie added with a smirk.

"Oh shut up Sophie, keep your nose out. I'm sorry Molly, I didn't mean to upset you, but he did let you down, there's no getting away from that."

"I know Mother, but you don't have to be so brutal about it. Look, he's back, and we are being professional about things, so stop going on about him. He's nothing to me anymore, and neither am I to him. So to answer your question Sophie, he doesn't care."

"Bullshit on all counts," Sophie whispered, just loud enough for Molly to hear.

Molly blew out her cheeks and rolled her eyes. "Come on, let's go. I think Sophie's had enough, and I've had enough of Sophie to be honest."

"Just making a point that's all, and if it's hit a raw nerve, well that's not my problem."

Molly lowered her head, not wanting her mum or Sophie to see the tears that were now threatening to fall. Sophie was right that a nerve had been hit, but it was her mother's comment that had done the damage. Joe had made it clear six years earlier that he didn't care about her one bit, and it still hurt.

***

Two hours later and the three women were sitting in a local Tapas Bar. The frostiness caused at the wedding shop had thawed slightly, but Molly was still smarting a little. She didn't know why she'd asked Sophie to come along, she had an opinion on everything and it wasn't usually one that Molly wanted to hear.

"So, what do you want to drink?" Molly asked, skimming the wine list. "Shall we order a bottle of the house white?"

Sophie, realising that she'd upset her sister, decided to try to be pleasant over dinner. "That sounds lovely Moll. You pick one, whatever you'd like is fine with me"

"Yes, Molly just order what you think." Wendy held eye contact with Sophie, silently warning her to keep up the better behaviour.

Suddenly Sophie's resolve disappeared out of the window, jumped on a bus and left town altogether.

"Bloody hell," she hissed. "Molly, look at who's just come in. It's only Joe, Christ he's even sexier in the flesh than I remembered. Are you sure you don't want to trade Rob for him?"

"Oh Sophie," Wendy cried dropping her head into her hands. "Couldn't you have just pretended you hadn't seen him?"

"Oh for God's sake, Mother, get a grip." Sophie stood up and waved in the direction of the door. "Hey Joe," she called.

Molly's breath caught as she looked at Joe, who was accompanied by a tall, dark man who was almost as gorgeous as he was. Joe was looking particularly sexy in jeans and checked shirt, a leather jacket and a thick scarf to protect himself against the late January coldness. He was instantly recognisable and the handful of early evening diners in the restaurant had started to mutter amongst themselves, apparently unsure of whether to believe their eyes or not. Molly tutted - how on earth did he think that he, one of the best football players in the world, would be able to dine out without being noticed and probably approached by fans?

Suddenly Sophie's voice bellowed out Joe's name again. This time Joe looked around and spotted the three of them. He momentarily stopped in his tracks, and then started walking, with his companion, in their direction. With each of Joe's approaching steps, Molly felt her heart beating to a faster rhythm. By the time he'd reached the table, Molly's stomach was lurching, and she had to hide her hands beneath the table in case he saw how much they were shaking. Joe half smiled at Molly and then, when he looked at Sophie, a huge grin stretched across his face.

"Hi Sophie," he said, bending down to give her a peck on the cheek. Then suddenly he realised what he'd done. "Sorry, it's just lovely to see you again. Mrs Pearson." He turned to Wendy and nodded. No kiss was offered.

"Hey Joe, good to see you," Sophie replied, squeezing his hand. "Molly said you were looking hot, but I didn't expect you to look *this* hot."

"No, I did not," Molly blasted.

"Sophie always was a big joker. Don't worry, Moll, I still don't believe anything she says."

"Anyway, enough about you, who's your friend, he's very handsome?" Sophie looked around Joe towards his companion who had been hovering in the background.

"You remember my friend Ed Bryce, don't you Molly? He lodged with my Mum and Dad for the first year of his residency here; he's here for a conference so we thought that we'd catch up." Joe placed his hand on Ed's back.

"Hi Molly, lovely to see you again. It's been a long time." Ed leaned down to kiss Molly's cheek.

"Ed, how are you, great to see you too. How is Katie, it was Katie wasn't it, and you had a little boy?"

Ed gave a small smile. "Hmm it was, but we're not together anymore. I'm married to Lucy now," suddenly his face lit up like a beacon. "Nate's just turned seven and he lives with us, and we've just had a little girl, Tilly."

"Oh that's lovely; it sounds as though you're very happy."

"I am, extremely. Anyway, I'll go and get our table, nice to see you again Molly."

As Ed walked away, the wink at Joe and pat on his back didn't go unnoticed by Molly.

"Oh he's married then," Sophie sighed, staring after Ed.

"Very married," laughed Joe. "In fact he's sickeningly in love with his wife, so sorry Sophie." Joe had to smile at Sophie, whom he'd always found funny.

"Never mind," Sophie sighed. "Another one bites the dust. What about you though, Joe? Don't you have a girlfriend then?" She gave him a wink.

"No, I was seeing someone in Spain, but it didn't work out." Joe glanced at Molly, but she was looking down at the table.

"Oh that's a shame, isn't it?" Sophie nudged Molly, almost knocking her off her chair. "Poor Joe."

Throwing Sophie a withering look, Molly turned to Joe. "What are you doing here anyway?" she asked, now sitting on her shaking hands.

"Having an early dinner, the same as you."

"I mean, what are you doing here without any protection?" Molly shook her head in despair.

"He's having dinner Moll, not sex. Ignore my sister Joe she just can't seem to switch off from work." Sophie gave Molly a dig in the ribs with her forefinger. "Anyway Mother, is there anything that you wish to say to Joe?"

"Sophie," Molly hissed.

"No, it's fine Molly." Wendy looked up at Joe. "I'm pleased you've done well for yourself Joseph, but I can't quite forgive you. Molly may have to because of her job, but I don't."

Joe's eyes flashed with anger. "Look Mrs Pearson, I didn't come over for an argument and I understand how you must feel, but at the risk of getting my head bitten off, I didn't do anything wrong, despite what you may wish to believe. I don't want to be rude, but I'm a little sick of being blamed for something I didn't do." Joe cut Wendy off by turning to Molly. "I come here quite a lot to eat, it's near to the hotel, and I don't get bothered by anyone...usually." He gave a little wry smile. "Anyway, I'll let you get on with your meal. It was great to see you again Sophie, and you Mrs Pearson, and I'll see you soon Molly."

"Hah, not if she sees you first." Sophie laughed at her own joke and slapped Joe's arm.

Molly gave her a withering look. "Yes, I'll see you soon."

Once Joe was seated with Ed in a quiet corner of the restaurant, Molly punched Sophie in the arm.

"What did you have to say all that for, in fact, what did you call him over for in the first place? You totally embarrassed me. I'm supposed to be retaining some level of professionalism in all of this."

Sophie started to chew on a breadstick. "Oh get a sense of humour Molly. If you weren't so uptight I wouldn't have to act like such an idiot would I?"

"Oh just look at the menu and shut up, the pair of you," Wendy snapped. "Anyone would think you were children, not grown women."

"Sorry Mum," they both chimed, and then buried their heads in the menu.

***

Throughout the meal, Molly surreptitiously glanced in Joe's direction. She tried to tell herself that it was to check he wasn't being hassled by anyone, but she knew she was kidding herself - she just wanted to look at him. She'd hardly seen him over the last couple of weeks. It had been her choice, but now he was nearby she realised that she preferred to have him close, she liked to be able to look at him, to drink him in. All the time she hadn't seen him, she'd kept her mind occupied by thoughts of Rob and their wedding, and had pushed any thoughts of Joe to the back of her mind. Now though, now all she could think of was how gorgeous he looked.

The last six years hadn't aged him at all. He was still beautiful, his deep blue eyes still crinkled at the corners when he laughed and his smile still lit up his face. He'd lost that boyish roundness as his cheekbones were now more pronounced, and from what Molly could tell from the way his clothes fitted him, he still had an incredible athletic body. She sighed, and tried to re-focus on what her mother was saying about table decorations.

"You okay Moll?" Sophie reached across the table and took Molly's hand. They'd finished the meal, their Mum had gone to the ladies, and Sophie had noticed Molly was lost in her thoughts. "I'm sorry if I upset you earlier, about the dress and calling Joe over. I know I should grow up."

Molly looked up and gave a watery smile. "Oh I'm used to you being an idiot. I'm fine, just tired."

Sophie glanced in Joe's direction. "Look, don't bite my head off, but is that all it is? You're not having second thoughts about getting married are you?"

Molly didn't snap back with a denial, she merely shook her head, keeping her eyes on the table. "No, don't be silly."

"Oh dear, I do fear the lady doth not protest enough. Is it Joe?"

Now Molly snapped. "No, don't be ridiculous, I'm just tired." She turned away so that Sophie wouldn't see the tears welling in her eyes.

"Okay," Sophie sighed heavily. "Look, I know I can be a prize prat at times, but I'm here if you want to talk."

"I know," Molly said. "Thanks."

Wendy chose that moment to come back to the table.

"Are we ready to go then?" she asked.

"Yes Mum," said Molly, gathering her thoughts together.

Wendy looked from one daughter to the other. "Are you two being nice to each other?"

Sophie nodded. "I've just apologised for being stupid earlier. I shouldn't have called Joe over, after all it's over between him and Molly. Isn't that right Moll?"

"Yep, all over a long time ago," Molly replied, trying to believe that she was telling the truth, even though the thudding of her heart told a different story.

CHAPTER 8

"Blimey Molly, what was that in aid of?" Rob asked as Molly appeared from under the duvet.

"Just wanted you to go off on your course remembering what you have at home." Molly winked as she slipped out of bed and into the en suite. "Are you coming for a shower then, or what?"

"Fuck me, all this before seven thirty on a Monday morning." Rob chuckled as he jumped up and followed Molly.

For the last couple of days Rob hadn't known what had hit him – Molly had been insatiable and there had been no arguments. He guessed that she was probably feeling more relaxed now that everything was more or less organised for the wedding, or maybe she was making that 'effort' that she kept banging on about, but whatever reason he didn't care, he was certainly reaping the rewards.

Molly, on the other hand, knew exactly why Rob was getting more sex than a nineteen year old in Magaluf – guilt. After seeing Joe in the restaurant on Saturday, he occupied her thoughts constantly. It was as if she'd been possessed by him, even Googling him to see whether she could find out who on earth the woman was that he'd been seeing in Spain? She'd also sent an email to Marcus on the Sunday evening, relieving him of his 'Joe duties' as he called them, making up the excuse that Joe's agent insisted that because of Joe's high profile it should be Molly who dealt with him. Her finger had hovered over the delete button on her phone but when Rob walked in, she panicked and hit send. She'd worried about it all evening but it was too late, the message had been sent and there was no way she could retract it now.

***

"Have a good week, and don't miss me too much." Standing at their front door, Rob kissed the tip of Molly's nose.

Molly smiled up at him. "I'm looking forward to the peace and quiet," she joked.

"You'll be bored without me to look after." Pulling Molly closer, Rob kissed her. "And don't forget, if you go out don't speak to any men." He smiled, trying to make light of the comment. "Although if you go out with Sophie she'll probably be the one who gets the attention."

Molly frowned knowing that he was being serious about talking to men, and about Sophie getting more attention. "I won't even be going out; we're too busy at work we've got an away game midweek."

Rob's face darkened. "Yeah, well don't let those players take the piss either and don't forget I'll Face Time you every night at eight."

Molly hugged him. "Okay, but don't worry if you can't. Try and make the most of it, I know it's only an appraisal writing course, but you may meet some people that could help you move up the ladder."

Rob sighed, rolled his eyes and gently pushed her away. "Okay, I will, and I will definitely Face Time you, so make sure you're free at eight every night."

Molly bit at her bottom lip, wishing she hadn't made the comment about his job. She didn't want to appear pushy; it was just that he needed to move on from his dodgy mates and his dodgy little practices before he got himself into serious trouble.

Molly watched as Rob walked to his car, and sighed as she thought about their relationship. Despite their bedroom antics over the weekend he didn't make her feel the way Joe used to. He had made her feel beautiful and desired, and she didn't feel that with Rob. At first things between them had been great, perfect almost, but once they became engaged Rob started to show a different side to the funny, charming and kind self that Molly had first fallen for. He made her feel inadequate and less than desirable. Then there was Joe – all the feelings rushing around inside her were stupid. It was obviously because he'd been her first love, and yes he was gorgeous, and almost every woman on the planet wanted him, but he'd broken her heart and she should hate him for it.

With a quick beep of the horn, Rob drove off and Molly waved goodbye. As he disappeared around the corner she realised, with a heavy heart that the feeling that was currently tugging at her chest was one of relief and a knowledge that she probably wouldn't miss him at all.

***

She had been in the office a couple of hours, catching up on some paperwork, when Mrs Mac, the laundry lady, came bustling in. Her usually happy face was shadowed by a large frown.

"Hi Mrs Mac," said Katie, who sat at her desk opposite Molly's. "How are you today?"

"Not very happy, Katie." Mrs Mac flopped down onto a chair. "It's that bloody Grimaldi fella again."

"Oh no, what now?" Molly dropped her head back and closed her eyes.

"I'm sick of it Molly, you need to speak to him. I've asked Mr Ribero but he just pretends he can't understand what I'm saying, and Bruce the first team coach, just laughs at me. He's getting on my wick."

Katie passed Mrs Mac a cup coffee and gave her a friendly pat on the shoulder.

"Here you go, if we had some I'd have put a brandy in it for you. It looks as though you need it."

"Tino is becoming the bane of my life." said Molly as she searched in her drawer for some biscuits. "So what's he done this time?" She found the biscuits and offered the packet to Mrs Mac.

"He keeps bringing his washing in for us to do," said the older lady, munching on a digestive. "I've told him 'no' about five times, but he charmed Helen last week and then Julie yesterday. I wouldn't mind, but it's what you find in his pockets – it's not pleasant." Mrs Mac screwed up her face.

"Oh who's this you're talking about?" Marcus and Rosetta had just walked in and heard Mrs Mac complaining.

"Tino Grimaldi," Katie explained, a grin on her face.

Despite being one of the most difficult players to deal with because of his sheer stupidity, it was that same stupidity that many found endearing, making Tino everyone's favourite.

"Oh he's alright," Rosetta smiled. "He's harmless, just a bit dense, that's all."

"Well you come and empty his pockets then," Mrs Mac said. "Yesterday it was a pair of dirty socks and I mean filthy, they were hard and stunk. Then last week I found some women's knickers in one pair of jeans and a piece of half eaten toast in another pair."

Everyone, except Mrs Mac, started to laugh loudly.

"Were the knickers clean?" Marcus asked, still laughing.

"Marcus, really do you have to?" Molly threw a pen at him in disgust.

"Well I'm glad you all find it funny." Mrs Mac sat back in the chair with arms firmly crossed over her ample chest. "So what are you going to do about it Molly? I'm not doing his washing anymore, it's not part our job anyway, and I don't see why he thinks it is."

"I'll speak to him; I've got to go over to the training ground anyway, so I'll tell him this morning. Has he been rude about it, does he demand you do the washing?"

There was now a glimmer of a smile on Mrs Mac's face. "No, that's the problem; he's so bloody nice about it. He buys us cakes and flowers, and then starts talking all sexy in Italian to the girls, and well they just give in and take the washing off him."

"Ooh what does he say?" Rosetta asked. She was fluent in Spanish and Italian and was interested in how Tino was charming the ladies.

"Oh lots of things but there's one he says...ooh let me get it right, la ragazza sexy con grandi volgari. That's his favourite."

Rosetta started to laugh. "How come you remember it word for word, Mrs Mac? You don't fancy him yourself do you?"

Mrs Mac shook her head. "No, *I do not*. I know it because he says it all the bloody time, especially when he's got a big wash that needs doing."

"What does it mean, Rosetta?" Katie asked.

"Well, it can only be to you Mrs Mac because it means; you sexy girl with big boobies."

Even Mrs Mac couldn't help but join in with the laughter this time.

"Why the cheeky little bugger, just wait until I see him." She held a palm against her reddened cheek.

"Say this to him Mrs Mac, he'll soon go running – I'll write it down for you, but you need to say; come circa alcuni sporchi sesso sulla lavatrice?"

"What does that mean?" Marcus grinned at Rosetta, knowing that it was probably rude.

"Oh now that would be telling." Rosetta wrote it down on a piece of paper and passed it to Mrs Mac. "I don't think Tino will bother you again after that, although knowing Tino he might."

"Anything is worth a try love. Anyway, I'd best be off, so you'll speak to him then Molly, just in case this doesn't work?" she asked brandishing the piece of paper.

Molly nodded her head. "Yes I promise, I'll speak to him today, but get practicing your lines just in case."

***

An hour later Molly was at the training ground. She was on the way to the offices in order to meet the Manager, to talk about hotel details for the following evening's away game – then she'd have words with Tino. Thoughts of Tino brought a smile to her face. He was a real handful, who needed dealing with on a weekly basis, but at least he made her job fun. It was better than some of the players she'd had to deal with over the years. At least

Tino was harmless and hadn't been accused of receiving stolen goods and dealing cocaine, like one player they'd had at the club a few years earlier.

As she reached the double doors into the gym, Molly decided to cut through to get to Mr Ribero's office. She knew she wasn't supposed to walk on the gym floor in her stilettos, but everyone who cared was outside helping to defrost the paths down to the training pitch – God forbid one of their £40 million assets slipped and injured themselves. She pushed the doors open, and then walked on tiptoe across the gym.

"Naughty girl," a deep, sexy voice she recognised called from behind her.

Molly halted. Her stomach flipped.

"Hi Joe."

She turned around to see Joe, standing in front of her in nothing but his shorts. Her legs started to tremble as she felt a heat envelope her body and her nerves fizzing with excitement. Joe's shorts were extremely low on his narrow hips, revealing his taught, well-defined, six pack, and v-shaped pelvis with a smattering of hair leading up to his navel. He stood with his hands on his hips, emphasising the broadness of his chest. His arms were tanned and muscular and bare of any tattoos, unlike most of his team-mates. His golden skin was smooth and shimmered with a light perspiration. He had a couple of day's growth on his chin, his blonde hair was messed up in a boyish fashion, and his cobalt blue eyes shone like precious jewels. He looked wondrous, and Molly could do nothing but stare and cross her legs as the heat reached her groin.

A small smile crept on to Joe's lips as if he knew her secret. "You're not supposed to be in here in high shoes," he said, walking slowly towards her as his eyes raked up and down her body.

"I know." Was all Molly could manage without taking a huge gulp.

Joe stopped a few paces in front of her and smiled widely now.

"Where are you going anyway?"

"Oh, erm to see Mr Ribero about the hotel for tomorrow night," Molly said, trying desperately to shake herself out of her trance. "Why aren't you outside with the others?"

"I was here early to do some extra gym work; no one is due for another half hour. Come on Moll, you should know that. Weren't you the one who gave me the schedules, and also the lecture on being late?"

Molly gave a small laugh. "I suppose I was, yes. Well, I'd better let you get on then."

"I'm pretty much finished if you fancy a coffee?"

Molly's face reddened as she shook her head. "Oh no, I can't, I shouldn't be late for..." her voice tailed off as she turned around and nodded towards Mr Ribero's office.

"Okay, no problem, another time maybe."

"Yes, maybe. I'll see you tomorrow on the coach then."

Joe left, waving a goodbye to Molly.

Molly, rooted to the spot, blew out a long breath, as she realised that her breasts were pushing against her blouse and the little niggle that Joe had talked about was starting to hit a little harder every day.

CHAPTER 9

♥

"Molly, you have all hotel details, yes?" Mr Ribero was standing at the front of the luxury coach talking to Molly. They were waiting for the last few players to arrive for their mid-week away game in London that evening.

"Yes, I've got the booking details here, why?"

"You can ask them to put me away from players, yes?"

Molly nodded. "Yes, if you wish."

"Good, I need sleep and not want to be near Faustino or Alexi, they snore like pigs." He chuckled and shook his head. "Ah I funny man, yes?"

As Mr Ribero wandered off to find a seat, Marcus nudged Molly.

"God, he hilarious, yes?"

Molly giggled.

"Ah bless him," she said. "At least he's jolly, not like the last one. You couldn't even get him to say good morning to you."

"Who are we waiting for Molly?" Jack, the driver, called over his shoulder.

Molly looked down at her list and silently called off the players' names, but she already knew exactly who was missing.

"Just Joe, he came in early to do an interview for City TV and they got a little bit delayed. He shouldn't be too much longer."

At that moment, Joe came running up and climbed on board. Molly and Marcus were sitting in the front seats, and Molly was holding onto the rail in front of her, so as Joe pulled himself up the steps their fingers touched. Both of them snatched their hands away, as if they'd had an electric shock.

"Sorry," Joe said. He coughed nervously.

Marcus, misunderstanding his apology, smiled and said. "No worries Joe, it wasn't your fault the interview was delayed."

"It's fine," Molly whispered hypnotised by his gaze, her eyes never leaving Joe's.

"That's okay then," Joe replied, directing his response at Molly.

As he moved past her, Joe's breathing became heavier, his eyes lingering on her face. His mouth twitched into a brief smile that caused Molly to take a sharp intake of breath.

Her stomach flipped and a small smile crept to her own lips as Joe took his seat. Molly felt like a schoolgirl again, hugging a secret crush to herself – a young girl yearning for the school heart throb and getting excited when he merely glances at her. But this wasn't a sweet and innocent infatuation; this was starting to become a heart pumping, blood heating desire.

"Okay Jack," Marcus cried, completely oblivious to what was happening in front of him. "Let's get going."

***

Fortunately for Molly, Marcus liked to sleep on the coach. He wasn't a very good traveller, so to avoid feeling travel sick he always tried to catch a nap. Molly was relieved, she was distracted thinking about Joe, how he'd looked yesterday and how a quick touch of his fingers had sent shock waves through her body, and when he'd looked into her eyes earlier, her crotch had practically throbbed with desire for him. Also, if she glanced up at the coach's rear-view mirror, she could just about see Joe, who was sitting three rows behind playing cards with Jimmy Cavanagh. He looked gorgeous yet again, so much so that Molly felt sure she had actually felt drool on her chin. He'd taken off the jacket of his charcoal grey club suit, rolled up the sleeves of his pale blue shirt to reveal muscular, tanned forearms, and loosened his tie. Molly almost groaned with desire every time she caught sight of him.

After about two hours, Molly could sense that the players were starting to become restless. They were getting louder and moving around the coach and quite a few missiles were being thrown. She decided to ask Jack to stop for half an hour to give them time to stretch their legs. They'd left at nine that morning so had plenty of time.

As she stood talking to Jack, something hit her on the backside. Molly was going to ignore it as she was used to that sort of messing around from the players, but then something happened that demanded her attention.

"Who the fuck did that?" she heard a familiar voice roar.

Molly turned around to see Joe on his feet, staring angrily up and down the coach. The rest of the players were open mouthed, Joe was one of the mildest mannered players in the league, never mind the club, and so his shouting had shocked them. Then at the back of the coach a couple of younger players started to laugh, bringing their baseball caps down in front of their faces so that Joe wouldn't see.

"I asked a question, who the fuck did that?" He demanded again.

Molly moved towards him, holding onto the seats as she walked precariously up the aisle.

"Joe, it's fine. I'm used to the fact that they're a bunch of idiots" Molly laughed trying to make light of the situation, and also attempting to divert attention away from the fact that Joe had come over all 'He Man' about her.

"Hey Joe, you're not giving our Molly one are you?" Greg Pounder shouted from the back of the coach.

From the corner of her eye, Molly saw Joe tense and start to dart forward. She quickly put her arm across his body, stopping him from going for Greg. The two team security guards had left their seats at the front and were now standing like a wall behind her.

"Leave it Joe," Molly hissed, giving him a stony stare. "He's a prat." She turned to the two burly men behind her and shook her head. "It's fine."

"Joe, you sit down and Pounder you apologise to Molly." Bruce Roberts the first team coach was now also on his feet.

"Sorry Molly," said a suddenly less cocky Greg. "I didn't mean anything by it."

"It's okay Greg; it just makes a change to have a gentleman on board." She looked at Joe and smiled. "So who *did* throw something at my arse anyway?" she asked.

"Sorry Molly." A hand was raised towards the back of the coach, it belonged to Seamus Bryant, an eighteen year old who'd recently moved up from the youth team.

"Seamus!" A few of the players chorused, and peace was once more restored as Jack pulled into the motorway services.

***

Finally, by lunchtime, the coach pulled into the car park of The Dog Inn Country Manor, the plush Surrey hotel where they would be staying for the night. The players trooped into reception and waited for Molly and Marcus to book them in and collect the room keys.

"Okay boys," Molly called." Normal room shares apply unless anyone wants to swap. *Does* anyone want to swap?"

"I do." Greg Pounder called.

Molly knew what he was going to say. Being the comedy genius that he was, Greg always declared that he wanted to room share with Molly.

"Are you sure you want to say it Greg?" she asked without looking up from her list.

"No, best not eh?" Greg called back.

"Right, come and get your key cards from Marcus."

As the players milled around Marcus, Molly moved aside and sighed with relief. She was always glad once she'd got them safely booked into the hotel without losing anyone en route. She turned her own key card over in her hand. She was in room 406 on the floor above the players, so was grateful that she would get at least eight hours away from them.

"Nowhere near us then," Joe commented as he looked at Molly's card.

"What? Oh sorry, no." Molly put her hand to her neck as she felt it prickling with heat.

"That's a shame; I thought we could have watched a bit of telly together."

"Joe, you've just nearly had a go at a team mate for being disrespectful to me, now you're doing the same." Molly couldn't help but smile despite her indignation.

"What's wrong with wanting to watch Coronation Street with you?" Joe laughed at the frown that was beginning to crease Molly's forehead. "What's the matter?" he grinned.

"You know what," Molly said. "Now go to your room and have a nap like a good boy." She turned to the rest of the team. "Right boys don't forget you need to be back down here at three for your pre-match meal," Molly shouted above the chatter, disappearing into the crowd of players and away from the temptation of Joe.

***

Later that evening, the team were back at the hotel. Everyone was on a high, as not only had they won the game comfortably, but the win had taken them to the top of the Premiership. Everyone was buzzing from the win, as well as the fact that Mr Ribero had allowed the players one drink in the bar before bed.

Molly sat at the bar with Marcus, listening to them all replaying the game, exaggerating every pass, every kick and every goal.

"I don't quite remember the third goal in the same way, do you?" Marcus smiled at Molly, nodding towards a group of three or four players who were celebrating loudly.

"No, it was more of a tap in than the goal of the season that Fernando thinks it was. Anyway…" Molly sighed, jumping down from her stool. "I'm off to bed. I've had enough of this lot for one night, and it looks like Mr Ribero is ready to send them all up for the night too."

Molly and Marcus laughed as they looked at the manager who

was standing, hands on hips, watching his players. He particularly had his eye on Jimmy Cavanagh, who was dancing rather badly to the music being played in the bar.

"I'll stay and help the boss round them all up. I'll see you in the morning."

"Okay, thanks Marcus, see you in the morning."

As she walked past the crowd of players, a hand reached out and gently took her arm; it was Joe.

"You're not going to bed are you?" he asked.

Molly looked at him shyly, wondering whether he ever looked anything but gorgeous, and tonight he'd played some sensational football, scoring twice and setting Fernando up for the third. Suddenly she felt nervous talking to him, aware that the other players may be watching after the incident on the coach. She moved a few steps back.

"Yes, I'm shattered, and we've got to be back on the road by nine in the morning, so I need to get some sleep."

"The offer still stands to watch some telly together." Joe took a drink and licked his lips.

That simple movement sent Molly's blood pressure into orbit, as she thought about what how his lips and tongue used to make her feel. It was then that she knew that she had to get away from Joe. "I'd better go, see you in the morning."

"Okay" smiled Joe "that's a no then. Goodnight."

Molly turned and made her way to the elevators as quickly as possible.

***

Once back in her room, she sank onto the bed, breathing heavily. Her hands were shaking, and her heart was thundering in her ears. She folded her arms around herself and rocked gently.

"Oh shit," she whispered. "What the fuck am I going to do?"

She was done for. The little niggle was now shouting at her to listen, like an insistent child. Joe was right, she still wanted him, and she wasn't sure she had the strength to keep pushing him away. It had happened so quickly - the turnaround from wanting to push him away to now just wanting him, badly.

CHAPTER 10

♥

Molly paced her hotel room and wondered what to do. She was due to face time Rob in a few minutes, but how could she when she felt so wound up? He knew her well enough to know instantly that there was something wrong. What on earth could she possibly tell him? That she was still attracted to Joe and it was all she could do to stop herself from jumping is bones every time they met? No, she couldn't tell him that. She took a few deep breaths and then picked up her iPad ready to contact Rob. If he asked what was wrong then she'd have to think of something on the spot. She had sat down and started to prepare herself when right at that moment her phone beeped loudly to announce the arrival of a text. She was so tense with nerves that the noise almost made her fly out of her seat. She picked up her phone and saw that the text was from Rob. Molly's hand went to her mouth – Christ, could he read her mind or something? She clicked on the message.

Hi Moll having a drink in the bar then going for food so will ring you in morning instead

Typical of Rob, Molly thought – he had insisted that *she* was never late for their face time, yet because he was busy it was okay for *him* to cancel. However, knowing that she didn't have to speak to Rob flooded her with a sense of relief. She threw her phone onto the bed, kicked off her shoes and decided that a lovely long soak in the bath could only help. As she pulled her blouse out of the back of her skirt, there was a knock at the door.

She stopped, dead still, and held her breath for a few seconds. It wasn't unusual for a player to get locked out of their room and come knocking at Molly's for help, but she knew that this wasn't such a time – she had no idea how she knew, but she knew beyond doubt that it was Joe at the door.

She moved towards it and with shaking hands reached for the handle. The knock came again; it was quiet and coaxing, daring her to open the door. Molly's resolve was weakening, but she knew that if she opened it she would be passing a point from which she could never return. She quietly backed away from the door, holding her breath, hoping that Joe would think she was asleep. The knock came again, this time a little more insistent. Molly bit at her thumbnail and lowered herself onto the edge of the bed. She needed Joe to go back to his own room, because she knew if he didn't the craving she had for him would over power any feelings of common sense.

"I know you're in there Molly. Just open the door, please." Joe's voice was low, but pleading.

Molly covered her face with her hands, and groaned quietly.

"Go away Joe," she cried.

"No, I won't. Molly you want me as much as I want you, you know you do. Please open the door."

"Joe, please don't do this. Go back to your room."

There was silence for a few seconds, and Molly held her breath.

Finally Joe spoke, his voice full of emotion. "I love you; have never stopped loving you and I think you feel the same way. I can't be without you anymore, my heart aches when I look at you and all I want to do is kiss you and hold you. Please Molly, you're all I can think about."

Molly's breathing was heavy, and her hands were shaking as she stood up and walked to the door. Placing her palm flat against the dark wood, Molly took a deep breath and paused momentarily before taking two steps back into the room.

"Molly, please."

Suddenly anxious to come face to face with him, Molly moved forward. She snatched at the handle and pulled the door open.

Molly's resolve didn't just weaken, but absolutely crumbled as she pulled Joe into the room by his belt loop. Their mouths crushed against each other as Joe landed hard against her. He kicked the door shut behind him as Molly entwined her fingers in his hair and kissed him hungrily, marvelling at the sweetness of his taste. Desperate for each other, their passion soared fast and high as Joe reached up under her blouse, his fingers gently caressing her soft skin making Molly moan with pleasure into his mouth. His kisses became more insistent as he cupped Molly's buttocks and pulled her against his erection. Thinking only of the tingling sensation between her legs, Molly put her hands behind her back, and unzipped her skirt, letting it fall to the floor. She started clawing at Joe's belt as she tried to unbuckle it. As soon as she succeeded, Joe pushed his jeans down his thighs with one hand, all the time keeping up his kisses, holding tightly onto Molly. Finally, he pulled back and looked at her standing in front of him in just her blouse, lace underwear and hold up stockings.

"What's wrong?" Molly looked scared as her finger tips gently touched his cheek. "I thought you wanted this."

"Of course I do, more than anything. I just want to be sure that you do. Do you?"

Molly nodded, her fingers trembling as she moved them to the hem of his t-shirt. "I know it's wrong," she whispered hoarsely, "but I want you Joe, I need you." She pulled Joe's top over his head, and then slowly ran her hands across his bare chest, before dropping her head to lay gentle kisses along his collarbone and up his neck.

Joe, unable to hold back any longer, practically tore the buttons off Molly's blouse and deftly unfastened her bra. Her breasts sprang free of the fabric and Joe ran his finger along their soft curves, stopping at Molly's nipple that instantly hardened as he circled it slowly. Molly moaned gently and clung to Joe's shoulders as he placed his hands under her bottom, encouraging Molly to wrap her legs around his waist, kissing her constantly as though it would kill him if he ever stopped.

"I want you now," Molly breathed into his ear.

"Christ Molly," Joe groaned. He laid her down on the bed. "You're beautiful, you know that don't you?" He stood at the end of the bed gazing at Molly, his desire for her evident.

Joe pulled off his jockey shorts and leaned down, slowly peeling away the rest of Molly's underwear and her stockings, stopping now and then to place gentle kisses on her thighs and stomach. When they were both completely naked, he knelt down on the bed between Molly's legs.

"Are you sure?"

Molly bit her bottom lip and nodded, pulling Joe to her. She shifted her hips up to meet him, and taking her lead, Joe laced his fingers with Molly's and slowly slid inside her.

"Molly," he whispered. "I love you."

"I love you too," she cried, her body burning with pleasure.

***

As birdsong started to fill the early morning darkness outside the window, and Joe's soft, rhythmic breath blew against Molly's shoulder as he slept, she brushed away the tears of guilt that lay on her cheeks. She felt sick in her stomach, and her heart felt as though it was in a crushing grip, thinking about what she'd done to Rob. Having sex with Joe was a terrible thing to do, but spending the whole night with him made it seem a whole lot worse; it wasn't just a moment of madness. Molly drew in a ragged breath and turned her head to look at Joe – she let out a small sob; it was real, it had happened and he was in her bed. They had spent most of the last seven hours reacquainting their bodies with each other, revelling in their mutual need and desire, and it was as though the last six years had never happened; that they'd never been apart. Molly hadn't wanted to think about whom Joe had shared his bed with since they had been apart, but he'd obviously used the time to improve his expertise. They'd always been passionate, enjoying some incredible sex, but last night had surpassed everything that had ever gone before.

Molly lifted her head to look at the time on the clock next to the bed: 5:30. She sighed, wiped her eyes and then gently touched Joe's tanned bicep. Part of her didn't want him to go, part of her felt happy about what had happened, but she had to be alone to come to terms with what she'd done, and to figure out what she did next.

"Joe," she whispered, shifting herself around to face him.

Joe stirred and slowly opened his eyes, smiling at her sleepily. "Morning beautiful." He kissed the tip of her nose, and gave her a smile.

Molly gasped remembering it as his contented, post-sex smile; it was heavy eyes and sleepy. Instinctively she touched his cheek.

"Hmm, fancy a replay of last night?"

She closed her eyes - maybe if she couldn't see him the desire to say yes would go away.

"You have to go Joe, we shouldn't have done this." She tried to get free from his arms, but Joe held her tightly.

"Hey, what's wrong?" He gently took a strand of her hair and wound it around his fingers.

"This, this is wrong." Molly pushed her palm against his chest. "What we did is wrong."

"Don't say that, there was nothing wrong about last night. Everything was exactly how it should've been - perfect."

"Please, don't make this any more difficult than it already is. I've done something terrible, and what's worse I knew exactly what I was doing." Molly covered her face with her hand and let out a sob.

"Hey, hey, come on, don't get upset, please." Joe gently took Molly's hand away from her face, and kissed her palm.

Molly stared at him wide-eyed. "I feel like shit Joe, I can't even blame it on drink, I knew from the moment you knocked on that door what would happen, how deceitful it was, yet I still let you in."

"We're both to blame, I guessed that you were struggling being around me, and despite promising to stay away, I didn't – I couldn't."

"But you're not engaged are you? I bloody am!" she cried, snatching her hand away from Joe's. "And, what on earth are you going to tell Jimmy, he'll wonder why you weren't in your room all night?"

Joe shifted slightly in the bed, allowing Molly room to sit up. As the covers dropped to reveal her naked body, she suddenly felt awkward and reached across for her blouse that was next to the bed. She pulled it on, fastening just enough buttons to cover her breasts.

Joe looked at her, his eyes full of sadness.

"Jimmy won't be a problem," he said quietly. "He always takes a sleeping tablet when we're away, so when I left he was deep in the land of nod. He'll still be fast asleep now, which means I can sneak back in and he'll never even know I wasn't there."

Joe moved into a sitting position, so that his face was level with Molly's

"What's changed sweetheart? Last night was amazing, so why are you being like this?"

Molly was silent for a few seconds, while she picked at an invisible thread on the duvet. Finally she looked at him.

"Because I should have kept away from you, I shouldn't have even wanted to share the same airspace as you, but I didn't did I? Oh no what did I do? I let you into my room, and I hate myself for it."

"Moll, we both know it's not that simple."

Molly clutched at the duvet with both hands. "Yes it is, and what about Rob? What's going to happen when he finds out?"

"He doesn't have to find out."

"What we just carry on as though this never happened? What was it then, a quick shag for old time's sake, is that it?"

Joe sat forward and knelt in front of Molly, grabbing hold of her hands.

"Don't you dare think that, you know that's not true. I love you more than anything, or anyone I've ever loved my whole life and I would never do that to you, and you damn well know it."

As Molly dropped her eyes from Joe's intense stare, her body gave an involuntary shiver as she caught sight of his naked body and his morning arousal. Quickly she darted her eyes back to his face.

"This is such a mess," she cried. "My head is mush and all I can think about is how I've betrayed him, we're supposed to be getting married."

Joe picked up Molly's hand and laced his fingers with hers. "I'm not asking you to make any decisions now, because I understand how difficult this is for you, and I'll accept whatever you decide, but you have to know I want you with me always, because I love you."

Large tears started to roll down Molly's cheeks, as the enormity of what she'd done and what she had to face, hit her once more. She'd done exactly the same thing that for the last six years she'd hated Joe for. She'd cheated and betrayed the man she was getting married to.

Joe's thumbs gently swept away the tears. "Don't cry Molly, please. I'll never mention this again, and I promise to stay away from you if that's what you want."

"No," Molly gasped, realising she couldn't stand that. "I don't want that, but I feel so awful about Rob. I've cheated on him, and I hate myself for it, it's just that I love you, probably never stopped."

"I feel sorry for Rob, I do, but you know what I'm going to say – leave him so we can be together…but only when you're ready."

Molly looked at Joe, and with her lip quivering and her eyes welling with tears, she let herself be pulled to his chest.

"We'll work it out, I promise," he whispered.

Molly didn't answer, but let her tears fall silently, as she clung to Joe, knowing that nothing would ever be the same again.

CHAPTER 11

♥

Molly made her way nervously into the reception. After lots of talking and crying, Joe had finally left her room at 6:45 am, and although he'd sent her a text to say he'd seen no one on the way back to his room and that Jimmy was still sleeping soundly, Molly was dreading the thought that someone might have realised what was going on, particularly as her eyes were a little puffy from crying earlier..

"Morning, sleep well?" Marcus asked, walking into the reception area, dragging his overnight bag behind him.

"Brilliantly," Molly replied, a little over-brightly. "Really, really well, I was in bed within ten minutes of being back in my room, and you?"

"Hmm not bad, I hope the rest of our party are just as perky. I hate it when they're grumpy, especially when we're on a coach."

"I know what you mean, but..." In the distance, Molly could see Joe, sitting in the bar with a couple of other players; the sight of him was terribly distracting, and she couldn't help but allow a small smile to touch her lips as she recalled the night they'd had in her bed.

"But?" said Marcus, raising his eyebrows expectantly.

"Oh, yeah...but they won so they should be okay."

"You alright?" Marcus asked.

"Yes, sorry I just thought I saw someone from the press in the bar near the boys. Anyway, let's get them all checked on the coach and back home."

***

The come down from the euphoria of winning the previous evening meant that everyone was pretty much shattered, so the journey home was much quieter than the one the day before. Joe had feigned a headache and insisted that he sit near the front where he could be quiet. The others didn't realise that all Joe actually wanted to do was to be near Molly. For the two of them though, it was a horrendous journey as they were so near to each other without being able to touch or speak about what had happened.

Half way home, Molly's phone rang; it was Rob. Molly looked around at Joe, but he was sat back in his seat with his eyes closed and arms folded across his chest. She thought about dropping the call, but she had to appear as normal as possible to Rob.

"Hiya," she answered.

"Hi, sorry I didn't get to speak to you last night."

"It's okay, how was your night?"

"Good thanks, we had a few drinks in the bar and then went for a curry. So, what did you do last night?"

Molly's emotions were at odds with each other – she felt exhilarated from what she did last night, and hugging such a delicious secret was exciting, but there was also a suffocating fear rolling around in the pit of her stomach.

"Not much," she replied. "Just a bath and an early night. The manager let the lads have one drink, so I left them to it, although I'm sure most of them had more than one."

"Oh okay. Look, I'd better go, we're just on a break from yet another riveting talk," Rob laughed.

"Okay, I'll see you on Friday. What time will you be back?" Somewhere in the back of her mind she was trying to figure out how long she'd have with Joe without having to face reality.

"We finish at three and it takes about three hours from Glasgow, so sixish I would think, unless I stop on the way. Why, will you be waiting for me with just an apron on?"

Molly laughed but dodged the question. "Okay, see you about six on Friday then. Take care."

"Will do, oh and Molly if you don't fancy wearing an apron a nice little mini skirt will do, in fact anything other than your old maid knee length ones."

Molly feigned a laugh. "Okay, bye."

Molly ended the call and hugged the phone to her chest and wondered what the hell she thought she was playing at. Now she'd spoken to Rob her throat was dry, and her palms were sweating, and she was reminded of the fear that she'd had as a child, when she'd got lost in town while shopping with her Mum. That day though, she'd been found by a lovely lady in Marks and Spencer, and had been given a biscuit and some orange juice while she waited for her Mum; whereas now no one could help her, not even Joe, and certainly not her Mum – she had to sort this one out herself.

**

When they arrived back at the ground, Mr Ribero announced that after they'd watched a DVD of the previous night's game, the players could have the rest of the day off. So, Molly decided, she and Marcus could have some time off too. She checked in at the office first, to make sure that Katie and Rosetta were okay and as everything was running smoothly then went to see Becky; the one person whom she knew wouldn't judge her for what she'd done.

Becky no longer worked at the club, and had finished after having her first baby just over two months earlier. She'd stopped chasing after footballers when she met her husband, Pete, and her life was now the epitome of domesticity, and she felt infinitely happier than when she spent her time chasing after men who only wanted a quick fling.

"Hi, come in," said Becky, pulling Molly into a hug. "Kettle's on."

As soon as Molly had phoned to say she was calling round, Becky knew something serious must have happened if she was taking the time off work, despite the fact she was probably owed it tenfold.

A few minutes later, both of them were on the sofa cradling a hot mug of tea each.

"Are you sure it's okay me coming round? I'm not stopping you doing something with Harry, am I?" Molly took a sip of her tea and glanced at the sleeping baby in the Moses basket next to them.

"No, all he does at the moment is eat and sleep. I'll have to feed him in a couple of hours though, he's just had one feed before you got here. So," Becky said pausing to rub Molly's arm gently. "What's wrong?"

Molly rubbed at her eyes, and tried to hold back the tears that she felt stinging.

She sighed, there was no point delaying it, she may as well come straight out with it. "I've slept with Joe," she blurted out.

"Okay," Becky nodded thoughtfully, showing no surprise "And how do you feel about it?"

Molly placed her palm against her stomach. "Sick."

"Do you regret it?"

Molly shook her head slowly. "No, and that's one of the reasons why I feel sick. It just felt right, as though that's how life should be. It was amazing, he's amazing. It was always good before, but now..."

Becky's mouth twitched into a smile. "He's an athlete Molly, I wouldn't expect anything less. Plus he's one of the world's most fanciable men; you don't get that title by looking like Shrek. So, how did it happen?"

"He came to my room and like an idiot I let him in."

"Well it was bound to happen sooner or later, so even if you'd managed to stay away from him last night, I doubt you'd have lasted much longer."

Molly frowned. "I have tried to stay away from him you know."

"That's the point Moll; you had to try to stay away, so you obviously knew something could happen. As soon as you told me that you'd asked Marcus to deal with him, I knew you still had feelings for him." Becky leaned forward and squeezed Molly's hand. "Moll, he was your first love, anyone would find it difficult."

"But I should have tried harder, I should've thought about Rob."

"Yes you should, but come let's be honest; things aren't right with him are they? You're as excited about the wedding as a group of Hells Angels at a knitting circle. It's only a few months away, so what are you going to do?"

"I don't know, I haven't even thought about the wedding, but I do love Rob."

"Really, are you sure about that, have you ever really loved him? And what about Joe, how do you feel about him?"

"I love Joe, probably never stopped, but he cheated on me, and I'm not sure I'll ever trust or forgive him." Molly let out a hollow laugh. "Hah, how stupid is that after what I've just done?"

"Well it is a little hypocritical, but this is Joe we're talking about, however, missy you've not answered my question about Rob." Becky looked at Molly expectantly, but no reply was forthcoming. "Okay, do you want me to be honest?"

Molly nodded.

"He was always second prize. I know that he helped you to trust men again, and I do believe you did love him, but not for a long time. You told me almost a year ago when you first got engaged, albeit when you were drunk, that you were having doubts and now, added to that, Joe is back."

Molly ran a finger around the rim of her mug, staring down at the rust coloured liquid. Becky was right; she had been having doubts about her relationship with Rob for a long time. She had already begun to accept that he wasn't 'the one', she had loved him because he had helped to mend her broken heart, but love born from gratitude wasn't the same as deep, heartfelt love. You couldn't build a lifetime on it.

"So, how did you leave things with Joe?" Becky interrupted her thoughts.

A deep crimson coloured Molly's cheeks. "We argued for ages about it, but I couldn't say no, Becky. I tried, I told him it was wrong and we had to stay away from each other, but I don't think I can."

"Are you going to carry on seeing each other?"

Molly chewed at the inside of her mouth and shrugged.

"He agreed to give me some space, but I know if he rings me I'll be there like a shot. I know it's wrong, but being back in his arms, was so…so fantastic and safe. Shit, I can't believe I'm doing this. Do you think I'm a bitch?"

"No, you're not. I'm not condoning what you're doing, and I'm not judging you either, but you haven't half got yourself into a bloody mess."

"I know and I don't know what to do, I'm so confused?"

"Well don't do anything yet, I mean don't make any decisions. Okay you had one night of amazing sex with your first love, and like I said, he's always been the one, but don't use him as an excuse to leave Rob. If you want to leave Rob, then do it, but try and stay away from Joe until then"

"Easier said than done, I have to deal with him, that's my job, and now they've erected a bloody fifty foot billboard picture of him right opposite my office window, apart from which he's like a bloody drug, I don't think I can stay away."

"Pull the blinds down, although if it's that one of him in his undies I can see why it'd be a distraction."

"Becky, that's my… that's the man I've just had sex with you're talking about." Molly poked Becky in her side.

"Ooh you nearly said my man then didn't you? This is going to be difficult whatever you decide, you do know that don't you?"

"Yes," Molly sighed. "I do, and I honestly haven't got a clue what to do. I love Joe, but there's also the fact that he cheated on me, well it broke me Becky, you know that. I don't know whether I can get past it, no matter how hypocritical that may be."

Becky smiled warmly as she pulled Molly into a hug. "I know, which is why I'm always here for you, no matter what you decide to do."

"Well that's good," Molly sighed. "Because I have a feeling that if I choose to be with Joe, my parents are going to disown me and may never speak to me again."

CHAPTER 12

♥

After spending a couple of hours chatting with Becky, and cuddling baby Harry, Molly went home, fully determined to put some space between her and Joe. Even though last night had been phenomenal, every time she thought of Rob she felt sick and ready to burst into tears. Even though their relationship had been faltering for a while, she didn't want to hurt him, so decided to give herself some time to think carefully about the situation.

The only problem was that Joe didn't seem to be on the same wavelength, and just as she was getting undressed to take a shower, he sent Molly a text message.

Hi beautiful been thinking about you all day. I know we agreed that I'd give you space but any chance we can meet up? Sorry if I'm pressuring you but I can't get you out of my mind xxxx

Molly sighed, Joe was taking a tremendous risk texting her a message like that. She hadn't told him that Rob was away, so for all he knew Rob could have picked up her phone and seen the message. She sat on the edge of the bed, staring at the text and biting her thumb nail, after a couple of minutes she started to smile as her memory replayed her night with Joe and the thought of seeing him and doing it all again sent a shiver over her body.

She hesitated for merely a few seconds before typing.

You promised but you always were persistent!! I shouldn't but just imagining that cute little smile of yours makes me do stupid things. Where and when? Xxx

A few seconds later her phone beeped a return text.

Going to look at an apartment – fancy coming with me? Can pick you up from work at 5 to make it look official xxx

Molly replied.

Not at work took afternoon off, but might be a good idea anyway so it looks like business. Meet you on car park at 5 xxx

Joe's reply was a smiley face and three more kisses.

At five, having quickly checked her appearance, Molly jumped out of her car as soon as she spotted Joe's pulling onto the car park. The February evening was cold, and the wind took her breath away as she walked towards his car. She walked sedately, in case anyone was watching, but inside she was running, desperate to be in his arms again, all thoughts of Rob locked away in a drawer at the back of her brain.

"Hi" she said breathlessly as she jumped into the passenger seat of Joe's car.

"Christ" said Joe, his eyes roaming hungrily over her, "you look gorgeous." He leaned in for a kiss, but Molly quickly put her hand out.

"No, not here, someone might be watching."

"Shit, sorry I should've thought. You just look so bloody beautiful."

"Gorgeous and beautiful, thank you." Molly smiled, with a blush to her cheeks.

"Let's go and look at this apartment." Joe thrust the car into gear and drove away from the club.

***

All the way to the apartment, Joe clutched Molly's hand and

continually stroked the back of it with his thumb. They barely spoke, just glad to be with each other, and enjoying the electric anticipation of what was undoubtedly going to happen.

Just over half an hour later they pulled up outside a gated apartment development, set in beautifully manicured grounds. There were two, white, three storey buildings, and along the spot lit drive, through some large, mature trees, a huge glass conservatory, lit with fairy lights, twinkled in the early evening darkness.

"Wow," breathed Molly, "it's beautiful."

Joe picked up a small key fob from the dashboard, and pointed it at the gates that then swept open.

"I know, it's only six apartments and the top floor ones are 3 bedroom penthouses." Joe pointed through the trees. "That conservatory up there, that houses the swimming pool and gym, and behind that, which you can't see from here, is a private fishing lake. So, did I do well in finding it?" Joe started to laugh, remembering their day of apartment hunting.

"Yes, you did." Molly put her head on one side and frowned at Joe. "Did you already have this up your sleeve when we spent the day looking?"

"No, I swear I only heard about it yesterday," he protested.

"So why are you laughing?" Molly swatted a hand at Joe's arm.

"I'm just remembering what a bad mood you were in, that's all."

"If you say so. Come on then, show me what you're spending, ooh...half a million on?"

Joe started to laugh again. "God you're good. Not quite half a million, just under. It's the show penthouse that we're going to see, and it's fully furnished so I have an option to buy all the furniture as well if I want to. They've only been finished a month, and there's only one sold so far, some pop star who's bought it as third home, or something just as ridiculous," he looked at Molly and twinkled a smile, a look that sent her stomach on a rollercoaster ride. "Which means that it's just us here tonight."

"No estate agent then?" she asked, her groin started pulsating with excitement.

Joe shook his head. "I'm a famous footballer. They trust me and I told them I was bringing my parents to have a look around after a meal out, so wasn't sure what time it would be. Plus, they know where to go if I trash the place."

"We'd better be good then," Molly replied, knowing that was probably the last thing they were going to be.

As Joe drove up the drive, Molly gazed at his profile and felt her body react – heat pooled between her thighs and her breasts swelled. She was amazed how her levels of desire sky-rocketed just by looking at him, but she was also scared because she knew that she was falling deeper and deeper in love with him again.

***

"Oh. My. God." Molly lay back on the Egyptian cotton sheets, breathing heavily as she came down from her orgasm.

Half an hour earlier, Joe had let them into the luxurious penthouse, and within seconds they were ripping each other's clothes off, desperately looking for one of the bedrooms.

"Fucking hell Moll that was just…fuck." Joe, unable to find any words worthy of what they'd just experienced kissed Molly gently as he traced a pattern up and down her arm with his fingers.

"Mmmmm." She moaned in appreciation, barely able to speak, but with a wide smile on her face.

"I agree." Joe lay back onto the bed and pulled her into his arms.

After a few minutes, he broke the silence. "I know I said I wouldn't pressurise you, but we could do this all the time you know," he said, raking his fingers through her long, dark hair.

"I know," Molly whispered. "And I know I have to make a decision, but I can't just yet, it's difficult with the wedding so near. Can we just change the subject?"

"No, we can't, the fact that the wedding is so near is exactly why you should start thinking about what you're going to do. It'll be worse the longer you leave it, and the closer to the wedding you get; that is of course if I'm the winner."

"Joe! I know I have to make a choice, but you make it sound like a race or something."

"Hey," Joe turned over on his side to face Molly. "I'm not trying to make a joke about it, I know it's going to be hard, and I know that you aren't doing this lightly."

"Honesty, I'm not, it's just that I don't want to hurt either of you. God, I'm such a bitch, the kind of person I've always hated. I'm like those pathetic, horrible people on daytime television who always come out with the bullshit, 'but I loved them both.'" Molly mimicked a whiney voice. "Urgh, I hate the person I'm becoming, and I hate you for coming back here." She dug her finger in Joe's ribs, making him cry out.

"Ouch, don't injure me, the boss will kill you."

"Hmm and Rob will kill us both if he finds out." Molly smiled at Joe, but inside felt dismal and wretched. "Seriously Joe, this is really hard for me, I'm not that sort of person who cheats …well I wasn't, now look at me. "

"I don't want to share you Moll, so I'm not going to give you an easy way out of this and just have an affair with you."

Molly pushed the hair from Joe's eyes. "I know, and I couldn't do that anyway, although isn't that exactly what this is?"

"Hmm, I suppose. Listen, just for tonight, let's pretend that no one else exists, and we live here." Joe pulled Molly further into his arms and kissed her gently.

"I just hope the estate agent doesn't turn up with any more prospective buyers." Molly started to giggle, realising that it was a terrible thing to do having sex on the "show" furniture.

Joe read her mind and laughed. "It's shameful isn't it, having sex on a viewing? I'll have to buy the place now, and the bed."

"Well," Molly whispered close to Joe's ear. "If you're buying the bed, we may as well make as much use of it as possible." She trailed a finger up Joe's thigh, and let it linger near his groin. "Ooh," she giggled, pulling the duvet over them both. "Nice to see we're on the same wave length."

CHAPTER 13

♥

They spent almost three, passionate hours together at the penthouse, and before they left they made sure that everything was back to normal, doing their best to make sure no one would realise the bed had been taken for the test drive of its life.

On the way back to the club, they talked nonstop about everything; Joe's restaurant, Molly's job, her sister's love life, Joe's parents, but avoided the subjects of Molly cheating on Rob and Joe cheating on Molly; yet both issues were like two big, fat, white elephants sat cross legged in the back of the car listening in.

As they finally pulled up on the club car park, Joe turned off the engine and let out a sigh.

"Here we are then, time to say goodnight. Are you sure you don't want to go somewhere else for a while?" Joe gave Molly a thin lipped smile, knowing what the answer would be.

Molly shook her head. "Where would we go? We'd get spotted at your hotel and neither of us wants to be front or back page news. As for my place, well obviously that's a no no."

"Christ no, that wouldn't be right. Anyway, where does Rob think you are, did you say you were out looking at apartments with me?"

"No, he's not home; he's on a course this week…oh shit!" Molly shot a hand to her mouth. "I was supposed to face time him at eight o'clock, what time is it now?"

"Ten to nine," Joe answered, looking at his watch. "Just say you got tied up with one of the players." A small smile briefly touched his lips.

"That's not funny Joe. Oh God, I need to go, I'll tell him I was at Becky's and lost track of time."

"Becky who you used to hang around with? Blimey how is she?"

"Joe!" Molly shouted, leaning down to pick up her handbag from the foot-well. "I don't have time to reminisce, I have to go. I'll speak to you tomorrow, somehow."

"Okay, and maybe tomorrow night we can go somewhere …if you're on your own."

Molly nodded as she searched in her bag for her keys.

"We'll talk tomorrow Thanks for tonight, it was lovely." She smiled at Joe and squeezed his hand. "I would kiss you goodnight, but someone might be watching."

"I know, night beautiful, I'll see you tomorrow."

Molly got out of the car and walked across the car park, desperately forcing herself not to run back, and give Joe a long lingering kiss goodnight.

***

"Don't worry" said Rob, "It's not a problem. I had some work to do for tomorrow anyway."

The fact that Rob was being so reasonable added further weight to Molly's already guilt laden heart.

"You do look tired, Rob. I hope you're not working too hard, or partying too hard, for that matter."

Even via the screen on her iPad, Molly could see his eyes were ringed with dark circles.

"No, Mother I'm not partying too hard, I promise. There's a lot of work to do in the evenings, so just trust me to behave," he replied snippily. "How's Becky anyway, is she still breast feeding, you should've face timed me from there if she is, give me chance to look at a decent pair for a change."

"You are a shit at times, do you know that?" Molly used all her self will not to simply reach across and disconnect him.

"What? For God's sake, it was only a joke. You're always saying yourself you wished your boobs were bigger."

"You shouldn't be joking about other women's boobs, especially Becky's." Molly chose to ignore the comment about her own breasts. "I'm going to go, I'm knackered and you've got work to do."

"Oh don't be like that, it was a bloody joke."

Molly felt tears of anger brimming in her eyes.

"I know, you said." Molly coughed to hide the waver in her voice. "Anyway, don't work too hard, okay."

"Okay, I'll speak to you tomorrow; hopefully you'll be in a better mood."

"Maybe," said Molly, "Night." She smiled weakly and waited for him to disappear from her screen, before turning off the iPad.

Molly flopped back against the sofa and covered her face with her hands. Why did she let him get to her like that, or was he right? Had she simply lost her sense of humour? Perhaps the problems they'd been having were all her fault. Maybe she was being too sensitive about his comments and too snobby about his choice of friends and maybe their relationship was more real than hers and Joe's would ever be. She and Joe had been nubile youngsters brimming with confidence of what life had to offer them, and now, six years on, they were fooling themselves that life could be like that again. The tears that had pricked her lashes a few moments ago now started falling freely down her cheeks, as a tightness started to crush at her heart.

"What the hell am I going to do?" she cried to the empty room.

She pulled her knees up to her chest as her sobbing got louder and the pain she felt hit harder. She thought of Rob and how good they had been together, perhaps if she tried they could be that good again, she had loved him, but Joe...well Joe was someone she couldn't stay away from. He'd been in her heart all this time but she just hadn't wanted to admit it and now he was back it was impossible to ignore how he made her feel, or how she felt about him. Molly knew that if she'd been giving someone else advice on the same situation she would've said that she couldn't possibly want Rob if it had been that easy for Joe to get her into bed. When she thought about Rob it was obvious that the relationship was all but over. Her time with Joe showed her that life with Rob wasn't what it should be – what it had been once. On the face of it, it was simple: she *had* to decide between them, and soon. It was a difficult choice between what had been and what could be.

CHAPTER 14

It was Friday evening and Molly was waiting in anticipation for Rob to arrive home. At the beginning of their relationship, after any time apart, the anticipation would have been about the fantastic sex they would have once they were back in each other's arms, but tonight Molly's feelings were totally different. She could never be intimate with Rob again. She'd made her decision; tomorrow she knew she would be breaking his heart.

***

The previous afternoon, she'd told Marcus and Katie that she was going apartment hunting with Joe and his agent, so if anyone spotted them they would have a valid reason to be together – the idea of Joe's agent going along had been a spur of the moment thing that seemed pretty viable.

Joe drove and refused to tell her where they were going, but eventually she realised that they were heading for Joe's restaurant. When they arrived the street was deserted, it was early evening, just after the shops had closed, so luckily no one was around.

"What are we doing here?" Molly asked as she unbuckled her seatbelt.

"You'll see," Joe said, giving her a dazzling smile. "Come on."

Molly followed Joe into the restaurant, and as she as she

stepped inside, realised why they were there.

A table had been laid for two people and in the middle were a dozen tea lights twinkling in the darkness. Around the room were more candles, of varying shapes and sizes, all burning away brightly. Music played quietly in the background, and as she listened Molly felt an emotional tug at her heart.

"It's our song," she gasped, remembering the nights they'd spent listening to Chasing Cars on repeat. "I haven't listened to it since…"

"Oh shit," Joe cried moving towards the iPad that was on the bar. "I'm sorry I didn't think."

"No, Joe, please leave it on." Molly caught Joe by the hand and pulled him to her. "It's a lovely thought, and you know how Snow Patrol always got me in the mood." Snaking her arms around Joe's neck, Molly kissed him slowly and deeply, arching herself towards him.

"God I love you," Joe whispered, gently pulling himself from Molly's embrace. "I never stopped. I just wanted tonight to be perfect, and I'm sorry if I messed up by playing the song."

"Honestly you didn't, and this all looks gorgeous. You've gone to a lot of trouble, but how did you manage to light all the candles before we got here, the whole place could've gone up in smoke?"

"Don't worry, Luna and Gabi were here, they left about ten minutes ago, and there should be something to eat for us as well in that basket over there." Joe nodded towards a large wicker hamper over by the bar.

"They know about me then?" Molly asked, surprised that Joe's business partners knew about their situation.

"Of course they do. They've had to listen to me talk about you for hours on end." He noticed the fearful look in Molly's eyes. "Don't worry, they know the situation, and anyway who are they going to tell? They don't know anyone here, and I promise they won't sell their story." He meant it as a joke, but Joe realised as soon as he said it that Molly wasn't amused. "God there I go again, messing things up, I'm such an idiot at times."

Molly's stomach flipped when she saw the worry etched across his handsome face. She knew she couldn't be mad at him. "Forget about it, let's have a look and see what's in the basket."

With the excitement of a child at Christmas, Molly pulled Joe with her in the direction of the hamper, knelt down and carefully pushed up its lid.

"Oh my god," she said, staring into the basket with wide eyes. "Look at all that food, *and* Champagne *and* strawberries dipped in chocolate. Did Luna make all this?" she asked, getting to her feet and carrying the basket to the table.

Joe nodded proudly. "Yep, she's an amazing chef. Spain's loss is our gain. She's made paella, chorizo salad, and a frittata, which officially is Italian I know, but she does such an amazing job of it we thought it would be wrong to leave it out just for the sake of a thousand miles or so."

"What's this?" Molly pulled out a plate of food, wrapped in pink tissue paper and tied on top with a pink bow.

"Open it and see." Joe stroked her cheek gently, his bright eyes watching her face closely. Gently Molly pulled at the tiny bow and gasped as the layer of tissue paper unfurled itself to reveal a plated pie. On it, made of pastry, were the words "I Love You".

"Is this what I think it is?" she asked, clutching at Joe's arm.

"Yes it is. I know it's a bit cheesy, pardon the pun, but I know how much you love it," he smiled. "It's not one of my mum's admittedly, but Luna makes a mean cheese and onion pie as well."

"Oh Joe, thank you so much. This is all so lovely and thoughtful."

Molly caught hold of the edges on Joe's jacket and pulled him to her, kissing him gently.

"I really ought to thank you properly, so how can I do that?" she asked dropping a kiss on Joe's neck while pulling his jacket off. "What can possibly repay you for all of this?"

Joe held his head back and groaned as Molly continued kissing up his neck and along his jawline, while pulling his shirt out of his jeans. She slowly unbuttoned it and ran her hands along his taut stomach and up to his shoulders before pushing his shirt down his arms, and pulling it over his hands. She then started to drop little kisses along his chest and shoulders before moving behind him and kissing him across the top of his back.

"Just say when I've thanked you enough, won't you?" she whispered.

Coiling her arms around Joe's waist, Molly unbuttoned his jeans and then slowly and purposefully unzipped them, while she nibbled at his ear. Joe groaned as she then slipped her finger into the waistband of his jockey shorts, and ran it along his stomach, her nail scratching gently across his skin.

As Joe's erection pushed against his underwear, he took Molly's hand and started kiss from her wrist up to the crook of her arm, she moaned quietly as the touch of his lips on her sensitive skin sent her on fire. Then tracing a pattern with his tongue, back along her arm to her wrist, Joe drew her around to face him. He slowly lifted the hem of her t-shirt, pulling it over her head and throwing it to the floor. Molly's long, dark waves were now pulled to one side, exposing the smooth silkiness of her neck and shoulder, allowing Joe to run a finger slowly down them. He admired the swell of her full breasts in her black lace bra, and cupped them gently, feeling her hard nipples through the lace. With the blood pounding in her ears as his touch sent her senses reeling, Molly pushed her head backwards to reveal more of her neck. As he kissed up from her throat, Joe lifted his hands and pulled the straps from Molly's bra down her arms, allowing her breasts to escape. Molly reached behind her and unfastened the clasps and let it slide to the floor. Her hair had fallen forward and was now covering her chest, so Joe swept it back and dropped his mouth to circle her nipple, making her cry out in ecstasy.

She clung to Joe's shoulders gently pushing him away from her so she could look into his eyes. "I want you now, *please*, Joe."

Their desire overtook them, and suddenly they were tearing at the remainder of each other's clothes, discarding them as quickly as possible. Joe pulled a chair out from the table and sat down, with Molly's hand in his. She took his lead and sat astride him. . "I love you so much," he whispered, gazing at her face. "Whatever you decide always remember that."

He dragged his thumb slowly across Molly's full lips while his other hand moved up her leg toward the apex of her thigh. "You are so bloody beautiful."

"Christ Joe," she murmured, desire prickling at her skin. "Now, *please*."

He lifted his hips, and gently guided himself inside her, eliciting a soft moan from Molly. Joe gently nipped at her breasts while she raked her fingers through his hair, curving herself into his body as they both moved in a slow, sensual rhythm, each thrust bonding them together. Joe swept his hands slowly down Molly's body and then, taking hold of her hips, pulled her closer to him, burying himself deeper inside her. Molly dug her fingers into Joe's back, clinging to him, following his rhythm. With every kiss and touch their desire increased, their pace quickened, their breathing became heavier, their bodies, fused together, became hotter, tenser, until finally, unable to hold back any longer, they both let out a cry of ecstasy, and collapsed, trembling in each other's arms.

Molly rested her head on Joe's shoulder as she breathed heavily, a light perspiration glistening over her olive skin.

"That was amazing," she said. Her mouth found Joe's and she kissed him tenderly, her skin still tingling.

Joe hugged Molly tightly to his chest and sighed.

Finally, he spoke. "I can't lose you again, Moll. Doesn't this prove how much we are supposed to be together? That was more than just sex, and you know it."

Molly's eyes filled with tears. "I know" she replied. "And I know I have to speak to Rob and I will, but not tomorrow, I'll do it on Saturday when I get home after the match. I can't do it on his first night home, and once he knows he might try to cause trouble and you've got a game to play. Are you okay with that?"

Joe nodded. "Yes, if that's what you want, I don't want to pressure you."

"You're not pressuring me. Deep down I've always known it

would come to this, but I just couldn't admit it because of what happened...you know with *her*." Molly lowered her head, unable to look at Joe.

He placed his hand under her chin and lifted it until she was looking into his eyes.

"I swear to you Molly, I didn't cheat on you. I admit I was at a party where she was, that was the room I was photographed coming out of, but nothing happened between me and her, or me and anyone else for that matter."

Molly nodded slowly and bit her bottom lip. "Okay," she said. "I believe you."

"I have never and will never lie to you, and I will make sure that every day of your life you realise how much I adore and love you, okay?"

"Okay" said Molly again. "You've convinced me. So, shall we get some of that food now? I could kill for a piece of that pie."

Joe let out a laugh. "Okay, let's eat, and then maybe later you can thank me again."

***

As Molly recalled the previous night with Joe, she felt her body start to respond to memory of the pleasure he'd given her. After they'd eaten, they'd talked about things they would do in the future, when Molly should move into his apartment, the holidays that they would go on, places they would visit, they talked about everything before finally making love once more in the fading candlelight. As she remembered their conversation it struck Molly that she'd avoided the subject of how and what she was going to tell Rob. The thought of it had picked away at her brain all evening but she'd tried to push it to one side. It had been a wonderful surprise from Joe, and he'd made so much effort that she didn't want to spoil it, but, she realised with horror that she was quite happy to spoil Rob's life. Molly knew people would hate her, but Joe was the one she needed to be with. Joe was the one she could not be without.

Just after six, the headlights shining through the lounge window announced Rob's arrival. Molly immediately felt sick, her hands started to shake and thousands of butterflies in hobnail boots danced a tango in her stomach. She took a deep breath and made her way to the hall to greet him.

"Hi," she said brightly as Rob came through the front door. "Good journey?"

Rob put down his suitcase and, with arms open wide, stepped towards Molly.

"Hi." He pulled Molly into his arms and kissed her.

Molly responded inasmuch as she kissed him back, but there was nothing else, no passion, no feeling. Rob's kisses used to thrill Molly to her core, making her desperate for more and wanting to tear his clothes off, but they hadn't for a long time and now even more so, they left her feeling hollow, empty except for a deep grief in the knowledge that this part of her life was almost at an end.

"What's wrong" asked Rob. "That's not my usual welcome home."

Molly's heart hammered faster. Should she tell him now?

"Oh" she said limply, "Just period pains, you know how it gets. I'm glad you're back safely." She put her arms around Rob's waist and hugged him.

"Ah, is it really bad? Why don't you make us a coffee and put some brandy in yours."

Molly nodded. "Okay, go and sit down and I'll bring it through."

"Okay, thanks. I'm knackered, the motorway was a nightmare."

***

A few minutes later, Molly handed Rob his coffee and sat down on the armchair opposite to him.

"So, are you feeling happier than the other night?" He looked at her guardedly.

Despite her determination not to be so sensitive, she was immediately infuriated. They hadn't spoken since, just a couple of text messages saying good morning and good night to each other, so their argument had gone unresolved.

She gave him a thin lipped smile and nodded.

"So it was a bad journey then?"

"There was an accident northbound," said Rob. "You can imagine all the 'rubber neckers' going southbound slowing everything down. Anyway, what did you get up to last night? We had some sort of mock awards dinner."

"Really, did you win an award?"

"Don't laugh, but I won Best Dancer."

"Best Dancer? Are you sure they gave it to the right person? So it wasn't all work, work, work then?"

"The evenings were pretty fun, lots of beer and throwing some shapes in the local nightclub. Anyway, you've still not told me what you did last night, anything exciting?"

"Oh nothing much, just watched some T.V. Tell me about your week instead; I bet it's been far more interesting than mine."

***

The next morning, as the light sneaked in through the crack in the curtains, Molly groaned quietly. She had to be up in half an hour, and she'd had very little sleep. Her mind hadn't stopped going over how she was going to tell Rob, and the guilt of what she was about to do pulled at her heart. She'd also lied about having her period just to stop Rob from pouncing on her in bed, but she hadn't been able to stop him wrapping both his arms around her for most of the night.

Suddenly Rob stirred and, not wanting to have to tell any more lies just yet, Molly snapped her eyes shut and pretended to be asleep. She heard Rob yawn, and then felt him turn over to look at his watch on the bedside table before getting out of bed. He didn't go to the bathroom as she'd expected, but padded out of the bedroom and then downstairs.

Molly turned onto her back and sighed heavily. She had to tell him today, but the thought of what she was going to say and how she was going to say it filled her with dread. After about ten minutes, she heard Rob's tread on the landing as he came back upstairs. As he walked through the door, Molly smiled and stretched out her arms as though she'd just woken.

"Morning," she said. "You're up early,"

"I fancied a cup of tea," said Rob, holding up two mugs. "I made you one." He placed the mug on Molly's bedside table and then he reached under his other arm to retrieve some envelopes that he'd tucked there. "Oh and there were two of yours in my post that you'd put to one side while I've been away, you must have missed them." Rob dropped the mail onto the bed.

Molly picked up the envelopes and then passed the rest to Rob as he climbed back into bed. "It's just junk mail from a credit card company, and ah let's see, oh yes I've won a prize." She threw the letters down onto the floor and reached across for her tea.

As Molly sipped her drink, Rob opened one of his letters and started to read it. After a couple of minutes he threw the duvet back and, still holding onto the letter, flew out of the bedroom. Molly heard him run back down the stairs and shut the lounge door. Perplexed, she got out of bed and went to the landing and listened. She could hear his muffled voice, obviously talking to someone on the telephone. Panic set in as it suddenly struck her that the letter must have been about her and Joe. There was no doubt in her mind; someone had found about their affair and told Rob before she'd had the chance, but who? Molly continued to listen but couldn't make out what Rob was saying exactly. His voice was reasonably calm, but surely if he'd heard about her infidelity he'd be shouting by now. After a few minutes, Molly heard the lounge door open and she watched as Rob, head bowed, slowly made his way back upstairs.

"Everything okay?" she asked.

"What?" Rob looked up at her, the letter still in his hand.

"Everything okay?" Molly repeated and nodded at the envelope.

"Oh, sorry," he said. "Yes it's fine, nothing urgent. I'll tell you when you get home after the match."

"Are you going to the game today?"

Rob looked at Molly quizzically. "Of course, why?" As a

season ticket holder he attended every home game.

"It's just that letter seems to have upset you."

"No, I'm fine. Are you getting in the shower now, or having your breakfast first? If you are I'll jump in before you?" He placed a hand on Molly's cheek before brushing her messy, bed hair away from her face.

"Erm, no I'll get in the shower now if that's okay?"

"Yep, go for it, I'll put some toast on." Rob smiled, kissed Molly's nose and retreated back downstairs, leaving Molly bewildered and worried about what exactly was in the letter.

***

"He can't know," Joe whispered. "No one knows, we've been really careful." After the game, in the player's lounge, Molly had managed to attract Joe's attention and nodded towards the corridor outside. Joe had followed her out, and Molly had dragged him into an empty office just along the landing.

"Something in that letter upset him Joe. What if someone wrote and told him about us?" Molly dragged a hand through her hair, worry etched all over her face.

Joe took hold of Molly's hand and gently pulled her to him, landing a soft kiss on her forehead.

"Baby, you said it yourself if he knew he'd probably have caused a scene. He'd be up here now offering to fight me for you."

"Joe, it's not funny." Molly pulled away and started to bite at her thumbnail.

"I'm not trying to be funny. Look, just go home as normal, and when you can, tell him. If you don't want to do it tonight, then fine, whenever you're ready, and stop chewing your thumbnail. I can't believe you still do that."

Molly dropped her hand to her side and gave Joe a sarcastic smile.

"I'm going to tell him tonight as agreed. I can't keep avoiding him."

"Do you want me to come home with you, to make sure you're okay?"

"Christ no, that would just make things worse, and it wouldn't be fair on him." Molly leaned her forehead against Joe's and groaned.. "I just wish it was over already."

"I know, and I'm sorry you have to do this, but once it's done we can get on with our life together. Just ring me when you've done, and let me know you're okay. Promise?"

Molly nodded. "I promise, but I'll be fine, it's Rob I'm not so sure about."

***

When Molly let herself into the house just after 7pm, she found Rob in the lounge. He was sitting in darkness, still wearing his coat, shoes and scarf.

"Hi," Molly said tentatively as she leaned down to turn on the lamp next to the sofa. "Have you just got back?"

Rob shook his head. "No, been back about an hour."

"Okay, so why do you still have your coat on?"

"Sit down Moll, please," said Rob, ignoring her. "We need to talk." He nodded at the armchair.

Molly's heart quickened and her mouth suddenly became dry. He *must* know, she thought, he must be about to tell her he knows everything.

"Wh-what's wrong?" she asked, sitting down.

"That letter I got this morning." Rob fished in his coat pocket and pulled out a crumpled envelope, showing it to Molly.

"Yes, what about it?" Molly's voice quivered.

"I got some news today, and well, it's the worst news I've ever had in my life."

Molly didn't know how to react. Normally she'd have rushed and pulled him into an embrace and told him everything would be okay. But this wasn't normal, he was probably about to tell her what a bitch she was for cheating on him. As Molly looked at Rob's crumpled face, she didn't care if he pushed her away, she had to comfort him and tell him how sorry she was for what she'd done. She moved across to the sofa and sat next to him, taking hold of his hand and squeezing it tightly.

"Rob love, what news did you get?"

A shuddering breath caught in Rob's throat as he turned to Molly, his eyes glistening in the lamplight.

"I have cancer Moll." Rob's eyes dropped to the envelope in his hand, and he passed it to Molly. "I have Non Hodgkins Lymphoma."

CHAPTER 15

♥

Molly grabbed the letter from Rob and ripped it out of the envelope.

When she had finished reading it she waved the letter in of Rob's face. "What the hell does it mean, and why didn't you tell me you'd been tested?" she cried, tears streaking her face.

"It was a routine check-up for the Health Insurance that work provides – we have to get a check-up every year. The doctor who did the tests felt some swelling under my arms, so he insisted I had some blood tests." Rob's face was emotionless as he stared past Molly.

"They can cure it though; they've caught it early enough haven't they?" Molly grabbed both of Rob's hands.

"I don't know, not until I see the consultant next week."

"Right, I'll take the day off and come with you."

Rob shook his head. "No, I'll be better on my own. I won't be worrying about you if I go by myself."

"I can't let you go on your own," Molly said. "I'm coming with you."

Rob managed a weak smile. "Okay, if you insist."

"I do. We're going to fight this and you are not going to let it beat you, I promise." Molly said as she pulled Rob into a tight hug.

Rob clung to Molly as she gently rocked him, and as she tried to soothe his quiet sobs, all thoughts of Joe and their life together disappeared – floating from her mind like feathers in the breeze.

***

Molly spent the following day spent in a daze. She didn't take her eyes off Rob, watching and waiting for him to break down, but there was no sign of him doing so. He'd been quiet, watching T.V. and reading the Sunday papers, and refused to discuss his cancer.

Then, at about five in the afternoon, Rob announced he was going to play snooker with a couple of friends.

"Don't you think you should stay at home?" Molly asked, watching Rob shrug on his coat.

"No, I'm carrying on with life as normal, so I'm going to play snooker."

"Rob, you've hardly spoken about it, shouldn't we talk instead?" Molly grabbed his hand.

Rob shook her hand away. "Stop worrying, and *don't* tell anyone else about it just yet. I don't want anyone to know until I've see the consultant, okay?"

Molly nodded. "Okay, if you say so. See you later then."

After he'd left, Molly broke down and sobbed. She was so scared for him, and what he was going to face over the next few months of treatment, and yet he seemed so matter of fact about it all. She'd watched him sleeping most of the night, amazed that he'd been able to, but he must have been mentally exhausted because he did, albeit fitfully.

Wiping her eyes, Molly suddenly thought about Joe for the first time since Rob had given her the news. She knew Joe would be worried and wondering what had happened, but she wasn't sure she should call him. Rob had asked her not to tell anyone and telling Joe would be betraying him once again, but he needed to know why she hadn't finished things yet – saying it's not the right time just wouldn't be a good enough reason as far as Joe was concerned, even though he'd promised not to pressurise her. Then it struck her, how could she end things with Rob at all now? It would be too cruel.

Molly picked up her phone, and dialled Joe's number.

He answered almost immediately. "Hi beautiful, are you okay?"

"No," Molly choked, before starting to cry again.

"Molly, what's wrong, has he hurt you? I'm coming round, shit I don't even know where you live exactly, what's your address?" His voice was full of concern.

"No Joe, you can't and I'm fine." Molly took a deep shuddering breath. "I haven't told him yet."

"What's wrong then, has something else happened? Please Moll, you're scaring me"

"I can't tell him, I'm so sorry."

"Okay, you need more time, that's fine. We knew it wasn't going to be easy." Joe's voice was getting more anxious. "Whenever you're ready is okay with me."

"You don't understand," Molly cried. She blew out a huge breath, to try and stop anymore sobs escaping. "I need to see you, I can't tell you over the phone like this.

"Tell me what?" Joe's voice was quiet.

"Where are you?" said Molly, ignoring Joe's question.

"I'm over at the apartment," he said. "They're letting me rent it until the sale has gone through. It was supposed to be a surprise, for you."

Molly put a hand to her mouth, stifling a cry of despair. "Okay, can I come over now?"

"Of course you can, are you okay to drive or do you want me to come and get you?"

He knows, Molly thought, he knows that I'm going to break his heart.

"I'll be fine, I'll see you in about half an hour."

As soon as she'd ended the call, Molly picked up her keys and left the house. She couldn't wait because if she didn't do this now, she'd never do it and that wouldn't be fair to either Joe or Rob.

Molly arrived at the apartments and parked her car out of view, around the back of the building, before making her way to the front entrance. She found Joe waiting for her by the door.

"Hi," he kissed Molly passionately before taking her hand and leading her into the lift.

Once inside he held her to him, and she began weeping uncontrollably, her shoulders shaking as wracking sobs escaped her body. When they got to Joe's penthouse, the lift doors slid open onto the landing, and Joe practically carried Molly into the apartment.

He pulled her down onto the sofa pulling her onto his knee and held her tightly, until finally her cries started to subside.

"Okay?" Joe asked, handing Molly a tissue.

"I'm sorry, I shouldn't have done that to you." Molly took the tissue and wiped her eyes and nose.

"That's okay, I'm guessing I might be joining you soon. You're not going to tell him are you? You've changed your mind and chosen him haven't you?"

Molly shook her head. "No, Joe, it's not like that. I love you and I want to be with you, but..." Her voice trailed away to silence, so deep was her sorrow.

"But, you're not leaving him." Joe dropped his head against her shoulder and sighed. "What's happened?"

Molly took a huge breath, steadying herself before telling Joe.

"I promised him I wouldn't say anything to anyone, but I have to tell you so that you understand why I'm doing what I'm doing. He must never know that I told you this. Rob has cancer."

Joe stared at Molly, the colour draining from his face, and he was unable to speak for a few moments.

"Shit, Moll. When did he find out, is it terminal? Christ that's awful."

"He got the letter yesterday morning. It's Lymphoma, that's all I know until he sees the Consultant on Tuesday." Molly wiped her eyes as more tears escaped.

"I don't know what to say." Joe hugged Molly to his chest and gently stroked her hair. "Where is he now?"

Molly let out a hollow laugh. "Playing snooker, believe it or not. He won't talk about it."

Joe held Molly away from him and gazed at her, his eyes taking in every inch of her face.

"You can't leave him can you?"

Molly shook her head. Her bottom lip quivered. "No. I'm so sorry Joe. I have to be there for him, maybe when he's better I..." What was the point even saying that, Molly thought, it could be years before she felt it was okay to leave him. She lifted her hand and caressed Joe's face. "You do understand, don't you?"

Joe nodded. "I do, I wouldn't expect you to do anything else. Will you still marry him?" There was suddenly fear in his eyes.

"God, I haven't even thought about it. I don't know. I suppose until we know how bad things are..." Molly started to cry again.

"Hey, come on, please don't cry, baby. You'll do whatever is right, I know you will." As Joe realised that it was over, and that Molly would more than likely marry Rob, tears started to well in his eyes.

"What am I going to do Joe, without you, I don't know if I'll cope?"

"Of course you will, you're strong, you can do this."

"Why are you being so good about this, so calm? I thought you'd go mad."

Joe shrugged. "You weren't mine to start with," he sighed. "I was stealing you away from someone else, so maybe deep down I expected this to happen."

"But I *was* yours, I always have been. I love you so much, but I just can't..."

Joe kissed her tears from her cheeks, lacing his fingers in hers and savouring her scent with every kiss as if this would be the last time he would ever see her.

Molly, still weeping, moved her head slightly so that Joe's kisses landed on her mouth. She kissed him back tenderly, taking her hands from his and gently stroking his face. Their kisses suddenly became more desperate as they realised that this was the end, and after a few minutes Molly pulled back. She stood up and took hold of Joe's hand.

"I'm the worst kind of person in the world for doing this," she whispered, "but I need you to make love to me one last time, Joe."

Joe stood too, and pulled Molly to him. "Are you sure? I don't want you to regret it."

Molly looked up at him. "Never, I'll never regret what we've done, and it might be an awful thing to do but I know I'll regret it if we don't."

"Okay," Joe whispered. He kissed the top of her head and led her to the bedroom.

***

A couple of hours later, Molly cried all the way home. Joe had made love to her slowly and tenderly, and then afterwards held her tight, lying in silence except for the sound of their own breathing. She'd found it difficult to leave, holding onto Joe's hand all the way to her car, neither of them wanting to be the first to let go, until finally they had no choice. As she drove away from Joe, Molly watched him in her rear view mirror and then, when she reached the gates he had disappeared from sight and she thought her heart would break. She knew she would see him at work, but he wouldn't be her Joe anymore and she wouldn't be his Molly.

Rob still wasn't back when Molly got home so, emotionally and physically shattered, she climbed into bed, fully clothed, and fell asleep, wondering if she would ever feel happy again.

CHAPTER 16

♥

Molly woke the next morning to the sound of Rob showering. At first it felt just like any other morning, then suddenly the misery hit her like a landslide – Rob had cancer and she and Joe were over. Desperately wanting to turn over and go back to sleep to forget it all, Molly pulled the duvet over her head, but she knew hiding away wouldn't help anyone and she had to be strong and supportive for Rob. Poking her head out, she glanced at the clock, it was almost seven and time to get up so, still dressed in her clothes from the night before she stumbled out of bed and went to speak to him.

He was just climbing out of the shower as Molly walked in.

"What time did you get home?" she asked rubbing sleep from her eyes.

"About eleven. You were zonked so I didn't wake you. Are you okay?" As he reached for his towel, Rob eyed Molly thoughtfully.

"I suppose. What about you?"

"Okay, considering, although, I'm not looking forward to catching up on thousands of emails from while I was away." Wrapping the towel around his waist, Rob stepped past Molly, back into the bedroom.

Molly's mouth dropped open – emails were his only concern, how could that be possible knowing what he knew?

"Rob, will you please just stop." Molly grabbed his arm. "We need to talk about your illness; we haven't discussed it since you told me. I don't know how you're feeling, you haven't told me why you didn't say anything sooner, what you want to do about the wedding, do you feel ill, and have you told your parents? I don't know anything except that you've got cancer and I have a thousand questions running around in my head."

Rob rounded on Molly, his face hard, his eyes narrow.

"I'm fucking scared, how do think I feel? I didn't want you to worry when it might be nothing, so no I haven't told my Mum and Dad either. I don't feel ill, just tired and as for the wedding of course it's going ahead, why should we stop our plans just because I might drop dead in a few months?"

"Don't talk like that. You don't know that you're going to die." Molly took Rob's hand and squeezed it gently. "You can beat this" she whispered.

It didn't matter that she had been about to leave him, she didn't wish him harm and wanted to help him as much as possible, and her heart was heavy for him.

"I hope so Moll, I honestly do, but just at this moment I'm not feeling as positive as you. I'm sorry if the way I'm dealing with it upsets you but it's the best I can do at the moment." He pulled away from Molly. "Just go to work and try and forget about it until we find out more details tomorrow."

"Okay, if that's what you want, but don't bottle things up, it will make you feel worse."

"Not sure I could feel any worse to be honest, Moll. Now go and get your shower, or you'll be late for work."

***

When Molly came out of the shower, she noticed that the house was silent, and after calling his name she realised that Rob must have already left for work. It wasn't like him to go without saying goodbye unless he was sulking about something, which admittedly was often, but then things weren't normal anymore. As she dressed, Molly thought about Joe, wondering how he was, whether he felt as desolate as she did, or whether he was relieved it was all over. She desperately wanted to call him to find out but she knew that she couldn't - it had to be over, at least until Rob was better. Molly let out a sigh, thinking that even when Rob got better there was no saying she would feel as though she could leave, or even that Joe would still want her. No, she had to admit it to herself; it was over between them and her felt as though it was broken, all over again.

***

As she got to the football ground, Molly was surprised at the number of press hanging around outside the main reception. She recognised a couple of the regular, local press, and they nodded hello as she walked past.

"So, what do you know about all this then Molly?" asked Jim Marshall from the local radio station.

"About all what, Jim? I'm not sure what you're talking about?"

"Joe Bennett."

Molly's blood went cold, and a nervous shiver ran through her body.

"What about him? What's wrong?"

"That model he had a fling with has reared her head again; she reckons her son is Joe's."

Molly legs wobbled to the point that she thought they were about to give way beneath her. She reached out and held onto one of the metal post lights that lit the path up to reception. She felt her forehead prickle with sweat and her heart thudded a foxtrot.

"He's denying it of course and to be honest I believe him. She's on her uppers and just after a quick money making scheme if you ask me."

"Right," said Molly, "right." She was shaking and her face was white.

"You okay Molly?" asked Jim, holding a hand out to her. "You look as though you're going to pass out."

Molly shook her head. "No, I'm fine Jim, just a bit of stomach flu I think. Anyway, I'd better get inside and see if there's anything I can do to help. Have any of you spoken to Joe personally yet?"

"No, but I'm hoping that if he speaks to anyone it'll be me seeing as we've got a good relationship with the club, but I guess that's up to your press office."

"Yes, I suppose so. Thanks Jim, I'll see you soon." Molly staggered away, as fast as her shaky legs could move.

Once inside the building she headed for the ladies toilets and barely had the time to shut the cubicle door behind her before she started throwing up. Molly sat there for some time, her insides felt as though they were a dishcloth being wrung out and her heart ached in her chest. Maybe Jim Marshall was right, the model, Lara Jade, was just trying to make some money. Joe was now a massive star so she'd seen an opportunity, but would any mother be that cruel as to lie so publicly about who the father of their child was?

Eventually, Molly calmed down enough to let herself out of the cubicle. She tidied her hair and fixed her make up before slowly making her way down the corridor to her office. When she arrived the rest of her team were all there, flicking through the newspaper, reading Lara Jade's story.

"Molly, have you heard?" Marcus asked looking up from a double page spread of Lara Jade with her bosoms on show.

Molly nodded and coughed in an attempt to get rid of the huge lump in her throat.

"Yes, I've just seen the press on my way in" she croaked "I spoke to Jim Marshall. So, what's happening from a club point of view, has anyone from press been down to give us the club stance?" She quickly turned away, not wanting anyone to see the tears that were welling in her eyes.

"We've had an email to say no one is to talk to the press and that Joe is staying away from training today. Apparently he's holed up in his apartment with his agent."

"Okay," said Molly, straightening her jacket and determined to remain professional. "So we do as we're told. I don't want anyone from this department telling anyone about it, and if any of your family and friends ask, you tell them you know nothing. Am I understood?"

They all nodded, knowing that when Molly was this serious, you followed her instruction.

"Rosetta, aren't you down at the training ground this morning?"

Rosetta nodded. "Yes in about half an hour. I've got take Greg Pounder to the private hospital, he's come in with a black eye and bruises on his stomach, so the Manager has asked that one of us take him to get it checked out."

"Christ, what's he been up to?" Molly asked.

Rosetta shrugged. "He says he 'fell over', but it looks like he's been beaten up if you ask me."

Molly sighed. "Okay, well you'll probably be bombarded by the press about Joe when you get there. They'll be hounding everyone that turns up there today, so just give the no comment line."

"Okay will do."

"The rest of us just carry on as normal." Molly sat down at her desk and switched on her PC. She wasn't sure she could concentrate on work, but she could at least look as though she was.

At that moment Molly's mobile buzzed in her bag. She wasn't sure whether to answer or not, seeing Joe's name on the display, but she knew if she didn't he'd just keep calling and draw attention from the others.

"Hello," she answered dully.

"Molly, it's a lie I swear to you."

"Wait a second," said Molly. She got up and walked out into the corridor.

***

"Are you still there?" Joe asked after a few seconds.

"Yes, I was just getting out of the office. She obviously thinks something happened between you, otherwise why would she put her son through all of this?"

"I don't know Moll, but you have to believe me. I'm going to ask her for a DNA test. Tony, my agent is trying to get in touch with her now."

"Save yourself the money Joe, get Jeremy Kyle to do it for you," Molly snapped.

"Please Molly, don't be like that, I didn't sleep with her at that party."

"So you say Joe, I don't know whether I can believe anything that you've ever said to me."

"I haven't lied about cheating on you, and I haven't lied about how I feel about you."

Molly's brow furrowed. "That sounds as though you've lied about *something* though Joe, what have you lied about?"

There was a pause on the other end. "Nothing, I've lied about nothing."

The knot in Molly's stomach told her otherwise. "I swear to God Joe, tell me now what it is. I've got nothing to bargain with, except if you really do love me and want any chance of us ever being together once Rob's better then you'd better tell me what it is you've lied about."

"I didn't lie, I just didn't tell you. Please don't hate me for this, it was after we'd finished and I didn't think I'd ever see you again, but once I made my mind up that I was going to get you back, I knew I couldn't tell you."

"Now Joe."

"I did sleep with her, once, but it was about five years ago. We'd been finished about a year, and she turned up at a Turkish magazine party I was at. I got drunk and ended up back at her hotel room."

Molly was silent for a few seconds, and as the information registered her feeling of nausea returned. How could, knowing what that woman had done to them, whether her initial story was true or not?

"Why didn't she sell that story then? You were getting to be a big star, so why didn't she go to the papers about your return match?"

Joe sighed. "Christ Molly, it wasn't a return of anything, I've told you I never cheated on you. I don't know why she didn't go to the press, maybe she realised that if she sold that story they'd realise she lied the first time. What sort of story is "I slept with Joe Bennett, *again*"? It would have been a nothing story, not worth anything."

"So this child could be yours then?" Molly's heart slammed against her chest realising that if it was Joe's child, then there was no going back for them - ever. "No, Tony's found out the kid is going to be six next month, so he's too old. I couldn't possibly be his father."

"Look Joe, it doesn't actually matter when you slept with her. She forced us apart when she sold her story whether it was true or not. At the end of the day, you slept with the woman who broke us up."

"I know and I regretted it as soon as it happened, you have to believe me."

"I do believe you regretted it, but you still did it. I'm sorry Joe, it is well and truly over between us. I can't trust you, I think you slept with her when we were together as well, and I have a horrible feeling that this child is going to be yours. We shouldn't have started anything up again, that night at the hotel you should have stayed away, and I should have said no."

"Please Molly, he won't be mine, I know he won't," Joe pleaded.

"It doesn't matter anyway," Molly replied calmly. "We're bringing the wedding forward, so just forget we ever happened." With that Molly ended the call, and her relationship with Joe.

She didn't know why she'd lied to him about the wedding, to hurt him probably, but they were over anyway, and he already knew that it might happen, plus Molly wasn't terribly sure that even carrying on with the wedding was the right thing to do. She'd been about to leave Rob before he told her about his illness and he deserved much more than a pity wife. As she started back to the office, Molly's phone rang out again – it was Rob.

"Rob, what's wrong?"

"Hey, calm down, it's okay, well sort of."

"What do you mean?"

"I didn't tell you because I wanted to do it on my own, but I had my appointment with the Consultant today."

"You went on your own? You should have had someone with you." Molly ran a hand through her hair as she paced up and down the corridor unable to believe that he'd seen his consultant alone.

"Please Molly, just hear me out. I needed to do this on my own, I can't explain why, I just had to."

Molly took a deep breath and stopped pacing. "Okay, I get it, I just wish you'd told me. How did you manage to get in to see them today?"

"I changed the appointment on Saturday, when I got the letter. I was lucky they'd had a cancellation."

"So what did they say?"

"He explained everything that will happen, the treatment, the survival rates, everything I need to know."

"So the blood tests then are pretty conclusive, there's no chance they could be wrong?" Molly asked, already knowing the answer.

"No," sighed Rob. "It's definitely cancer. The good thing is it's not spread to any organs, but I do have it in two groups of lymph nodes, my groin and underarms."

"And what does that mean?" Molly wished she'd been there to ask her own questions, and maybe even take notes.

"It means it's not as bad as it could be. Look we'll talk about it all tonight, I promise."

Molly had to concede that Rob did sound more upbeat than earlier in the day.

"Okay, I'll be home about six, and we can talk then."

As she sat back at her desk, Molly realised she had no right to complain to Rob about not taking her to his appointment. She was about to leave him, so why should she have a licence to ask questions about his future? At least he sounded more positive, and maybe this would bring them closer together again. But her feeling were still at odds, she cared about him very much and she was scared for him, but the thought of being intimate with him seemed wrong and she didn't know whether that was guilt or lack of desire. As for loving him, how could she if she'd been about to leave him after one week with Joe? But one thing she did know for certain was that for now, at least, Rob was her priority.

CHAPTER 17

Molly and Rob spent the evening talking about what was going to happen over the next few months. They argued too, as Rob wanted to keep it from the rest of the family until he was in remission. Molly felt he should at least tell his own parents, but Rob was adamant that he wanted to face it alone. He didn't want Molly, or anyone, feeling as if they had to be there to hold his hand. He decided to have his head shaved, not so short that he'd look like the third Mitchell brother, but short enough that people wouldn't notice when it started to fall out. The final thing they had talked about was the wedding and although she was pretty sure she shouldn't have done, Molly found herself agreeing to bring it forward. She suggested that it would be better to postpone, because while she wanted to be there for Rob, she didn't want to marry him. But, it was what he wanted and yet again he persuaded her that it was the right thing to do. They agreed that it would be a quiet registry office affair, with just immediate family – the big party they'd originally planned could wait until Rob was better. Thankfully, the venue where they were to be married and have the reception was very understanding about Rob's illness, plus they had two brides on standby who had been desperate to have their weddings there but couldn't because they were fully booked. The excuse that Molly and Rob gave their families was that they'd decided to buy a bigger house and so the money they were spending on the wedding seemed extravagant – thankfully everyone believed them and agreed that a smaller wedding and a meal in a local restaurant would be much better. Everyone apart from Sophie, who seemed to think it was because Molly was "up the duff"

***

As far as Joe was concerned, Molly hadn't spoken to him for almost a week, since the story of his "love child" had broken. Each day the press attention had lessened, Lara had failed to produce any pictures of her son to indicate whether he looked like Joe or not and, according to some papers, had refused a DNA test. While this left everyone seriously doubting the validity of Lara's statement, it didn't make Molly feel any better about the situation.

The next time Molly saw Joe it was match day. Thankfully it was a home game, so they would only meet briefly in the player's lounge after the game. Nevertheless, her nerves were jangling and her thumbnail had almost been chewed down to the knuckle.

It was seven in the morning and Molly was alone in the office. She couldn't sleep, so had gone in early to make sure that the players' complimentary ticket requests had been met. She'd just finished marking the last one off her list when her mobile rang.

"Molly, I need you, I in trouble."

Molly groaned. "Tino, its match day, what have you done now?"

"It not my fault Molly. I not know where I was."

"Okay Tino, what's happened?"

"I go out in my car last night. I find pub and I go in for drink. I only going to have orange but I buy us all drinks, so I no able to drive my car."

"And, what else?" Molly just knew the best was yet to come.

"So I sleep in my car, I have what you call bag of sleeping in it so I very warm."

"Right."

"But this morning Molly, I have no wheels."

It could have been the lack of sleep, or the fact that she was so emotional that made her so hysterical, but when Molly let out that first roar of laughter she found that she couldn't stop. Her sides ached, tears slid down her cheeks and she almost wet herself, deliriously relishing Tino's misfortune and foolishness. Then after a few minutes, she heard his tinny, alarmed voice shouting.

"Go away, please, do not hurt me."

"Tino, what's wrong?" Molly quickly snapped out of her laughter.

"The young boy he stick fingers in air at me. Please Molly I scared."

Holding back more giggles, Molly blew out a breath and steadied herself.

"Do you know where you are, Tino?"

"No, pub has name of bird, but it all dirty I not able to read it." Tino's voice trembled with genuine fear.

"Hang on Tino, just give me a minute."

Knowing that many of the players consistently lost their phones, she had installed an app on her iPad that could find them. She typed in Tino's name and after a couple of seconds a map appeared on the screen, with the location of Tino's phone. Molly shook her head and groaned.

"Only you could go to one of the roughest pubs in the western hemisphere and think you could get away with it. Stay where you are and I'll be there in about twenty minutes."

"Thank you Molly, I love you."

"I know," said Molly.

***

As she pulled up behind Tino's car, Molly was amazed a crowd hadn't gathered around his neon green Lamborghini. Not only was it an unusual sight, but inside was a City player, alone in what was predominantly United territory. She started to laugh again as she saw the bricks holding the car up, wondering how on earth Tino had slept through the wheels being removed. She walked around to the driver's side and tapped on Tino's window.

Tino buzzed the window down. "Oh Molly I so glad to see you."

"You idiot Tino, what on earth were you doing coming here?"

"I play darts and I not know name, it game with little blocks with spots on."

"Dominoes - you spent the evening playing darts and dominoes with the locals, no doubt paying for their drinks, and they repay you by nicking your wheels."

Tino dropped his head and blushed.

"I sorry Molly. Please you not tell Mr Ribero or the boys, they take the pee from me."

Molly shook her head. "No I won't tell them. Come and sit in my car, the pickup truck should be here in a few minutes." Molly had called them on her way to the pub and had arranged for Tino's car to be taken to the dealership for new wheels to be fitted.

"I'll take you home."

"You very lovely woman Molly. La ragazza sexy con …"

Molly lifted her hand. "Stop, Tino. I know exactly what that means, and it won't wash with me, so don't even bother, besides I *do not* have big boobs."

"I sorry." Tino dropped his eyes and had the decency to look ashamed.

For the next five minutes, they sat in silence and waited for the pickup truck. Then once the Lamborghini was safely on the back, Molly drove Tino home to his city centre apartment.

"Do you want me to wait for you?" she asked as they manoeuvred through the early morning traffic. "You have to be at the club for a pre-match meal and warm up by eleven." She hoped he'd say no, it was still only eight o'clock and two more hours of Tino's company would surely send her crazy.

"It okay Molly I will come in my other car."

Molly sighed and shook her head; of course he had another car, probably just as ostentatious and twice as expensive.

"Tino, can I ask you a question? Why don't you just find a nice girl and settle down, someone who will look after you and make sure you don't do anything else stupid that could put you in danger?"

"I not find one woman who enough for me. When I marry I will love only one woman, but now too many women love me because I footballer, so maybe I wait until I finish football and only my wife love me. My woman will make me laugh and be sexy lady."

Molly smiled. Despite Tino's ego and his stupidity, at least he was honest.

"So you love the ladies but what else do you love then Tino? There must be something"

Tino nodded vigorously. "I love Llamas."

"Of course you do," Molly laughed. "More than you love the ladies?"

Tino thought for a second. "That is difficult, do I love Llamas more than I love sex and footballs? I cannot answer Molly."

"Well, you're different to most footballers, they just love the ladies, and as many of them as possible."

Tino put his head on one side to think. "Yes, but not all. The boys who already married at City, they good boys."

"Ah, so it's just the single ones who are naughty boys."

Tino laughed and nodded. "Yes Molly you right."

**

When Molly got back to the office, it was still empty. No one else was due to arrive until nine. She'd just turned on the coffee machine when Joe walked in. "What are you doing here?" she asked, just about managing to stop the coffee pot from dropping to the floor.

"I needed to see you. I was waiting on the car park for you to arrive."

"I thought we'd said everything there was to say." Molly turned away.

Even though he looked tired and drawn, it took nothing away from his handsome features and Molly had to summon all her strength to stop herself from touching him, from wanting to soothe away his problems.

"I haven't come to beg for your forgiveness, or to ask you to think about taking me back."

"What then?"

"Lara Jade is publishing a statement of retraction in the papers tomorrow."

"About her child being your son, or about you sleeping together?" Molly flicked on the coffee pot.

"About the child, she won't retract the other story. According to my solicitor if she does she'll have to pay back the money she was paid all those years ago and she obviously hasn't got it."

"So why has she suddenly decided to do a U-turn on the child story then? Surely she's been paid for that too?" Molly paused in spooning coffee into the pot, perplexed by Lara Jade's admission.

Joe shook his head. "No, the paper who published the story was still drawing up the contract so haven't actually given her any money yet. She's had to retract it because someone snitched to the paper that her boy is actually nine years old, he's small for his age so can pass for six. In fact I think they played her at her own game, and sold a copy of the boy's birth certificate to the newspaper."

"I'm pleased you're in the clear," said Molly, trying her hardest to concentrate on the coffee pot and not Joe. "You must be relieved."

"Not really, it doesn't alter the fact that I've lost you," he replied.

"We were over anyway; you know I have to be there for Rob." Molly couldn't help it any longer and moved towards him.

"You don't have to marry him, Moll, stay until he's better and then be with me."

Molly desperately wanted to tell him that was what she would do, but she knew she couldn't without hurting Rob, and that wasn't an option.

"It's what he wants and I don't know how to persuade him otherwise. I've tried to get him to agree to postpone it, but that was for my own selfish reasons, and I can't be selfish when he's so ill. Plus I don't know if I can trust you." Molly looked down at her shoes and scuffed at the carpet.

Joe sighed and threw his arms in the air.

"How many times do I have to say it?" he cried.

"I know," said Molly, "and I want to believe you, but it's not just then it's now. Practically every woman on the planet thinks you're gorgeous and wants you, and I'm just too insecure to be able to handle that, no matter how often you tell me that's not what you're like."

Molly felt her pulse quicken, that wasn't strictly true. Deep down she knew that she could trust Joe, she knew beyond doubt that he loved her and would never risk losing her again. What supposedly had happened six years ago, when he was young, she knew wouldn't happen again.

"I'm just not getting through am I?" said Joe. He moved away and looked through the window to the icy February morning. "Okay, you win, but please don't marry him."

Molly lowered her eyes again, unable to look at him. They stood in silence for a few seconds, neither knowing what to say. Then Joe took something from his jacket pocket.

"I got this for you," he said. "I want you to have it." He handed her a small, black, velvet covered box.

"What is it?"

"Just a gift, it was supposed to be a housewarming present when you moved into the apartment, but I guess we'll just call it a parting gift now." Joe smiled sadly.

Molly flipped up the lid and inside was the most beautiful, delicate, heart shaped diamond pendant, on a white gold chain.

"I can't take this," she said. "It's beautiful; it must have cost a fortune. I don't deserve it and I can't take it." She flipped the lid back down and passed it back to Joe.

"I want you to have it, please," he pleaded.

"I can't," she said. "How would I explain it to Rob? It's obviously expensive and he'd know I couldn't afford it."

"He wouldn't need to know you have it."

Molly shook her head and smiled. "Come on Joe, he's not stupid. Please, take it and get your money back."

Joe put the box back in his pocket and sighed.

"I won't make you take, but I won't get my money back, just in case you change your mind, and I don't just mean the necklace."

"I won't and I'm sorry, about everything. I do love you, but this is how it has to be." Molly kissed him gently on the lips and hugged him tightly.

Joe eventually pulled away and smiled.

"Good luck with everything Moll, and don't forget where I am if you need me."

"I'll see you most days," she whispered.

"I know," said Joe, making his way out of the office, "but somehow that makes it much worse."

CHAPTER 18

♥

"I don't even want a hen night, and I can't believe Sophie has railroaded me into it" said Molly. She was sitting in the back of a taxi with Becky. They were on their way into town to meet Sophie and a few friends. Sophie had totally ignored Molly's wishes and organised a hen night the weekend before the wedding.

"Seriously Molly, why are you doing any of this?" said Becky, looking out of the window at the passing traffic. She shook her head. "I know I said not to use Joe as an excuse to leave him, but why bring the wedding forward, because not being with Joe is obviously making you miserable." Molly hadn't told Becky about Rob's cancer, just that she'd called it off with Joe and opted for a smaller wedding because they wanted to buy a bigger house. "It's like I said to you the other day, getting married on the rebound isn't going to help you forget him."

Molly sighed. "I'm not getting married on the rebound; I was supposed to be marrying Rob before Joe came back. I love him and want to marry him. "

"So you say," said Becky, arching an eyebrow. "Although that's a little different than what you said a couple of weeks ago. But, if it's what you want then I can't argue, can I?"

"It is what I want, but what I *don't* want is this sodding hen night. Sophie's only organised it because her own love life is so crap – she's just hoping to find some bloke to get off with."

Becky turned and smiled at Molly. "You never know. You might actually enjoy it once you get a couple of drinks down you."

***

It turned out that Sophie had done a fantastic job of arranging Molly's hen night. She had booked them into the VIP section of one of the classier bars in town, securing an area with comfy sofas and armchairs, waiter service and free champagne all night.

"I should give Sophie some money for all of this," Molly shouted in Becky's ear, trying to get her to hear above the thud of the music. "It must have cost a fortune, it's not cheap champagne they're plying us with.

Becky shook her head. She took a large sip of her champagne. "Nah, don't worry about it, she can afford it. How many poor barristers do you know?"

Molly looked over at Sophie, who was draping herself over the young waiter serving the drinks. "Christ, look at her, she's couldn't look or act any less like a barrister if she tried. You know, I think she's been lying all this time, and she's actually a Barista."

Becky laughed and watched as Sophie tried her best to get a handful of the waiter's bottom. "Yeah, I bet all this time she's just been the tea lady, and living a lie for the last four years."

"Ah bless her, she's a pain in the arse, but I love her. I'll get us some more drinks, and save the poor lad before she ravishes him." Molly sighed and indicated to the waiter that they wanted more champagne. He smiled gratefully, rushed over with the bottle and began filling up their glasses.

"Sorry about my sister," Molly shouted over the music. "She's been diagnosed as a raging nymphomaniac."

The colour drained from the waiter's face. He looked at Sophie, who tipped him a wink, and then back at Molly. He nodded gratefully.

"Thanks for telling me, I'll try to keep out of reach from now on."

"You do that," Becky chimed in. "Her last boyfriend ended up in hospital with exhaustion because of her *'appetite'*" she dibbed her fingers in the air. "In fact, one of her other exes is still in a nursing home, he never got over it."

"Shit," cried the waiter. He looked at Sophie again. There was a definite fear in his eyes this time. Again Sophie winked at him. He gave a feeble smile, the colour draining from his face. He turned and headed back to the bar. Molly and Becky collapsed in laughter as they watched him retreat.

"What are you two laughing at?" Sophie was suddenly at their side, looking in the same direction as Molly and Becky.

"Oh, nothing" Molly giggled. "Just having a little fun at someone else's expense."

"Oh okay, well listen, I don't like to be the one to piss on your chips Moll, but Joe and some of the team have just come in."

Molly felt the colour drain from her face as she looked over at the entrance to the VIP area. There, sure enough, was Joe, Tino, Jimmy and Charlie Gates, all dressed to impress, shaking hands with a couple of men who'd spotted them. Molly felt a buzz go around the place, and immediately about five or six rust coloured, willowy girls with hair extensions and false nails, gathered around them, practically pushing their chests under the noses of the players.

Katie and Rosetta rushed over to Molly, also having seen the new arrivals.

"Molly, do you think we should get some security down here?" Rosetta asked, glancing at the crowd that was now gathering around the players.

Molly, still staring at Joe, shook her head. "No, they'll be fine, I'll have a quick word with the in house security."

"No, you won't," Katie cried, "It's your hen night. I'll go with Rosetta, you shouldn't be thinking about work tonight."

"God, you three are like Mother Hens. They're grown men, and you can't protect them all the time." Sophie shook her head and sighed.

"I know Soph, but seeing as we are in the same place, we can't just sit back and let them get pestered all night." Molly turned to see Joe and his teammates pushing their way through the small crowd to another seated area. "Look, they're struggling already."

Molly quickly left her group and went over to the small throng gathered near the entrance. She pushed her way through, being sure to elbow a few pairs of enhanced breasts as she did. Finally, she reached the players, and managed to grab hold of Charlie's arm.

"Charlie," she shouted into his ear. "Do you need me to sort out security?"

Charlie turned and smiled when he saw Molly.

"Hey Molly, fancy seeing you here. Please, we're struggling to get through to the VIP area of the VIP area." He pointed to a raised seated area that was roped off.

Molly nodded and, looking back to Rosetta and Katie jerked her thumb towards the entrance and mouthed 'get security'. A minute later the players hadn't moved terribly far, but security were there, smoothly steering people away with little fuss. As the path cleared, Joe turned around to thank whoever was responsible and spotted Molly, obviously giving instruction to the security guys. His face broke into a huge smile. He stood aside and let his team-mates pass, then reached out and took Molly's hand.

He put his lips to Molly's ear.

"Thanks for that, I thought we were going to get mobbed."

The mere touch of his lips against her skin sent Molly's senses reeling.

"It's okay, but you know you can't just wander about the place without security anymore. You're not only famous in this city, but the whole world over and not everyone is going to want an autograph. Some people might want to punch you, or worse." As she lectured him, Molly took in every inch of his face, revelling in how gorgeous he looked.

"I know and I'm sorry. You shouldn't have to deal with this when you're not working. I promise I'll get my agent to sort someone out to work for me. Anyway, why don't you come over and have a drink with us?" His eyes were pleading with her, even if his tone wasn't.

"I can't, I'm with the girls." Molly nodded towards her group of friends, who by now had spotted the famous faces and were watching intently.

"That's okay, bring them all over. Is it someone's birthday?"

Molly felt her face redden. She struggled to speak for a few seconds.

Finally, she whispered into his ear. "It's my hen party, Joe."

Joe dropped his hand that had been resting lightly on Molly's waist. His eyes moved across to Molly's party and then back to her.

"Well" he said eventually. "I'm not sure what to say."

"I'm sorry Joe, I should have told you." Molly grabbed for Joe's hand at his side.

Joe shook his head. "It's okay. You said you'd brought the wedding forward, I just didn't think it would be this soon."

They stood silently for a few seconds, neither of them sure of what to say. Suddenly Joe let out a long breath.

"Go and get everyone, we may as well party together."

Molly shook her head. "No, it wouldn't be right, I couldn't."

Joe smiled, but it failed to reach his eyes.

"Please Moll, I'd like you to. Call me a masochist, but at least I'll be near you for a while and I might even be able to persuade you not to go through with it."

Molly opened her mouth to protest, but Joe held up his hand.

"I'm joking. Just go and get the girls and we'll have a good night, just as friends. No funny business I promise."

"Okay," Molly said. "But one thing, just make sure that Tino doesn't go near my sister; she'll eat him alive."

***

An hour later and Joe had already broken one of his promises to Molly – Tino was sitting on a sofa in deep conversation with Sophie. They'd hardly taken their eyes of each other and, after gradually moving closer and closer over the last half hour, Sophie was now almost on Tino's knee.

"Oh shit, poor Tino," Molly said to Becky.

"Hmm, I think Tino will survive, it's him I'm worried about."

Becky nodded towards Joe, who was pretending to be deep in conversation with another player. "We were chatting earlier and when he thought no one was looking all he did was stare at you, and he still is."

Molly glanced at Joe, who was indeed was looking furtively at her.

"I can't do anything about that, I'm sorry, I'm getting married."

"Molly, I have eyes you know, I've see the way you watch him too."

Molly shrugged her shoulders. "I'm just looking out for one of my players, that's all."

Becky laughed. "What, like you're looking out for Tino, Jimmy and Charlie? Bullshit, Miss Pearson."

Molly pushed her hair back. "I knew that this was a stupid idea. Why on earth did I think I could sit drinking with him, on my bloody hen night? I'm such a bitch. How cruel is it to do that to him, never mind how Rob would feel?"

"Maybe it wasn't one of the best ideas you've ever come up with, but I know you Molly. You're not a horrible person, and I can see that you love Joe just by looking at you. So the question is, my darling, why the hell are you marrying Rob?" Becky leaned closer to Molly and caught hold of her hand. "Come on, talk to me."

Molly shook her head, tears welling in her eyes.

"There's nothing to tell, honestly."

"Molly, the truth please," said Becky, wiping a tear from Molly's cheek with her thumb.

Molly took a shuddering breath. "I can't do this; I need to get some fresh air." Molly pulled her hand from Becky's, stood up and then ran towards a pair of double doors that opened out onto a balcony.

Outside the air was icy and Molly shivered in her sleeveless dress. She hugged herself in an attempt to trying to ward off the cold and moved across the deserted balcony to the glass barrier, she leaned over to look down at the murky water of the canal below.

"Molly, are you okay?" It was Joe, and he had her jacket with him. "Here put this on," he said, handing it to her. "Becky said you weren't feeling too well. I was worried when I saw you run out."

"Thanks" she whispered, slipping into her jacket. "You should go back in, I'll be fine."

"I'm not going anywhere." Joe took her hand and pulled Molly to him.

They stood inches away from each other, their eyes locked, their breath mingling in the cold air. Then, as Joe reached up to tuck Molly's hair behind her ears, his touch sent a shock wave through her body and she pulled away quickly.

"Just go back in" she said. "I'm okay."

"No, I won't." Joe moved forward and filled the space between them that Molly had created.

Molly held her hand against his chest. "Joe!"

"This is ridiculous. You don't want to marry him, I don't want you to marry him, so why are you?"

"You know why."

"But he'll more than likely get better and then what? You'll be married to someone you don't love."

"I do love him," Molly snapped.

"Bullshit, you care about him and feel guilty about what we did, but I don't think for one minute you love him."

"You don't know that, you've not been around for the last six years so who are you to tell me how I feel? You know how hard it was for me to betray him, and how difficult it was having to make a choice."

"Oh yes of course, poor you having two men fighting over you?" Joe sighed, turning his back to her.

"How dare you!" Molly turned Joe around by his shoulder. "You were the one who came back here, I didn't come looking for you, and you were the one who came knocking on my bedroom door after flirting with me, standing there in just your shorts with your bloody body on show."

"I was in the gym first, you shouldn't have even been there.

Anyway, you could've said no."

"You know I tried. I was happy with Rob until you came back."

"Well you can't have been that happy could you?" Joe cried.

That one was like a punch between the eyes from Mike Tyson, hitting the spot and flooring Molly because she knew it to be true.

"And don't you think I feel like shit about what I did? Of course I do, the bloody superstar Joe Bennett clicks his fingers, and I drop my knickers – not something to be proud of is it? All while my fiancé is suffering from cancer, I feel like the biggest bitch on earth."

Joe sighed and shook his head. "But at the time you didn't even know that he had cancer. Molly, we have a history together, we are meant to be together, the fact that we got together again so quickly proves you should be with me."

"Oh yes, of course, I forgot. We were so serious about each other that you felt the need to sleep with that slapper. That's how much you wanted us to be together, wasn't it you... you...prick!" Molly poked Joe in the shoulder.

Joe's eyes widened. "I've told you again and again, I didn't sleep with her while we were together. I am a prick though, for even thinking that you'd be sensible about things and realise you were wrong."

"*I'd* realise *I* was wrong? You admitted to me that you slept with her."

"Christ Molly, were you not fucking listening to me? I slept with her long after you'd thrown your hissy fit and finished with me."

Molly couldn't believe what she'd heard and poked Joe again.

"I did not throw a hissy fit, you broke my fucking heart you dick."

"Oh so I'm a prick and a dick am I?"

"Yes and a cock," Molly cried.

"Very mature Molly, I don't even know why I thought that you'd be grown up about it, I really don't."

"Grown up about it? Do you know how awful it was, hearing

about what you'd done? I was going to give up everything to be with you, I wanted to spend the rest of my life with you. You broke my heart, Joe. How dare you tell me I should be more grown up about it?" Molly felt tears drop to her cheek, and rubbed them away with the back of her hand.

"My heart was broken too. You didn't believe me, you wouldn't let me explain properly, and you even blocked my bloody number on your mobile. When you told me not to come home I thought my world had ended. I was stuck in Turkey and all I wanted to do was come home and talk to you and you wouldn't even let me do that."

Molly thought for a few seconds about what Joe had just said.

"You are such a liar. You never asked me to see you. After that phone call you called a couple more times, but not once did you try and come home."

Joe looked shocked.

"I did. I spoke to your Dad and told him what flight I'd be on and he said you weren't interested and that you'd gone away with Becky so wouldn't be there anyway."

Molly's mouth fell open. "You're lying."

Joe shook his head. "No, I'm not. I even remember your Dad's words, he said, "forget it lad, she's not interested and anyway, she's moved on and is on holiday with Becky, having a great time by all accounts.""

Molly felt sick as she looked at Joe's pleading eyes. She knew just by looking at him that he was telling the truth. Maybe if he'd come home and she'd seen his face she'd have believed him then too.

"He never told me that," she whispered. "I never went on holiday with Becky. I spent every night for almost two months crying in my bedroom, I certainly wasn't having a marvellous time."

"Please tell me you're joking," Joe said taking hold of Molly's hand.

She shook her head slowly. "No, I thought you didn't care because you only rang me a few times and then when I blocked your number you didn't try anymore. In my head, three measly phone calls meant you were guilty because you couldn't face me."

"I wrote to you, as well. Don't tell me you didn't get that either."

Joe could tell by the look of shock on Molly's face that she hadn't received his letter.

"Your bloody parents have caused all this," he cried as he paced up and down. "We could've sorted this six years ago if it wasn't for them. We could have been married with kids by now."

A smile crept to Molly's lips, despite the deep ache she felt in her chest and stomach.

"A bit presumptuous," she said drily.

Joe stopped pacing and looked intently at Molly. "Glad you think it's funny, but I'd actually bought a ring. I was going to propose the weekend the story came out."

Molly gasped and put a hand to her mouth, stopping a deep moan of pain escaping.

Finally, Joe spoke quietly, barely managing to stop his own tears from falling. "You know me Molly. There's no way I would ask you something so important and then sleep with someone else."

"Why didn't you tell me?" asked Molly. "Why didn't you just come home anyway?"

"You didn't even have an email address for me to write to and you wouldn't speak to me or see me, so how could I? And you obviously didn't get the letter. The club threatened to sack me if I left training and I was willing to let that happen but what was the point if, according to your Dad, you weren't there? I should never have believed him and just got on that plane."

"I'm so sorry Joe." Molly reached out and wiped a tear from Joe's face.

"Surely you must see that we should be together" he said catching Molly's hand.

Molly sighed heavily. "I need to speak to my Mum and Dad."

"Let me come with you."

Molly shook her head. "No, I have to do this on my own, and

if you're telling the truth then I'm so sorry, but it can't change anything, I still have to marry Rob. He probably deserves better than me, but I can't let him down again."

Joe nodded. "I know that nothing I say is going to change your mind, but maybe you should tell him about us and let him decide. Lying kept us apart for six years, so telling the truth might mean we can be together."

"Joe, it would crucify him, I can't," Molly blew out a breath. "And if I'm honest, I'm probably too selfish and cowardly."

"If you were selfish you wouldn't be marrying him. Please just think about it."

Molly nodded. "Okay, I will; but I need to speak to my parents before I do anything else."

Molly gently pulled away from Joe; feelings of desolation, regret and pity running through her head. She knew that she wouldn't tell Rob, and she was now leaving the man she truly loved behind.

CHAPTER 19

♥

After Molly left Joe, she dragged Becky and Sophie outside and explained everything to them, including Rob's cancer. They agreed that she should speak to her parents but Becky and Sophie thought it would be better left until the following day, when she had a clearer head. Molly knew this made sense, but the urge to find out the truth was too great and was determined to go there and then. Knowing what Molly was like, Becky and Sophie made it clear that they went along too, to make sure things didn't get too heated.

"Bloody hell, Molly. Why didn't you tell me before? I know Becky's your best friend but I'm your sister." Sophie gently squeezed Molly's hand as they sat in the back of a taxi on the way to their parents.

"I didn't know about Rob" Becky commented.

"I'm sorry Sophie, I just couldn't tell anyone, the more people that knew the more likely it was that Rob would find out." Molly looked away, a blush of shame touching her cheeks.

Sophie sighed heavily. "I understand, but despite my usual demeanour I do know how to behave sensibly and keep a secret when necessary, I'm a barrister for goodness' sake. Anyway, what are you going to do about Rob and you know who?"

"Nothing changes, I'm still getting married. I have to do this for him."

"Hmm, all very noble, Moll, but also a little bit shit. You can't marry someone because you feel sorry for them and that's what you'd be doing.

"Sophie's right. Perhaps you should tell Rob like Joe suggested. That way he can make up his own mind. You might find he doesn't want to marry you."

"I'm damn sure he won't if he finds out," Molly replied, "but I can't put him through that. He needs to get better, and something like that could be really damaging."

"Postpone then, just insist that you wait until he's better," Sophie begged.

"I can't, I've tried. We talked and argued about it, but he insisted we get married as soon as possible. There's no way he'll postpone. He's even persuaded his consultant not to start his treatment until after the wedding."

"What? You can't be serious." Sophie looked as though her eyes were about to explode from her head.

Molly nodded. "That was my reaction too. He only told me last night. His consultant, said it's fine as we're getting married next week."

"Have you spoken to him?" asked Becky. "The consultant, I mean."

"No, Rob told me not to interfere with any of it – he's adamant that he's doing this his way, or no way."

"What does that mean?" Sophie ran a hand through her hair and sighed.

"If I interfere in any of his decisions, then he'll stop the treatment." Molly started to bite her thumb nail nervously.

Becky reached across and slapped Molly's hand from her mouth. "He can't do that, why is he being pig headed?"

"Because that's what he is at times; an obstinate idiot who thinks he has to deal with everything on his own." Molly shrugged. "Do you remember when he was made redundant and didn't tell me until he'd got a new job?"

"God yes, then when you had a go at him about it he didn't speak to you for a week." Becky recalled. "But wanting to do his treatment alone is ridiculous, he needs your support."

Sophie shook her head despairingly. "Bloody hell Molly, you've got yourself into a real mess."

Molly rubbed her eyes. "I know, and it might just start getting a whole lot worse once I speak to Mum and Dad." At that moment, they pulled up outside their parent's house. Sophie paid the driver before joining Becky and Molly on the pavement. They all looked up at the house, and saw a light was still burning in the lounge. It was almost 11pm. but thankfully their parents Wendy, and Graham, were night owls.

"Are you sure you want to do this now?" Becky asked, pulling Molly into a hug.

"Yes," she whispered. "I have to know why they lied to me."

"Come on then titch, let's go and see the oldies and find out what they've got to say." Sophie grabbed hold of Molly's hand and led her up the drive.

***

Molly confronted her parents in the living room and at first they denied everything, claiming that Joe was still lying. Then Wendy tried to deflect from their guilt by accusing Molly of being deceitful and cruel by having an affair with Joe.

"Mum, this isn't about Molly, it's about the lies that you and Dad told. Whatever Molly's done, she's done because she loves Joe, and she's marrying Rob because she loves him too."

Molly felt her face flush, as Sophie's statement wasn't strictly true - she cared about Rob and felt guilty for what she'd done, but she didn't love him in the way she loved Joe.

Wendy threw her hands in the air. "You can't possibly love two people, that's a stupid thing to say and an excuse to do as you damn well please."

"You love both of us don't you?" Sophie asked.

"That's different. A mother's love is totally different to that for the opposite sex. I couldn't even imagine loving anyone else. I love your Dad, and that's it."

"Your mother is right, it's a good way of excusing the fact that you can't keep your underwear on." Graham pointed at Molly accusingly.

"Don't you think I know what I've done is wrong? Of course I do, but Joe was my first love Dad, and if you hadn't interfered I may well have been marrying *him* next week. You had no right to make that decision for me."

Graham shook his head and put his arm around Wendy's shoulder. "We did what we did to protect you. You were too young to be so involved, plus you'd have hated it in Turkey without us around."

"Huh" Sophie groaned. "That's the crux of the matter. You just didn't want her to leave you, did you? You potentially ruined her life just to make you feel better, to keep your own nest full. I was at Law School and you couldn't stand the thought of not having anyone here to control."

"Watch your mouth Sophie" snapped Graham. "You may well be a grown woman but you're still my child and I will not have you speaking to me or your mother like that."

"She's right though Dad, all you've ever done is control us and tell us what we've done wrong. Not once have you said that you're proud at what we've achieved." Molly glanced across at her sister, realising that she should have made more of an effort to be closer to her. They could have been allies growing up.

"Yes we have" Wendy said. "Your dad and I are extremely proud of both of you, even if we don't always say it. We did what we thought was best for you."

"Hah!" Sophie scoffed. "You actually believe that don't you? What a load of crap. You did what was best for *you two*."

Becky, who had been silent so far, stepped forward. "Look, before we start delving into family history, I think you need to remember why Molly is here."

"Becky's right," Molly said "and I don't want to say something that I'll regret, so just tell me why you lied to Joe and obviously hid his letter?"

Graham sighed. "We didn't want you to be anymore hurt than you already were, and like your Mum said, we thought the best thing was for you to forget about him."

"Dad, how on earth could stopping him from explaining be good for me? Do you know how much it hurt me? It felt as if my insides had been ripped out?" Molly started to sob as she recalled those awful days spent crying in her bedroom. "How could you let me go through that? How could you just let me believe he didn't care about me while all the time he really wanted to come here and sort things out and that he'd written a letter to me, which I suppose *you* read?"

Wendy and Graham both looked at each other, their faces crimson.

"Oh God" Molly sighed. "You bloody well did, didn't you?"

"You two are unbelievable." Sophie said, giving her parents a filthy look. She shook her head and walked into the kitchen.

"Do you still have the letter?" asked Molly, staring at the T.V. that was flashing away silently in the corner. Wendy and Graham said nothing. "If you do, I think you'd better get it. It's the least you could do."

Wendy nodded to Graham and touched his elbow.

"Go on love, go and get it."

"What about…?"

"Yes," said Wendy. "That too."

As Graham left the room, Molly turned and glared at her mother.

"What else are you hiding from me?" she demanded.

"Just wait until your dad comes back." Wendy turned and walked over to the sofa and sat down.

Sophie came back into the room, carrying a tumbler of amber liquid. She passed it to Molly.

"Brandy" she said. "I'm guessing you need it."

Molly smiled gratefully at Sophie and squeezed her hand. As Sophie and Becky moved to sit at the dining table, at the far end of the room, Graham came back in holding two white envelopes. He passed them to Molly.

"He sent me two?" Molly put her glass down on the sideboard and stared at the letters.

"No, he didn't." Wendy held her hand out to Graham, who

took it and sat next to his wife. "The other one is from someone else, some teammate of his at the time."

Tears dropped from Molly's chin onto the envelope, smudging the fading address.

"I need to be alone for a while," she whispered and left the room.

As Molly pushed open the door of her old room, her breath caught in her throat, as the pain of losing Joe, all those years ago, came back, just as gut wrenching and raw as if she'd had that heart breaking telephone conversation with him, only five minutes before. It had been her first experience of loss of any kind, and this room was where she had cocooned herself for weeks on end, refusing to talk to anyone, and only leaving her bed to go to the bathroom or to work. She couldn't eat, or sleep properly, and would lie in bed listening to a mix CD of 'their songs' on repeat, and clutching a photograph of Joe. A smile touched Molly's lips as she remembered how the CD had met its demise. Sophie had been home from university, and after hearing 'Dry Your Eyes' by The Streets, for the hundredth time, had flipped. She had stormed into Molly's room, snatched the CD out of the player and thrown it like a Frisbee out of the bedroom window.

Pushing the memories away, she sat on her old bed and, with trembling fingers, she first opened the envelope with Joe's writing on. She read it carefully. In it Joe said that he was lost without Molly, and swore to her that he'd not slept with anyone, nor had he even looked at another woman since he'd met her. He begged her over and over to see him in person, so he could explain face to face and so she could see that he wasn't lying. Finally she reached the last paragraph and, as she read it, Molly started to sob silently.

"You have to believe me, I adore you and I know we're only young, but I want to spend the rest of my life with you. This isn't how I had planned to do it, but please marry me. I have the ring and have had it for weeks. I was going to ask you when you were next over for the weekend, but that bitch sold her lies, and I didn't get chance. Please, please Moll, believe me and marry me...."

He finished by continuing to declare his love for Molly, and begging her again to see him. All of it was heartfelt, and Molly knew that he was telling the truth. She folded the letter and pushed it back inside the envelope.

She then took the other letter, which she saw was dated three months after Joe's, and took a quick look at the signature; it was from Danny Grey, who had been Joe's only English teammate at the time. Danny's letter told her that he'd got her address from a parcel that she'd sent to Joe, which he still kept in his room. He said that he'd thought of calling her but just didn't have the nerve, so a letter seemed better. Molly gasped as Danny then delivered a massive shock; he knew for a fact that Joe hadn't slept with Lara Jade because it was actually Danny who had. He hadn't spoken up because he was married, with a child on the way, and couldn't stand the thought of his wife finding out. It had been a monumental, drunken mistake, but as he wasn't a rising star like Joe, Lara Jade obviously didn't think she'd make any money selling a story about him. Danny went on to say that Joe still didn't know about him and Lara Jade, but he knew he'd have to tell him and just had to work up the courage. He begged Molly to get in touch with Joe but asked if she would pretend she believed him and not mention Danny's involvement, not until he'd told his wife at least. Danny then finished by writing that Joe was always talking about his love for Molly, so she had nothing to worry about. He would never cheat on her.

Molly now let out great wracking sobs as she curled up into a ball, clutching both the letters to her chest. Distress and grief cried out for the life she could have had with Joe if only her parents hadn't been so controlling, or Danny had been braver and admitted all this in the first place.

Eventually, Molly's tears subsided, and she wiped her eyes and nose on the pillow – leaving her mother some washing was the least she could do. Molly sat up and reached for her handbag, she pulled her mobile out and called Joe. He answered on the first ring.

"Are you okay?" he asked.

"Not really, I've seen your letter."

"What, they still have it? All these years and they've never shown it to you. Where are you now?"

Molly let out a sigh. "In my old bedroom, such happy memories," she added sarcastically.

"I'm coming round to tell them what I think of them. I'm sorry, Molly but I hate your parents for what they've done."

Molly closed her eyes, wondering whether or not to tell Joe about Danny's letter, but she knew she had to otherwise she'd be as bad as her parents.

"I got another letter too," she whispered.

"What other letter, what are you talking about?"

"They kept another letter from me, one from Danny Grey."

Joe was silent for a few moments. "Danny Grey? Danny my team mate at Galatasaray?"

"Yes, the same one."

"What did he write to you for?" Joe asked.

"He wrote…please don't go mad and do anything stupid."

"Sweetheart, please just tell me."

Molly took a deep breath. "He wrote to tell me that it was him who slept with Lara Jade, he kept it a secret because of his wife."

"You are fucking joking. I'll kill him when I find him" Joe roared on the other end of the line. "When did he write to you, why the fuck didn't he tell me?"

"Joe, please calm down. He wrote about three months after it happened, and I can understand why he wanted to keep it secret, he was protecting his wife – she was having a baby."

"I can't calm down Moll. We might have had a baby by now if he'd just been bloody honest with me. I would've kept it a secret, as long as he told you."

Molly heard a bang in the background, followed by a groan from Joe.

"Shit!"

"Joe, what's wrong?" Molly asked.

"I've just punched the cupboard door, Christ that hurts."

"Are you okay?" There was silence. "Joe, are you okay?"

"Yes," Joe finally sighed. "Fuck that hurts."

"Have you got some frozen peas that you can put on it?"

"Molly, I'm fine. I'm just so fucking angry."

Molly shifted back on the bed and leaned against the wall. "I know. I don't know if I'll ever speak to my parents again."

"Why didn't Danny just tell me?"

"Is he still with his wife, do you know?" Molly hoped he was, at least it would mean something positive had come from such a mess.

"As far as I know, I think he's got a couple of kids now. Last I heard he was coaching in Scotland, we lost touch after Galatasaray. I wish I hadn't now, this might have come out sooner."

"Well, it didn't, so we just have to accept it."

Joe sighed. "Shit, what do we do now?"

"Nothing, it can't change anything, you know that." Molly let a sob escape as the tears started again.

"Please Molly, don't cry. I can't stand this, let me come and get you, I can get a taxi."

"I can't, I have to go home. Rob will be expecting me soon. I said it wouldn't be a late night. God, I just feel so sad, about everything."

"This is awful. We could've had such a good life together."

"I know" Molly whispered. "I have to go."

"I love you."

"I know." Molly ended the call quickly, not wanting Joe to hear her crying anymore.

Molly lay back down and started to sob once more. After a few minutes, she sat up and was blinking sadly at the letters, when there came a quiet tap on the door. Becky and Sophie popped their heads through the gap.

"Are you okay titch?" Sophie sat beside Molly on the bed.

Molly nodded and wiped her nose on the sleeve of her jacket.

"I believe him. I could tell from the letter that he wasn't lying. Plus…" she laughed emptily. "His friend wrote to me as well, admitting that it was him who actually slept with that stupid slapper."

Sophie and Becky gasped.

"No way!" Becky joined them on the bed.

"Yes way. He couldn't admit it because his wife was expecting a baby, but he wanted me to know so that I'd make it up with Joe."

"But that pair of control freaks down there decided to keep it from you. Was it open?" Sophie asked.

Molly nodded. "Yes, they both were."

Sophie shot up and made for the door.

"Sophie no" Molly cried. "Leave it, forget about it. Nothing is going to change what they've done."

"But what about you and Joe? This proves he didn't do anything wrong, surely you can believe and trust him now." Becky smoothed Molly's hair away from her face.

Molly smiled sadly. "I know, but it's too late. I can't let Rob down."

"Molly, this is bloody stupid." Sophie thumped the heel of her hand against her forehead. "You can't marry him. You don't love him the same way you love Joe. You're marrying him out of pity."

"Sophie's right" Becky said. "You can't go through with this."

"I can and I am going to. Please, don't give me a hard time over this. Joe understands, so why can't you two?"

"Un-bloody-believable." Sophie cried. "And what about those two downstairs, what are you going to do about them? Invite them along to the wedding and act as though they *haven't* ruined your life?"

"I don't know Sophie; I don't know how I feel about them. I know I can't keep them away from the wedding, how would I explain that one to Rob?"

"Well" Becky sighed. "I just hope you know what you're doing, because I sure as hell don't."

"It's what I have to do, there's no other choice, and I'm just going to make it work as best I can."

CHAPTER 20

♥

In the taxi on the way back home, Sophie and Becky tried to fill the silence with by chatting, but Molly just stared out of the window and silently tried to make sense of what had happened and how she ended up making such a mess of her life, but no answers came to mind.

The first one out, Molly shoved a ten pound note into Becky's hand.

"Well thanks for a great night girls" she said, smiling weakly at both of them.

"Do you want us to come in with you, or I could stay over?" asked Sophie, hanging out of the taxi window.

"No, I'm fine honestly. I'll speak to you tomorrow." Molly turned around and made her way up the drive.

At the front door pausing to take a deep breath, Molly rubbed the streaky mascara away from under her eyes.

"I'm home" she shouted into the darkness of the hall.

"In here." Rob was in the lounge watching T.V.

Molly slowly opened the door and plastered a smile onto her face as she stepped into the room.

"Hi."

Rob looked up at Molly and smiled.

"Good night?" he asked.

Molly nodded and kicked off her high heels before flopping

down on the armchair.

"It was good, Sophie did a great job. I'm knackered though."

"You're a bit later than I thought," said Rob. "It's nearly one." Did you go on somewhere else?"

"No, we just stayed in the bar." Molly didn't look at him, but stared at the T.V. "What's this you're watching?"

"The new James Bond film, it's quite good."

Molly feigned a yawn. "Oh okay, I'll go to bed and let you watch it in peace then."

"Okay, I'll be up soon."

Molly got up from the armchair, just about managing to keep her tears in check until she'd closed the lounge door behind her.

***

Molly smiled up at Rob, desperately trying to look as happy as he did. The last week had seemed like a never ending nightmare. Thankfully, Joe had been away on International Duty all week, so she hadn't had to deal with him, but facing Rob had been just as tormenting. Molly had worked hard to pretend nothing was wrong, talking animatedly about the wedding and acting like the happy, but nervous bride to be. Rob had wondered why her parents hadn't been in touch during such an important week, but Molly made the excuse that she'd asked them not to as it made her even more nervous.

It seemed as though no time had passed since she confronted them about the letters, and now she suddenly found herself standing in front of the registrar with Rob, having just said their wedding vows.

"So Robert, you may now kiss your bride."

As Rob took Molly in his arms, his brother and friends whooped and cheered while the rest of the forty strong party of close family and friends clapped politely, all except Molly's parents, Sophie and Becky; all of whom looked down at the floor.

After they'd had some photographs taken, everyone made the half hour journey to a beautiful baroque style restaurant for their small reception.

As they sat in the back of the Bentley taking them to the

restaurant, Rob held Molly's hand tightly.

"Happy?" he asked, kissing Molly on the cheek.

Molly nodded enthusiastically. "Hmm, are you?"

"Very, just can't wait to get you alone later." He now kissed Molly passionately.

Molly kissed him back, telling herself over and over "Be happy, be happy". After a couple of minutes, Molly pulled away.

"You'll mess my hair up." She gave a little laugh and touched her hair that had been taken into an intricate knot at the nape of her neck.

Rob laughed and hugged Molly to his side. "You look beautiful, by the way, although there's not enough boobage in that dress, if I'm honest?" He laughed and winked.

"Oh well, sorry about that. You look pretty handsome yourself." Molly touched his cheek and realised he certainly did look handsome, in his charcoal grey suit, crisp white shirt and purple tie.

"Well, we make a great couple then, don't we, and we're going to have a great life together."

Molly couldn't speak, but merely nodded, hoping that Rob was right.

***

A little later at the restaurant, Sophie grabbed Molly for a quick chat and to check that she was okay.

"I tell you something Molly, when the registrar asked if anyone knew any lawful impediment I thought Joe was going to come striding in like D'Artagnan brandishing a sword and challenging Rob to a duel" Sophie giggled.

"Ssh, someone will hear you" hissed Molly.

"There's no one in here, I checked already."

"Are you sure?" Molly pushed open both toilet doors just to be sure. "That would really finish my week off."

"How are Eva and Adolf doing anyway, have you spoken to them?"

Molly laughed emptily at Sophie's name for their parents. "Well it was slightly tense with Dad in the car on the way to registry office. How was your journey with Mum?"

"Very quiet. A positive bonus as far as Wittering Wendy is concerned. To be honest, I thought you'd travel with Rob."

"I thought about it, but I knew he'd question it too much." Molly puffed out her cheeks and slowly let the breath out. "Do you think he realises there's something wrong?"

Sophie shook her head. "No, you've been brilliant. I don't agree with what you're doing, but I do understand why, especially when I saw how happy he looked. I guess you've just got to make it work, and try and forget Joe."

Molly bit at her bottom lip and nodded. "I know, and I'll do whatever possible to make him happy. I do care about him but..."

Sophie hugged Molly to her. "I know Titch, he's just not Joe, but this is the life you've chosen so make it a good one."

"Thanks Sophie." Molly turned and kissed her sister on the cheek. "I know we don't always see eye to eye, but you've been brilliant this week. I couldn't have got through today without you and Becky, but especially you and your support over Mum and Dad."

"Well that's what big sisters are for. Come on, get that smile back on your face and go and dance with your husband."

***

Molly moved around the restaurant, thanking people for coming and showing off her wedding band to those who asked. It wasn't anything fancy, just a plain, simple, white gold band, not at all like the diamond studded one that Rob had wanted her to have. It had seemed a little excessive; bearing in mind she'd broken her vows before she'd even taken them. Earlier, when Sophie was talking to Becky, she'd suggested that it was because Molly knew she'd be getting divorced at some point, so didn't want to waste any money.

Molly eventually reached the main table where she expected to see her husband, but he was missing.

"Where's Rob?" she asked Sophie, who was chatting to David, Rob's best man.

"In the bar" David said. "He's watching the England match. I did warn him that he was pushing it." He winked and turned back to Sophie.

Molly headed for the bar. Her heart was hammering, and she could feel a heat at her cheeks. She wasn't mad at Rob for watching the match, but she was anxious because Joe was playing and her new husband would be cheering him on.

"Hi" she said, tapping Rob on the back.

"Oh, busted. You don't mind do you?" Rob pulled Molly to him and kissed her.

"Sorry Molly, it was me that dragged him in here." Rob's elder brother, Gary, looked at her sheepishly.

"It's okay, I don't mind. Did we win?"

Rob shook his head. "No, we lost 3-1, we were awful. Joe Bennett missed a penalty."

Molly was glad that Rob's eyes remained fixed on the screen. It meant that he couldn't see the flush of red in her cheeks.

"He's had a terrible game to be honest" Gary added.

"Oh, really." She feigned disinterest.

"Here we go" Rob cried. "Let's see what he's got to say for himself."

Suddenly Joe's handsome face and tight, muscular body filled the screen; he was doing a post-match interview. Molly let out a quiet gasp, his body was almost perfection. He had no top on, just a Captain's armband on his bare arm, tight against his bicep, his chest was smooth and toned, and his stomach sculpted into a perfect six-pack. The camera moved up to his face and Molly could see tiredness and worry in his eyes; they were surrounded by dark shadows and had lost all their usual brightness.

"So Joe, not a good day, a missed penalty and a yellow card for you - *both* most unusual."

Joe sighed and ruffled his hair. "Yes John, it's just one of those days I guess. The main thing is we put everything right for the next game…"

Molly didn't hear any more. All she could do was gaze at Joe on the screen. At that moment, she just wanted to run to him and hold him and tell him everything would be okay. To stop herself from escaping, Molly held on tightly to the chair in front of her.

Rob downed the last of his drink and turned to Molly.

"Ah well, at least that performance is likely to be a one-off from him. I've never seen him so awful, have you Gary?"

Gary shook his head. "No, and thank God he never plays like that for City. Something's upset him. Women problems I'll bet." Gary and Rob started laughing.

"Well Molly would know." Rob nodded towards Molly.

"Eh? What do you mean?" Molly started biting her thumbnail.

"You see him every day, and you look after those players as if they're your babies. I bet you know what's wrong with him."

Molly shook her head. "No idea. I've not seen him all week; he's been with the England squad."

"Hmm, I bet." Rob laughed and gently poked Molly in the shoulder, before turning to Gary. "She never tells me anything Gary. I've tried getting the gossip, but she won't give it up."

"You know I'm not allowed, so get back to your guests and stop teasing me."

Molly pulled Rob's arm and dragged him back to the restaurant, desperate to move away from the pictures of Joe that were still flashing up on the T.V.

CHAPTER 21

♥

A week after the wedding, which was followed by a short break in Rome, Molly was back at work. The break had been *nice*, but nothing more than that. How sad, she thought, that what should have been the most romantic time of their lives, in one of the most romantic cities in the world, was just pleasant. They'd not argued and had an enjoyable time sightseeing, but Molly had just been going through the motions, wearing a smile like a mask and forcing a bounce into her step. Even though they'd had sex almost every night, there was no passion, no fire. They'd simply had sex. They hadn't made love.

Now, sitting at her desk, alone in the office, Molly was totally distracted – not only had Rob's treatment started that morning, but later in the afternoon she and Katie were due to escort some of the players, including Joe, to a local children's hospital. The thought of seeing him again filled her with equal measures of dread and excitement.

Earlier, she had sent Rob off with a bag of essentials to get him through the day: a bottle of water, tissues, a bag of boiled sweets, wet wipes, three magazines and the latest best-selling crime novel. He'd seemed more relaxed than Molly about the day ahead and had even been cracking jokes over breakfast. Molly had asked him to think again about letting her go with him, but Rob was determined that he wanted to be alone. As she pondered the situation her mobile rang.

"Hi Sophie" she said.

"Hiya Molly, I'm just on my way to court so thought I'd give you a quick call. How was Rob this morning?"

"Okay, quite calm to be honest, unlike me." Molly swung around on her chair, turning away from the window through which she could see Joe, plastered all over the giant billboard outside.

"Ah okay, that's good. Listen Moll, something struck me yesterday, and it's been playing on my mind."

"What?" Molly asked, sitting up straighter in her chair.

"Well, has he mentioned anything about his fertility after his treatment?"

"His fertility?" Molly stood up and closed the blind at the window. "What about it?"

"Well I remembered a case that I helped on when I was doing my pupillage at the chambers, for a woman whose husband had died from cancer. Because they knew the chemotherapy would make him infertile they'd had some of his sperm frozen, but as he'd died the clinic where it was stored wouldn't let her use it. So she took them to court."

"Oh no, that's awful."

Sophie sighed. "Molly, listen to what I'm saying. They knew the chemo' would make him infertile, has Rob mentioned that to you?"

Molly was silent for a few seconds as Sophie's words sunk in. "No."

"Well don't you think he should have, and if not why hasn't he?"

Molly couldn't answer. She had no idea why Rob hadn't told her or how she felt about the possibility of him becoming infertile.

"Molly, if you stay with him you may never have children, you do understand that don't you?"

"Yes," Molly whispered.

"So, that's just another sacrifice you're willing to make so that you don't hurt him is it?" Sophie's voice grew louder. "This is stupid Molly; you have to sort this out."

"You said at the wedding that you understood." Molly flopped down into her chair.

"For Christ's sake, I do, well I did, but this could jeopardise you having a family, and Rob hasn't even told you. Don't you think that's a little strange?"

"Yes, but he must have his reasons." Molly tried to think of a valid reason to offer Sophie, but couldn't.

"What reason is there to keep something this major from you? You have to tackle him about it, or are you actually going to see sense and leave him?"

Molly gasped. "No, I'm not going to leave him. I've only been married a week, and my reasons for marrying him in the first place haven't changed."

"Yes, but this is a really important piece of information that he's omitted to tell you."

"Maybe it's not so important to me." Molly rolled her pen up and down the desk distractedly.

"Bullshit Molly, all you've ever talked about is having a family one day. You've even picked your kids' names for God's sake."

"Yes well I'm not so sure I like Monica, and Chandler anymore, I was twelve when I picked them." Molly said.

Sophie tutted. "Molly this is serious. You married him out of pity, and now he's kept this from you. This is a fucking mess, and you have to get out of it."

Molly rubbed her eyes and gave a deep sigh. "Look, I hear what you're saying and I will ask him why he didn't tell me, but to be honest it's not something I'm concerned about at the moment."

"*What*, are you crazy? Please enlighten me on that reasoning."

"I don't know, I'm just not." She tried to keep her voice steady, but really didn't want to speak to Sophie about it any longer.

"I'll tell you why. It's because you've lost all purpose of your own life and you think it's all part of your punishment for cheating on him in the first place."

"That's not true. I'm just more worried about his health than whether I can produce a couple of kids."

"If you say so, but maybe deep down it's because you're not interested in investing anything in this marriage, which if that's the case then why stay in it at all? He'll get over it if you leave him."

"That would be cruel. You know I can't do that."

"Argh, you bloody infuriate me at times" Sophie sighed heavily. "Okay, but please don't let this go without speaking to him about it. It's too important."

"Okay," Molly replied impatiently. "I will. Now go to court and I'll speak to you later."

As she ended the call, Molly thought about why she wasn't as upset with Rob keeping it from her as she might have been. Maybe his health was more important to her than her own desires, or maybe Sophie was spot on, and Molly didn't actually care enough to be upset.

***

Later that afternoon, Molly and Katie were leading a small group of players down the stark white corridor of the hospital. They were visiting a children's ward to hand out gifts, have their photographs taken and generally cheer up all the kids. Joe was at the back of the pack, constantly watching Molly and waiting for an opportunity to talk to her about the letter. The other players had noticed that Joe wasn't particularly happy and had tried to cajole him into smiling with their usual jokes and banter, but a small smile was all they'd managed before he dropped back from the group and fell silent again.

***

Molly held the door open as all the players trooped into the ward. When Joe reached her, Molly's heart was beating rapidly, and her breath was ragged. Why did he have to look *that* gorgeous? His jeans were hanging low from his hips, the simple white t-shirt strained at his biceps, and his hair, cut short at the sides and longer on top, was sexily messy, crying out to Molly to run her hands through it – and his smell…God it was intoxicating.

Molly felt the pull of desire for him in her stomach as Joe stopped in front of her.

"Are you okay?" he asked, giving Molly a sad smile.

She nodded. "I'm okay."

"How was the wedding, did everything go well?"

Molly wasn't sure how to respond. Did she say 'oh yes the wedding and honeymoon were fantastic', or did she tell the truth, and say it was okay, but she was miserable without him?

"It was okay," she finally replied. "It went well, thanks."

"That's good." Joe dropped his head and scuffed his foot on the shiny floor. "Can we talk Moll? I think we need to." He looked up, his eyes pleading with her.

Molly looked down at the floor and shook her head. She wanted to do more than talk to him, she wanted to hold him and kiss him, to feel his body against hers.

"We can't Joe…I can't."

"Why? It's just talking, that's all."

"You know why."

Joe scrubbed his hands across his face and groaned. "For God's sake, we can't just leave it like that," he whispered. "*I* can't anyway. Please Molly, I don't feel like I can even breathe without you."

Molly shook her head. "Please don't say that Joe. We can't, it wouldn't be fair on Rob, and in any case…" She broke off and turned away, her eyes searching for the other players.

"What?" Joe insisted, standing in front of her.

She sighed and closed her eyes. "It wouldn't be just talking. I'd probably fall into bed with you again."

A small smile briefly touched Joe's lips. "Yeah? So?"

"So it would be wrong. It was bad enough doing it when I wasn't married to Rob, but now I am. I just can't, as much as I want to, I can't."

Joe placed his hand against Molly's cheek.

"Christ, what a mess,"

"You're not kidding."

"I don't know what to say or do that will make it better, I

honestly don't. So for now we'll just have to get through it one day at a time I suppose." Joe took a step away from Molly. "Come on then, we'd better go and cheer the kids up."

Molly smiled. "Thank you."

Joe shrugged and giving Molly one of his most beautiful smiles, walked away.

***

When they were all on the ward, Katie and Molly stood aside and let the players get on with talking to the children. Molly marvelled at the way their faces lit up like beacons, just from a simple handshake or a hand on the head from a player. Joe, however, was the most popular and all the children that weren't too ill clambered to speak to him.

At one point, he picked up a tiny little girl with blonde ringlets and bright blue eyes and Molly's heart stopped as he tenderly stroked the girl's face. He then said something that made her giggle and she threw her arms around his neck and kissed his cheek. Molly gasped as a thick thud of love for Joe hit her heart and took her breath away. He handed the little girl back to her mother and waved at her as he bent to speak to a little boy who was tugging on his jeans.

"Ah, how cute was that?" Katie nudged Molly.

Molly nodded, unable to speak, scared that if she did the emotion she was feeling would cause her voice to break. It was in that moment while watching Joe kneeling down and chatting with the boy that Molly decided she would leave Rob as soon as he was well. The feelings that she had for him were nothing compared to those for Joe, and while she'd done what she thought was right by marrying him, she now knew everyone else had been right in their opposition to it. She'd tried to kid herself that she'd done everything for Rob that her decision had been utterly selfless, but now she realised that she'd been a selfish coward. All she had done was delay the inevitable, miserable outcome.

***

Driving home, Molly must have been operating on autopilot

because before she knew what she was doing, she found herself parking behind Rob's car on the driveway. Throughout the journey home, she'd been worrying about how she would find Rob, anxious about how the day's treatment might have left him. In light of what she'd decided, Molly wondered whether she ought to raise the fertility issue and ask why he hadn't told her. She let herself into the house, hung up her coat and paused, listening out for any noise, but the house was silent. She went through to the lounge, which was empty, so she made her way back into the hall with a sigh. As she placed her foot on the bottom stair, she suddenly felt all her breath and energy rush out of her body. Her legs buckled, and she slumped down onto the stairs. Her heartbeat and breathing quickened like a steam train gaining speed. She held tightly onto the bannister staves, and tried to block out the sound of her heart drumming in her ears. Cold sweat spread across her body and tears surged from her eyes. She sat like that for what seemed like an eternity until eventually her breathing slowed, her heartbeat steadied and her tears stopped falling.

After pulling herself together, Molly made her way slowly up the stairs and opened the bedroom door. The room was in darkness, but she could make out a figure under the duvet. She tiptoed into the room with the intention of leaving Rob sleeping while she changed out of her work clothes.

Rob stirred in the bed. "Hi."

"Hey," she whispered. "How are you feeling?"

"Okay. Tired and a little sickly, but okay. What time is it?"

Molly looked across at the clock on her side of the bed. "Almost half past six. Do you want to stay there, or get up and have some dinner?"

Rob sat up, stretched and yawned. "I'll get up, but I'm not sure I could eat anything."

"How was it?" Her eyes were drawn to the cotton pads held by medical tape on his hand and on the inside of his arm, where the chemotherapy lines had been.

Rob shrugged. "Boring and depressing, but I don't want to

talk about it. Is that okay?"

Molly nodded. "Yes, that's fine, but I'm worried about you, so you'll have to tell me about it at some point."

"I know," Rob said, "but not tonight. How's your day been?"

Molly paused, wondering which parts of her day she should share with him – the fact that Sophie called to warn her about his possible infertility, or the fact that she'd spent an afternoon gazing at Joe and had decided to leave her husband. Taking a deep breath, she decided on Sophie.

"Sophie called me this morning, she's a little bit worried about something."

"Oh right, what's she worried about?"

Molly told Rob what her sister had said and how she found it strange that he hadn't mentioned the possibility that his treatment could leave him infertile. Rob listened, without interruption until finally Molly finished and flopped down onto the edge of the bed.

"Okay, I didn't tell you because I didn't want to worry you, but it's sorted anyway." He reached out and held Molly's hand.

Molly snatched it away. "Okay, I kind of understand that, but for God's sake this is important. You might not be able to father a child. Didn't you think that was something I *should* worry about?"

"Look, I made a mistake and I'm sorry, but it is sorted."

"Sorted? How is it sorted?"

"I made a sperm deposit last week when we got back from Rome. Although, you know we might be lucky, you could already be pregnant." Rob winked at Molly.

A cold sweat prickled at Molly's skin. She knew it wasn't possible as she was on the pill, but the thought still filled her with dread.

"Unlikely," she snapped. "So not only did you not tell me about the infertility issue, but yet again you made an important decision without telling me?"

"I just thought I was doing what was best." Rob threw his legs out of the bed and stood up. "But I got it wrong, so fucking shoot me, I'll probably be dead soon anyway." He stormed past Molly and walked to the en suite and slammed the door.

Molly sighed. She got up and banged on the bathroom door.

"Rob, can you not see that we should have discussed it?"

Rob pulled the door open and faced her, his hands on his hips. "I'm sorry, okay. I made a mistake. I thought I was doing the right thing not telling you, but obviously not. Haven't you ever made a mistake?"

Molly looked at the floor. "Of course I have," she said quietly, "but I just need you to see my point of view."

"I do, now I'm going to get a shower. I'm meeting the lads for snooker in an hour."

CHAPTER 22

♥

"If that's what I want to do, then I'm doing it, *okay*?"

"All I'm saying is perhaps you should wait and see what your consultant says first?" Molly turned her back on Rob and sighed.

She had been home half an hour and they had been arguing since she walked through the door. In fact, it was exactly the same as every other night for the past three weeks, with them disagreeing about everything, from Molly not stacking the dishes correctly in the dishwasher, to something like this – Rob insisting he go on a fishing holiday to France with his friends for a week. Molly wouldn't normally have protested, but wanting to go in the middle of his treatment seemed ludicrous.

"Just stop treating me like a baby." Rob pushed past Molly, almost sending her back onto the bed.

"Hey" she shouted to his back. "There's no need for that."

Rob stopped and turned to face her, his eyes narrow and his hands tightened into fists. "Well stop being a moaning bitch then."

As Rob slammed the bedroom door, Molly let out a scream of frustration. All she was trying to do was look out for him, but he seemed determined to do everything on his own terms.

She flopped down onto the bed and stared at the ceiling, listening to Rob banging cupboard doors in the kitchen below. There had been a brief hiatus from their rows around the time of the wedding, but they'd soon started up again. In fact they had got much worse since Rob had started his treatment, and while she understood it must be terrifying for him, she hadn't expected him to become as nasty and taciturn as he had. Lately they'd hardly said a word to each other, or when they did it was usually petty squabbling or, like tonight, positively blistering - heated enough to burn the paint off the doors.

Molly wondered if Rob had finally realised what she herself had over six months ago – their relationship had changed and had taken a deep descent into oblivion. Maybe he also knew that getting married had been a mistake. Whatever he was thinking he just wasn't the same person anymore, but then neither was she.

Turning onto her side and pulling her knees up, Molly thought about Joe, and a great fog of sadness enveloped her. She had only seen him a handful of times over the last three weeks and all had been strictly professional.

Lying in the dimming light of the bedroom, Molly had never felt as lonely or as empty. She had no connection with her husband, her own fault admittedly, and she had a self-imposed ban on the man she truly wanted to be with. Added to that, she didn't feel that she could tell anyone about her decision – she didn't want them saying "we told you so". Molly pulled the throw from the end of the bed, wrapped herself in it, and after a few minutes, the warmth, the silence and the darkness all helped to make her eyelids heavy. She felt herself floating into a soft cloud of sleep, when her phone suddenly shrilled on the bedside table next to her. Groaning, she reached over for it and saw that it was Mr Grahame, the club's Chief Executive. Pulling herself into a sitting position, Molly answered the call.

"Hi Mr Grahame, is everything okay?" He hardly ever called her outside of office hours unless there was a major problem with one of the players.

"Molly, I need you to get over to the City General as soon as you can. I'm in London meeting with the F.A. and just had a call from Joe Bennett's agent."

Molly almost doubled over as an invisible boot kicked her in the stomach.

She paused momentarily, afraid to ask. "Wh-what's wrong?"

"He's been burgled. He came home while they were there and they roughed him up a bit, but he managed to lock himself in the bathroom. Tony wasn't sure how badly hurt he is, he was on his way to the hospital when he called me."

"Oh my God!" She put a hand to her mouth.

"I'm sorry to ask you to do this Molly, but I know you'll get him sorted."

Molly took in a deep breath. "No problem Mr Grahame." She flung her feet to the floor and started searching frantically for her shoes that she'd kicked off earlier.

"I just need you to make sure he's okay, get him into a hotel for the night and let him have whatever he needs. I've got Karen onto Will from the press office and asked him to meet you there in case the press find out."

"Okay, Mr Grahame. I'm on my way."

"Good girl. Let me know how he is when you get chance. If…" Mr Grahame's voice trailed off and Molly could hear him sigh in the background. "If he's badly injured make sure no one finds out, get Will to put out a press release that he's got a few cuts and bruises, but nothing else."

Molly agreed and ended the call, pulling her club jacket from the wardrobe. She ran down the stairs in a daze, a sick feeling growing in her stomach. As she pushed open the lounge door, Rob looked up from watching the television.

"Where are you going?" he asked.

"There's been a problem with one of the players. I have to go and sort it out." She picked up her keys and her handbag and left, slamming the front door behind her.

CHAPTER 23

♥

"I'm here for Joe Bennett," Molly gasped, flashing her club identity card at the receptionist.

She doubled over, clutching her side and breathing heavily from running all the way from the only parking space she could find, which was right at the far end of the vast car park. On the way to the hospital, a ball of anxiety had bounced around her stomach and with every red light or slow moving car in front of her, it had grown bigger and bounced faster. She kept telling herself that he would be okay. He had to be – she couldn't lose him again, there was no point to anything if Joe wasn't in her life. By the time she got to hospital, her breathing was laboured, her hands were shaking and silent tears slid down her cheeks.

"If you press the green buzzer by the door, the nurse will let you through," the receptionist said. She smiled at Molly and pointed towards a door a few feet away.

"Thanks" Molly panted. She moved quickly across to the door and banged the palm of her hand on the large, green button. She tapped her foot impatiently and waited. After a few seconds the door was pushed open by a small, round nurse, in a washed out, pale blue uniform. She eyed Molly suspiciously.

"Yes?"

"I'm here for Joe Bennett, I'm from the club." Molly flashed her ID card again.

The nurse nodded and stood aside to let Molly through the door.

"I'll take you to him," she said.

Molly followed the nurse to the end of the ward and watched nervously as she pulled aside a pale blue curtain around one of the cubicles.

"He's in here."

Molly managed a weak smile of thanks, before ducking through the curtain. She rushed forward, unable to hold back her tears at the sight of Joe. His face was chalky white except for a black bruise around his left eye and a wide, scarlet flash of blood on his bottom lip. He was covered in a shroud like blanket that was pulled up to his chin and tucked around his shoulders.

"Oh my God, Joe!"

Joe opened his good eye and smiled.

"Hey Moll."

A breath of relief rushed from her lungs

"God, what did they do to you?" She ran her trembling fingers across his forehead, her eyes searching his face for any sign of pain.

Joe pushed the blanket down and dragged himself up the bed.

"No, lie down, you might be badly injured!"

"I'm okay, honestly. Look." Joe wiggled his feet and hands to show that he had no broken bones.

"What happened?" Molly pulled a chair closer to the bed and grabbed hold of his hand, stroking the back of it with her thumb.

"I got home and there they were, nicking all my stuff."

"How did they get in, and why didn't you just call the police?"

"I have no idea how they got in. The gate was closed when I got home but there was a Range Rover parked near the entrance door. I just thought someone was viewing one of the apartments so I didn't really give it a second glance and didn't call the police because nothing seemed strange. The front door was shut and I had no idea that they were in there until I went inside and one of them jumped me." Joe winced as he put a hand to his shoulder and flexed his arm. "I only went back because I thought I'd forgotten my wallet, but it was on the floor of my car all the time."

"Maybe now you'll get some security, like I keep asking you to do." Molly pulled Joe's hand to her lips and kissed it, needing to feel his skin against her. "Christ Joe, they could have killed you."

"Hey, I'm okay, and I promise I'll look into some security." Joe leaned towards Molly and brushed her tears away with his finger. "I'm glad you're here."

"I was so worried about you. Mr Grahame called and then every bloody traffic light I got to was red and then I had to park miles away and..." Tears started again as Molly relived her anxious journey.

"Moll, calm down, I'm fine – I promise." He shifted closer and kissed her gently.

Molly pulled away and smiled.

"Where's your agent by the way? Mr Grahame said he was on the way."

"He's gone with Will from the press office to decide what to release. I don't see the point in saying anything; it's only cuts and bruises." Joe shrugged and then nodded at their clasped hands. "Hey, you do know you're holding my hand, don't you?"

Molly blushed and started to pull her hand away, but Joe's grip tightened.

"Leave it where it is," he whispered "it's making me feel better."

"Oh God Joe, I thought you might be really hurt, or worse." Molly closed her eyes, her bottom lip trembling.

"Well I'm not. The nurse said I'm free to go home once they've stitched my lip."

Molly winced. "Ouch, that's going to hurt."

"I know, so you'll have to stay and hold my hand."

***

Joe's agent and Mr Grahame had agreed that Joe shouldn't return to his apartment until the next day, so Molly drove him to a hotel a few miles out of the city.

"I'd love to know how they got in" he said, touching the bruise around his eye. "They hadn't forced their way in, either through the gate or my door."

Molly shook her head and sighed. "They sound like they were professionals."

"I can't believe the cheeky bastards did it in broad daylight. They must have been watching the place to know I wasn't home."

"Well, I'm glad you weren't, they might have really hurt you otherwise." Nausea gripped Molly's stomach, as she thought about what could have happened.

As they drove along the quiet country road, they fell silent. Molly glanced at Joe from the corner of her eye, wondering whether he was going to ask her about Rob. She had made it obvious at the hospital how she felt about Joe, but he hadn't questioned anything. Then, as if reading her mind, Joe's hand reached across and gently stroked her cheek.

"How've you been?"

As he took his hand away, Molly immediately felt the coldness. She needed to feel his touch. She also knew that she had to be honest with him, after tonight and thinking the worse, she had to tell him the truth, always.

"I've been feeling a little bit rubbish, if I'm honest."

Joe's face broke into a smile. "That's good, not that you feel rubbish, but that you've been honest and not given me a load of crap that married life is great."

"It's not, believe me." She went on to tell Joe all about her rows with Rob. "He's not been violent to you has he?" Joe's jaw clenched.

"God no, he's not like that. He's called me a moaning bitch, but nothing worse than that."

"Well I'm not happy about that" Joe growled.

"He's scared Joe, it's no wonder he's lashing out." Molly glanced at him and smiled. "But thanks for caring."

"Of course I care. I love you. I want you in my life every day and in my bed every night." He turned to look at Molly and his voice dropped and became thick with lust. "I imagine what I'd do to you, how many different ways I'd show you that I love you and need you."

Molly pushed her legs together as a fire started in the pit of her stomach, and her groin throbbed at Joe's words.

"You have no idea how crazy you make me, do you?" Joe whispered.

Molly gripped the steering wheel so tightly her knuckles turned white, and stared straight ahead.

"I don't want to share you Moll, but I will if that's what it takes to have you in my life again."

Molly let out a small groan as she felt Joe's hand on her thigh – he moved it slowly up her skirt, only stopping when he reached the top of her stocking. His touch almost incapacitated her and she just about managed to pull onto the gravelled driveway of the hotel.

"I need you so bad, it hurts."

"Joe" Molly gasped.

Joe slowly rubbed the bare skin at the top of her thigh with the back of his hand, making Molly shift in her seat. Instinctively she lifted her crotch toward his hand, moaning quietly as her breasts strained against the buttons of her blouse.

Joe moved his hand back down her leg, letting his fingers linger as they traced the curve of her thigh.

"Stay with me" he whispered.

Molly shook her head. "I can't."

"I'm not going to take no for an answer, and the fact that your nipples are hard is telling me that you want to."

Molly glanced down; although she didn't need to look to know what Joe said was true. She could feel them tingling and that alongside the heat in her groin told her that he was right, she could if she wanted to, and God she wanted to.

"It's up to you. I understand if you don't want to, but I think you do." Joe unbuckled his seat belt and got out of the car.

As she watched him walk away, Molly placed her hand on her stomach that was doing a loop the loop, and clenched her thighs together, trying desperately to snuff out the fire that was burning between her legs. With an unsteady hand she picked up her handbag from the footwell and then got out of the car. She wasn't sure whether it was the crisp, cold night air that took her breath away, or the thought of what was about to happen.

***

As soon as they got through the hotel room door, Joe pushed Molly against the wall, his mouth instantly on hers, kissing her hard as his hand moved up her blouse and cupped her breast.

"Joe, your lip."

"Fuck my lip. Just the taste of you makes if feel better."

Molly pushed her head back, letting Joe's mouth move down her neck. She yanked off her jacket and unbuttoned her blouse. Joe started to kiss along the swell of her chest that was heaving with deep panting breaths. He kissed along her ribcage and down to her stomach, while his other hand pushed up her skirt. Molly reached out her shaking hands, grabbing for his shoulders, digging her fingers into the hardness of his muscles. Her hands went to the back of his neck and then quickly moved to his head, grabbing a handful of his hair as Joe's hand dragged down her underwear. When his fingers moved between her thighs she thought she was going to explode, and gasped at the sweet sensation that burned throughout her body. She reached out and pulled the buttons open on the fly of his jeans, and gasped as she discovered he was naked underneath. Briefly fluttering her fingers enticingly over his erection, Molly pushed Joe's jeans down, and arched towards him.

"Oh my God" she gasped as Joe moved his hand slowly between her legs.

"I love you."

"I love you too."

Groaning against Molly's open mouth, Joe lifted her, and as she wrapped her legs around his waist, moved inside her, taking her hungrily against the wall. Desperate and having been starved of each other, within minutes both their bodies tensed and shuddered to a climax, as Joe gently put his mouth against Molly's, swallowing up her scream of pleasure.

"You are amazing" he whispered into her ear, as he tried to control his breathing.

"What are we going to do?" Molly was panting, as out of breath as Joe.

He pulled his head back to look at her, cupping her face in his hands.

"What do you want to do?"

"I want us to be together, but we have to wait."

Joe kissed her forehead and then sighed. "Okay, as soon as his treatment has finished we'll tell him together."

"No, I have to do it alone, it's going to hard enough for him as it is."

"Will you tell him about us?"

Molly nodded. "Yes, I've lied to him enough already."

"Well until then, we'll have to be patient. It'll kill me being apart from you, but I'll wait because I love you."

"I love you too" Molly whispered as she clung to him, with tears of happiness escaping from the corners of her eyes.

CHAPTER 24

"What time did you get home last night?"

Molly looked down and stared at the toast on her plate. "About one, I think."

"What was the problem, or is it top secret as usual?" Rob pushed his own plate away and picked up his cup of tea.

Molly felt her throat constrict and her blood throbbing in her ears. Despite this she managed to look him in the eye.

"Joe Bennett was burgled and beaten up. We had to wait for him to get his lip stitched, and then he had to give a statement to the police and I had to find somewhere for him to stay so I dropped him at a hotel near to Wilmslow, then I called Mr Grahame..." Molly stopped, realising that she was babbling,

Rob blew out a breath. "God, is he okay?"

"Yes, apart from a stitched lip and a black eye."

"Have they caught them?" Rob took another sip of his tea, eyeing Molly over the top of his cup.

Molly shook her head. "No, but the apartments have CCTV at the gates and in the entrance hall, so they're hoping to pick something up from that."

"Hopefully they will, although if they're professionals it's doubtful."

"Do you really think so? Surely the police will find something on the CCTV."

Rob shrugged. "Maybe, but if they've targeted a gated apartment block, they must know what they're doing."

Molly's mouth fell open. It hadn't occurred to her that they may have targeted Joe; naively she had just imagined they had spied a chance on what were obviously the homes of wealthy people.

She started to flick through the newspaper.

"Do you think they could have been watching him, waiting to see when he went out?"

Rob stood up from the table, finishing off the rest of his tea. "I don't know, but I remember watching a documentary about it and a lot of burglaries are planned, especially if they think it's going to be rich pickings. Did anyone else get broken into?"

"Not as far as I know, but I don't think the other apartments have been sold yet?"

"There you go - a prime target. Anyway, I'm off."

"What time is your chemo' today?" Molly asked, catching hold of Rob's elbow as he passed her.

"One, so I should be home by five. Do you want me to start dinner?"

"God no, you'll be tired, and food is probably the last thing you'll want to look at. No, I'll sort it when I get home."

"Okay, whatever. See you later."

As the front door closed behind Rob, Molly realised that was the first civilised conversation that they'd had in days; also, she didn't fail to notice that despite their civility, Rob hadn't given her a goodbye kiss.

***

In the car, on the way back to his apartment from the hotel, Joe laced his fingers with Molly's whenever possible. At every opportunity he leaned across to kiss her cheek, or to stroke her hair, all leaving Molly feeling highly charged. She was craving for him yet again, but rather than do a U-turn back to the hotel, Molly held firm and drove to Joe's apartment where they were to meet his agent and Mr Grahame, who had flown back from London that morning.

Pulling up the drive, they saw that both men and the police were already there.

"Do you think they'll guess why we're late?" Joe asked, running a finger lazily along the back of Molly's neck.

She shivered with longing. "Stop it, someone will see."

"They're too far away. What about if I do this?" He circled her nipple on the outside of her blouse. It immediately sprang to life.

"Pack it in" Molly scolded, slapping his hand away, but with a wide grin on her face. "I'm supposed to be working, and you've already distracted me once this morning."

"I think you'll find I've distracted you, ooh let's see, six times as you were officially working last night too." He gave her his most dazzling smile.

Molly sighed. "And you can stop with the knicker dropping grin as well."

Joe started to laugh as he adjusted his jeans. He placed both his hands on his knees and looked away, through the side window.

"Okay, you win. I'll be good, but only until you're off duty and then I plan on making up for it."

"Whatever, Joseph, we'll see. Now, concentrate on what the nice policeman has to say."

As they got out of the car, Mr Grahame rushed over to them, his hand out ready to shake Joe's.

"Blimey Joe, that lip looks sore." He bent his head to take a closer look. "How many stitches?"

"Only three" Joe replied, touching his lip.

"Does it hurt much?"

"No, I put something on it last night that soothed it." His glance at Molly was so fleeting that no-one could have spotted it – except for Molly, whose cheeks flamed slightly.

"Well, at least it's nothing that will stop you from playing."

Tony stepped forward and peered at Joe's lip and eye. "Perhaps we should see what the club doctor says first. We don't want to risk the stitches bursting."

"I think it'll be fine," Joe said. "I gave it a pretty vigorous workout last night."

"Sorry?" Mr Grahame asked.

Molly stared at Joe, her eyes silently warning him that the burglars would be the least of his worries if he said anything.

"I Googled some lip exercises." Joe's face was serious as he addressed the two men. "They were very good and really stretched it out, so I think I'll be fine to play."

At that moment, Joe's lips were forgotten, as roaring up to the gates with the horn blasting, was a neon green Lamborghini. Everyone turned to the gate and en masse gave a groan.

"Tino."

"What the hell is he doing here?" Mr Grahame asked, shaking his head.

Joe pointed a small fob and pressed it to open the gate. They all watched as Tino's car sped up the drive and screeched to a halt in front of them. The wheels had barely stopped turning when Tino flew out of the car and rushed to Joe, grabbing him into a bear hug.

"Joe, I am so worried when Charlie he tell you have been buggered."

"Burgled Tino, it's burgled."

"I am sorry for that too. Did they hurt you bad my friend?" Tino moved back and held Joe at arm's length. "Oh my friend your eye it is bad, and your lippy."

"Oow!" Joe cried as Tino poked at the stitches on Joe's lip.

Stepping forward, Molly took Tino by the arm and guided him away from Joe, whose eyes were glistening with smarting tears.

"Shouldn't you be in the gym, Tino?" she asked.

"Mr Ribero he tell me I can come and see my friend. He say he sick of my crying." Tino turned and looked back at Joe. "My poor Joe, I will give you some clothes, they take your clothes, yes?"

"No, no, Tino, it's okay. They didn't take my clothes, and I'm not sure you're my size anyway." Joe shot a look at Tino's snake print shirt and cream trousers.

Tino nodded his head and shrugged.

"If you okay Joe, that is good, but I will help if you need it."

"I think Joe will be fine, now why don't you get back to the club. I'm sure the Manager will be happy to see you back." Mr Grahame moved across to Tino's car and opened the driver's door. "Go on lad, Joe is safe and sound."

Tino grabbed Joe into another rib busting hug. "You call me my friend if you are scared I will be with you."

"Thanks Tino, but I'll be okay, I promise."

As Tino sped away, everyone shook their heads in disbelief.

"Is that what you have to deal with every day, Molly?" Tony asked.

"Pretty much." Molly laughed as she watched the gates shut behind Tino's car.

"Remind me to give you a pay rise love," muttered Mr Grahame. "Right, Joe, let's go and see what these coppers have to say."

CHAPTER 25

♥

"So, are you okay for tonight?"

Molly looked around to check there was no-one nearby, before whispering into her mobile. "Yes, where are we going?"

"I thought I'd take you to meet Luna and Gabi. I need to go over some final details for the restaurant with them" Joe replied.

"Oh, okay."

"What's wrong, you don't sound very sure about it?"

"No, I am. I'm just a little nervous I suppose."

Joe started to laugh, and spent the next five minutes allaying Molly's fears that his close friends and business partners wouldn't like her.

***

Over the last three weeks, she and Joe had found time, and excuses, to see each other almost every day at either the club or the training ground. They'd also managed to get some time alone at Joe's apartment over the last two nights whilst Rob was away on his fishing trip, and had snatched a meeting at the team hotel when they had a match at Stoke. As much as they'd wanted to spend the night together at the hotel, they both thought it better if they didn't risk getting caught. Molly had given the excuse of a headache to go to her room instead of having drinks in the bar and Joe had gone to "make some phone calls" for an hour, before re-joining the team to continue celebrating another win.

Molly's home life hadn't improved any, in fact, things had got considerably worse. When he wanted to speak, which wasn't often, all Rob did was pick arguments with her. She still had no idea what was making him so grouchy, but whatever the reason, she didn't ask him because if he didn't want to raise it then she owed him that much – at least there would be no falling out and she could stay with him until he was better. Rob still hadn't told his family that he was ill and Molly knew without doubt that he wouldn't if she wasn't around, typically he'd want to deal with everything alone and she couldn't stand the thought of that. But deep down, she also knew that not asking him meant she could avoid having to face the truth a little while longer. As for Joe, he had been nothing but patient, loving and tender, offering her any support that he was able to.

The burglars still hadn't been found, the CCTV footage didn't give the police any clues other than there were two of them, both wearing balaclavas and nondescript, black clothes. The Range Rover that they were driving had been caught on camera too. It showed that within thirty seconds of Joe driving out of the gates, the burglars had driven in, but the number plates were covered and no one had noticed anything suspicious as a black Range Rover was pretty much de rigueur for the area. As Joe had thought, they had obviously been watching the place for a while as they knew exactly how long they had to get inside the gates once he had driven off. They also must have known that there was an exit loop on the gates, meaning that as you drove up to them on the way out, they opened without the need for a remote control, so there was no danger of them being trapped inside.

With Joe's swift return, they hadn't had the chance to take anything big, just some cash from a drawer, a couple of Joe's watches, some jewellery and his iPad, which made Molly petrified that they would return for the rest of his stuff, so she had been insistent that Joe hire some protection. Joe didn't think it was necessary, but to appease her now had an enormous, ex-Paratrooper called Denny looking after him when he went out alone in public. Molly had wanted Denny to live in at Joe's apartment, but he had argued he was merely a footballer, not a rock star, and there was no way that was going to happen.

***

"Seriously, they'll love you." Joe said as he dragged Molly up the path of his friend's house.

"Do I look okay?" She stopped in her tracks, pulling Joe to a halt as she took a deep breath, trying to calm the maelstrom of nerves in her stomach.

"Baby, you're beautiful. You look stunning in whatever you wear."

Molly leaned her forehead against Joe's chest and held onto him.

"Gabi and Luna are important to you; I just want them to like me."

Joe bent to look up at Molly and gave her favourite smile, the one that crinkled the corners of his eyes. "They will, I love you so they will too. Now, stop being silly."

Molly chewed at her bottom lip and nodded. "Okay. Let's do this."

A little over two hours later, and she wondered what all the nervousness and anxiety had been about. Gabi and Luna were absolutely lovely and had welcomed Molly into their home with open arms; literally grabbing her into a hug as soon as she stepped through their front door.

"You love him very much." Luna's rich, Spanish accent resonated sweetly as she looked at Molly with deep brown, hooded eyes.

Molly nodded as she glanced across at Joe, who was looking at some menu designs with Gabi.

"Very much. I always have." She looked back to Luna and smiled shyly.

"Well, he loves you very much too, he tell us every day for three years how much." Luna threw her hands up, a gesture of despair at having to listen to Joe talk about Molly. "I also see the way he looks at you. I have never seen him look at any other woman like that."

Molly gulped, not sure whether she liked Luna's forthrightness about Joe's love life in Spain.

"Did he have lots of women?" she asked, knowing that she might find Luna's answer stomach churning – but her inquisitiveness was winning an inner battle to know.

Luna shrugged, and jutting out her bottom lip, nodded her head from side to side, as though counting Joe's conquests in her head.

"I will not lie there were many women that he bring to the restaurant, but I do not think he slept with *all* of them."

Molly coughed nervously. "He said there was a woman he was seeing, but it didn't work out, who was that?"

Luna took a drink of her wine as she thought, and then shook her head. "No, no one. Oh many try to capture him Molly, but he was not interested, it was only ever you."

Molly looked over to Joe again, and this time their eyes met. His gaze was so intense it practically pinned her to the chair and took the breath from her lungs. She felt every nerve ending prickle and her body felt like an electric generator humming into life – only a look from Joe could make her feel that way.

Joe walked over and leaned down to kiss her gently on the lips.

"Are you ready to go?" he said, more a statement than a question.

Molly chewed on her bottom lip and looking up at him with wide eyes, simply nodded.

***

"Who the hell is that at this time in a morning?" Joe pulled his arm from around Molly and reached for his mobile.

Molly yawned beside him and rubbed her eyes. After leaving Luna and Gabi's the previous evening, they'd just about made it back to Joe's apartment before their desire for each other took over. She hadn't planned to stay over, but it was late and she felt so secure and happy in Joe's arms that she couldn't tear herself away.

"Tony, what the hell do you want at six in the morning?"

Molly, lay back and ran a finger down Joe's spine, never tiring of looking at his physique, and touching his golden skin.

"How did you know? Yes, she's here." Joe turned and looked anxiously at Molly.

Molly shot up and threw the duvet back. What the hell was he doing telling his agent that she was in his apartment – in his bed?

"Joe!" she cried.

Joe shook his head and put a finger to her lips.

"You have got to be joking, how the fuck has that happened?" Joe was silent for a few seconds listening to the voice on the other end of the line. "We *have* to stop it, I don't care what it takes or how much money you have to offer, just make it disappear, and tell them I'll sue if they go ahead."

Molly stared at Joe with questioning eyes.

"What's going on?" she mouthed.

Joe ignored her, his voice louder as he grew more agitated. "I know I should have told you, but it's complicated…okay, we'll speak later, and thanks." He dropped the phone onto the bed. "Shit, shit, shit," he groaned, banging his fist against his forehead to emphasise each word. "This can't be happening."

"What can't be happening? What the hell is going on?" Molly pulled at Joe's arm.

"I'm so sorry Moll, but one of the papers is running a story about us tomorrow." His hand reached out to her, but Molly shrank back from his touch.

"What, you and me?" Molly dragged both her hands through her hair and clutched her head. "About us being together?"

"Tony only got the heads up because he knows the sports editor. They've got photos of us." Joe moved forward and now grabbed Molly, cradling her in his arms. "I'm so sorry."

Molly pulled away again and stared at him, her lip trembling and her eyes wide and glistening.

"What photos have they got? We've been really careful."

Joe sighed and rubbed his eyes. "There are pictures of us talking at the training ground."

Molly gave a brief smile. "Pictures of us talking don't prove anything, where's the story in that?"

Joe shook his head. "It's the way we're talking. Apparently it's obvious in the way we're looking at each other something is going on. It's not just that…they've found out we used to go out together, plus they've got some photos of us from last night, in the entrance hall." Joe reached out a hand and cupped Molly's cheek, a look of defeat clouding his face.

When they had arrived home last night they'd been so desperate for each other that Joe had pinned her up against the wall inside the entrance hall and they'd almost had sex there, ripping at each other's clothes and kissing greedily – scenes that were perfect tabloid fodder.

Molly climbed off the bed and started to sob as she scrambled around the floor, picking up various pieces of clothing she'd discarded the night before. Her heart was beating so fast it felt as if it was revving up, getting ready to take off, and she felt as though she was about to vomit.

Joe jumped off the bed and grabbed Molly around the waist, pinning her arms to her side.

"Hey, calm down. Molly, please just breathe, come on please." Turning her around to face him, Joe pulled Molly into a tight embrace, gently rocking and wiping the tears from her face as he slowly pacified her.

A little while later, Molly sat on the edge of the sofa, clutching a tissue and staring through the window into the grey March morning. Outside, the world was just waking up, and everyone was going about their own lives, seemingly carefree. She wished that she could turn the clock back a couple of months, not to change being with Joe, but she would do everything differently. Now all she was going to do was hurt Rob in the most public of ways.

Joe came over and squatted in front of her, taking both her hands in his.

"Stupid question, but are you okay?"

Molly nodded silently, pulling Joe to her and hugging him tightly around his neck. He manoeuvred himself onto the sofa and, pulling Molly onto his lap, he gently kissed her forehead.

"It's going to be okay, we'll get through it. Tony might even be able to bury the story yet."

"No he won't, you know he won't." Molly whispered. "I don't care about me, its Rob I care about. He's coming home tonight and he's going to be coming home to *this*."

"I know, but I'll be there with you if you want me to be." he said, burying his face in her hair and taking in a deep breath.

"No." Molly shook her head. "I have to tell him by myself. I just don't understand how they've found out."

Joe gently pulled at Molly's thumb that had found its way into her mouth, before she had chance to start chewing at her nail.

"Neither do I, Tony thinks that some 'pap' got a lucky break when he was taking pictures at the training ground."

"But we've been so careful, especially on open training sessions, purely for that reason." Molly rubbed her temples, trying to ease the pounding in her head.

"He was probably in a tree with a long lens." Joe laughed, attempting to lighten the situation.

Suddenly Molly pulled away and covered her eyes with her hand.

"What about the club, what are they going to say?"

"Hey, look at me…please."

Molly dropped her hand and looked up at Joe.

"The club will be okay and if they try and punish you for this I'll threaten to put in a transfer request."

"You can't do that," Molly replied. "Then they really will hate me and want to get rid of me."

"Seriously, it's going to be okay. Tony is going to ring Mr Grahame and explain everything. We've just got to stay here until he tells us what he wants us to do."

Molly nodded and sighed. "Okay."

But she knew it wasn't going to be okay, not for a long time.

***

"I can't say I'm happy about this. I'm surprised at you particularly Molly, you're newly married, but what you lads get up to never surprises me." Mr Grahame was staring out of his office window, his back to Molly and Joe.

Molly twirled around her wedding ring as she glanced at Joe and grimaced. It felt as though they were in the Headmaster's office, about to find out whether they were going to be suspended for snogging at the back of the classroom.

Joe reached across for her hand. "Look Mr Grahame, we realise that this is a tricky situation for the club, which is why we were being so careful, also with Molly being married we were trying extra hard." Joe paused as he felt Molly flinch beside him. "But, as we said, this isn't just some sordid affair that's not going anywhere. We want to be together, we've loved each other for a long time."

Mr Grahame swung around to face them, his shoulders slumped and his hands deep in his pockets.

"So you said. But the fact of the matter is the tabloids and gossip press will only care about the fact that she's married and you're a rich, spoiled footballer who's seen what he wants and taken it."

"It's nothing like that though…"

"Molly, I know that, but all I'm saying is the press may not see it as some sort of Disney romance. And what about your husband, have you told him yet?"

Molly dropped her eyes, unable to endure the look of disappointment in her boss's eyes. "He's been on a fishing trip abroad, he's back tonight."

"Right, I suggest you get Marcus and the rest of the team up to speed with the details for Saturday's away trip, and anything else that needs sorting, and you take tomorrow and Saturday off. I'm sure when your husband arrives home you're going to need some time. After that we'll take each day as it comes. If you need next week then take it as a holiday."

"Thank you Mr Grahame." Molly's face flamed as she felt well and truly chastised.

"I'll get Will to come up with some sort of damage limitation press release, should we feel it necessary. Are you happy if we explain your history together?" Mr Grahame looked at them both in turn – they both nodded.

Molly knew that there was no going back now. She had to tell Rob the truth, so there was no point making up more lies for the press.

"I don't suppose Tony has managed to bury it by some miracle, has he Joe?"

"No, sorry Mr Grahame. Apparently, the story is worth much more than I could offer – priceless seemingly, but I don't know why."

Mr Grahame furrowed his brow. "Really, you don't know why…I really thought you had a bit more brains than that Joe. Okay," he sighed. "Keep me informed of what your plans are. I don't want to have to hear from some hack while I'm on the way to my car that you've eloped. I need to know everything."

"Thank you Mr Grahame, we do appreciate it." Joe got up from his seat, still holding Molly's hand.

"Let's hope it's a one day wonder, we've got an important run in to try and win the Premiership and I don't want any unnecessary distractions. I suggest you both tell your immediate colleagues so that they're warned before the story hits tomorrow. Now, both of you get out of my sight."

As they slipped into the hall, both Molly and Joe heaved a sigh of relief that at least that part was over.

"God, I was convinced he was going to sack me." Molly flopped down onto a chair. Mr Grahame was a fair man, much respected by everyone, but his loyalty was always to the club.

"I wouldn't have let him." Joe sat next to her and put his arm around her shoulder. "Unfortunately the worse part for you is to come, are you sure you don't want me there?"

"No, I'll be fine." Molly looked up at Joe and gave a weak smile. "I need to go and tell my team now, which should give them something to gossip about. What about you, when are you going to tell the squad?"

"Mr Ribero wants me to tell them this morning, when they're all in the gym. It's a good thing that you're not going to be here for the rest of the week; at least you can avoid all the jokes and banter about us."

"Hmm, I guess. Well, I'd better go." Molly quickly looked up and down the hall before landing a kiss on Joe's cheek. "I'll try and ring you later. Rob's back at about eight, so I'll tell him as soon as I can."

Joe's eyes narrowed. "If it looks as though it's going to get nasty, then promise you'll ring me straight away."

"I promise, now get to the gym before you get into any more trouble."

As Molly watched Joe leave, she felt a sense of relief. This was going to be awful for Rob, and she would have done anything to have avoided hurting him in this way, but at least now she would be able to start her life with Joe, and for that she was thankful.

***

Molly leaned back in her chair, waiting for someone to speak. All three of her team were open mouthed, staring at each other and then back to Molly.

"Well someone say something, I'm sure you've got lots of questions."

Marcus shifted uncomfortably in his seat and coughed nervously.

"You and Joe Bennett?"

Molly nodded.

"You and *the* Joe Bennett?"

"Yes, Marcus, me and *the* Joe Bennett."

"How long have you been…erm…you know?" Rosetta whispered as she leaned closer to Molly conspiratorially.

Molly sighed and wondered how much she should tell them. She was battling her conscience; they were her team and always loyal to her, so she should afford them the truth, but she also didn't want to lose their respect.

"Okay, well we went out together when he played for the club about six years ago, but we broke up when he went to Galatasaray. We hadn't seen each other since that day, so when he came back it was a massive shock, but we found that we still had feelings for each other."

"Ah, that's really romantic." Katie gazed at Molly and sighed.

"As much as it might be Katie, I should have stayed away from him. Not only was it not very professional, but I betrayed Rob."

"Oh shit, I never thought of that." Marcus turned to Rosetta and winced.

Molly pinched the bridge of her nose as her three colleagues all exchanged knowing glances.

"Okay, listen it's not something that I'm proud of, but Joe and I are together, and I am going to have to tell Rob tonight. I'm only sorry that I haven't been able to tell him first, but because the story is going to break tomorrow I won't be here and you all needed to know so that you're ready for their questions." She turned and looked through the window, and a smile touched her lips at the irony of a fifty feet high Joe gazing back at her under the huge tag line "I'm back and here to win".

Everyone fell silent again until finally Rosetta moved over to Molly, and placed an arm around her slumped shoulders.

"It's a bit of a shock, but we're here for you, as always. Is there anything else we can do?"

Molly shook her head. "Just say no comment, that's all you can do. The rest is down to me. It's my mess, and I've got to sort it out, I'm just not looking forward to it, one little bit."

CHAPTER 26

As she waited for Rob, Molly felt like a balloon stretched to bursting point. She was so anxious that even the distant sound of a siren sent her into floods of tears. Her stomach lurched and the breath rushed from her chest, as yet another set of headlights shone through the window, but moved on. She had never dreaded anything as much as this. If she rolled together her driving test, every exam she had ever taken and every interview she'd ever had, it could never be as awful as what she had to do now. Molly knew that everyone had been right, that she shouldn't have married him, but he was ill and she had wanted to be there for him – well that had certainly backfired.

Almost an hour later than expected, another set of headlights lit up the room, but this time they pulled up onto the drive. Molly's breathing quickened and she wiped her clammy, trembling hands on her jeans as she waited for Rob to come in. They hadn't spoken while he'd been away, there had been just a couple of text messages - one from Rob to say he had arrived, and a reply from Molly hoping he had a good time and to make sure he took his medication. Molly lay a hand on her chest and felt her rapidly beating heart, the long breath she blew out did nothing to slow it down.

Standing in the middle of the room, facing the door, she waited for it to be pushed open.

"Hi." Rob came in and flashed a weak smile at Molly. "Are you okay?"

Molly nodded and crossed her arms across her chest.

"Hmm, what about you, did you have a good week?" she asked as she started to chew at her thumbnail.

"Yes it was good to get away, you know…" He looked sideways at Molly as he moved over to the sofa. "Are you sure you're okay, you look a bit strange?"

This was it. It was time to knock down his whole world. Then it struck Molly, he might be glad, he certainly didn't seem to like her much at the moment, or maybe he already knew deep down. But no matter what, he shouldn't have to have his life laid bare in front of the whole country.

"I'm fine, sort of," Molly said quietly. She moved over to sit next to Rob. "I need to tell you something though."

"What?" Rob stared wide eyed at Molly, watching the tears falling silently down her cheeks. "What's wrong, why are you crying?"

Molly reached out to take his hand, but changed her mind and laid her palms against her churning stomach. She tried to speak but her throat was dry and her breath caught, causing her to let out a strangled sob.

"Tell me!" Rob demanded, his hand resting on Molly's shoulder.

"I'm so sorry, I didn't mean this to happen and I didn't want you to find out like this, but…" She took a large gulp of air, trying to control the sobs that were making her whole body shudder.

***

Rob's his eyes narrowed. "Find out what? Tell me."

"I'm so, so sorry Rob, I didn't mean to." Molly started to sob again, unable to continue.

He searched her face. "You've slept with someone else, haven't you?"

Molly nodded and wrapped her arms around herself.

"I didn't mean it to happen, but I was weak and stupid and it happened and…"

"Who the fuck is it, do I know them? Please don't tell me it's a player."

"I'm so sorry. You know I love you and I wouldn't do anything to hurt you, but I just, we just…"

Rob stared intently at Molly but she couldn't meet his gaze. He stood up and moved across the room and leaned against the fireplace with his back to her.

"Is it Joe Bennett?" he asked without turning around, his tone measured.

Molly didn't answer, but sobbed as she rocked in her seat, her arms wrapping even tighter around herself.

Rob turned to face her, his eyes wild. He moved across and squatted down in front of Molly, grabbing her chin and forcing her to look at him.

"I asked you a fucking question, is it Joe Bennett?"

Pushing his hand away, Molly nodded.

"Yes," she whispered. "I couldn't help it, he came back and I…"

Rob held up his hand. "I don't want to know the details. I don't care when it started, or when and where you've been shagging him, but it stops now." He stood with his fists clenched at his sides.

"No, I can't stop it, I love him and I have to be with him."

"What does that mean, you *have* to be with him?" he asked incredulously.

Molly let out a shuddering breath. "I love him and want to be with him."

"Why, is life with a cancer ridden bookie not exciting enough for you anymore? Why the hell did you marry me then?"

"It's not like that Rob, I loved you, and I just wanted to do what was right, but Joe and I just can't be without each other."

"Ah how bloody romantic, so his money doesn't matter then."

"No," Molly cried, scrubbing the tears from her cheeks with the back of her hand. "You know I'm not like that."

"I thought I knew you, but obviously I don't, you're just a lying, money grabbing slapper." Rob's jaw tightened as he took a step closer to Molly. "You make me sick."

"I can't help it, I've always loved him and I know that must hurt, but I did love you too, I still do."

Rob shook his head. "Please don't you dare give me the old 'I love you, but I'm not in love with you' routine, give me some respect. We've only been married a few weeks, why on earth did you go through with it?"

"You were ill, and you wanted to get married, so I wanted to do that *for you*. I ended things with Joe as soon as you found out about the cancer, but it was killing us both, and then when he got beaten up it made me realise how much I loved him."

"Oh great, so his bruises trump my cancer is that it?"

"Don't be stupid." Molly moved to him, but stood a few paces back, aware of the anger burning in his eyes. "It wasn't like that. I wanted to be there for you while you were ill and I did what I thought was the right thing by marrying you, but I know I was just being weak and cowardly and avoiding telling you. I was going to tell you once you'd finished your treatment."

"I thought that we were happy before I got ill, and before he came back, so how could you just let yourself do this, how could you just drop your knickers so easily?" Rob moved closer, with his nose almost touching Molly's, she shrank back as he spat the words at her.

"We *had* been happy, but I can't explain how he makes me feel, what I feel for him. I did try and stop it from happening, I honestly did." Molly's eyes dropped contact with Rob's.

He bent his knees to look up at her. "You hardly tried at all did you, how soon was it before he got you into bed? He's only been back three months so you can't have tried that hard. What was it days, hours, did he shag you at the Press Conference…you fucking tart."

Molly didn't see him move his hand, the first thing she knew was when her head jolted back, and her cheek started to sting.

"You bastard," she cried, clutching the side of her face. "You hit me, how dare you?"

Rob shook his head and smirked. "How dare I hit you, you've

just bloody ripped my heart out, but I can't slap you."

"No, no you can't."

Rob was silent for a few moments and then sighed.

"I'm sorry, I shouldn't have done that." Rob pulled Molly's hand away from her cheek and peered at it. "I'm just so angry with you."

Molly pushed him in the chest and moved towards the door.

"Where are you going? We need to talk about this."

Molly paused, with her hand on the door and looked at Rob over her shoulder. She sighed heavily, before moving back to the armchair.

"So, what happens now, are you going to him tonight?" Rob put his hands behind his head and stared up at the ceiling.

Molly didn't answer. She watched him closely and wondered how, in a few short months, she'd managed to mess his life up for him. He didn't deserve this; he was ill and had enough to worry about.

Rob broke the silence. "Well, are you, are you leaving tonight, because I assume you are leaving after declaring you *have* to be with him?"

"It's up to you, I can go tonight if you want me to, or I can go tomorrow."

"If it were up to me I'd make you stay and forget about the overpaid wanker, but it isn't. One thing though, why tell me tonight the minute I get through the door instead of after my treatment finished like you planned?"

Molly flopped back against the chair and closed her eyes, not wanting to see his face when he heard the words.

"I had to tell you tonight because tomorrow…well because tomorrow the press are going running a story about us."

"You are fucking joking." Rob paced the room. "I'll be a laughing-stock. Everyone will know what you've been doing behind my back."

"We tried to bury the story, but couldn't." Molly stood up and went to him. "I know I keep saying it, but I am sorry."

"Sorry doesn't cover this Molly. Do you realise that every part of our life will be out there? My family don't even know I'm ill yet. I'm going to have to tell them now, for fuck's sake." Rob lunged his hand across the fireplace, sending a vase and a photograph flying.

"I'm s…" Molly stopped herself apologising *again*, knowing that it certainly wouldn't help. "They might not find out, it's me and Joe they're interested in."

"And you don't think the jilted husband is a good story? They sure as hell will." Rob dropped down onto the sofa and held his head in his hands. "Why couldn't you just stay away from him?"

Molly's body, stressed and exhausted, gave way beneath her and she too collapsed onto a chair. For a long minute she and Rob sat in silence, looking at each other warily. Finally, Rob sprang onto his feet.

"I realise I can't make you stay," he said, "but if we put on a united front maybe the story will go away. What do you think? We could deny everything."

"We can't Rob, they have pictures." Molly winced as she remembered their steamy passion that had been caught on camera. "There's no getting away from the fact that Joe and I are together from the pictures they have."

"Christ, this just gets better and better." Rob rubbed his eyes wearily. "Okay, we deal with whatever they publish and maybe you're right, maybe they won't be interested in me. I can't deal with this anymore tonight, I'm going to bed. I'll sleep in the spare room and we can decide tomorrow what happens next."

"Okay," Molly whispered as she watched Rob disappear through the door.

CHAPTER 27

♥

Molly sat in darkness for almost an hour after Rob went to bed, worrying about what the following day would bring. She had called Sophie earlier in the evening and told her the latest news. This resulted in a full minute of silence from Sophie which was a record for her, being someone who was never short of something to say. When Sophie finally spoke she called her sister a prat, but told her that she would support her and would speak to a friend who specialised in media law to determine if there was any way the story could be shelved. However, she doubted it as "you're a pair of stupid idiots who allowed yourselves to be photographed in flagrante". Becky was a little more sympathetic but still thought Molly and Joe had been careless. Thankfully, Sophie had agreed to tell their parents about the story. Molly had barely spoken to them since she found out about the Joe's letter and she certainly didn't want to have to contact them and endure another lecture.

Closing the lounge door quietly, Molly sat down and dialled Joe's number.

"Hi, are you okay?" He answered almost immediately.

"It was awful," Molly groaned. "I've hurt him so much." She sniffed and wiped her nose on her sleeve.

"Sweetheart, please don't cry."

"I've never seen him so angry and upset."

"He didn't hurt you did he?" Joe asked anxiously.

Molly considered whether to tell him about the slap. "No, he didn't hurt me."

They spent the next hour talking about her conversation with Rob and how they were going to deal with the fall out the following day. Both agreed that it would be better if they stayed apart, at least for tomorrow, and then Molly would move into the apartment in the next few days. As she agreed to it, Molly's feelings were in turmoil. Just discussing it felt like another betrayal of Rob, but the thought of being with Joe all the time filled her stomach with butterflies and made her heart race – it felt like the countdown to the trip of a lifetime. Finally, with her eyelids drooping, Molly told Joe she was off to bed.

"God, I wish I could be with you tonight" he sighed.

"I know, but it won't be long now. Will I speak to you tomorrow?"

"Yeah of course. I'll call you first thing, before training."

"Okay, oh how did the team take it, by the way?" A small smile made its way to Molly's lips as she imagined some of the comments from the players at Joe's news.

"Hah, how do you think? They thought it was hilarious. A few of them gave me a pat on the back and made the usual coarse jokes. Tino even asked if we could double date with you and your sister."

"Oh God forbid! I know they mean well, but I can't help feeling it's all a bit disrespectful to Rob."

"Well to be fair, most of them did say they felt sorry for him, but were happy for us. We're a team, it's only natural."

"I suppose" Molly sighed.

"Listen, you go and get some sleep, and we'll talk tomorrow, okay?"

"Okay."

"Good, and don't forget I love you."

"I love you too" Molly whispered, hoping that tomorrow wouldn't be as bad as she expected.

***

Any plans Molly and Rob had the next morning of sitting down and discussing things were scuppered by the constant ringing of their mobiles. Joe called first, just to see how Molly was, and to let her know that they were indeed front page news. While talking to him, she opened up her iPad and went to the web edition of the newspaper running the story. Molly could see from the pictures that stared back at her that there could be no doubt she and Joe were in a relationship. They were talking, seemingly quite harmless, but gazing into each other's eyes and smiling warmly as Joe's finger linked with one of Molly's down at their side. The other photographs, in the entrance hall of Joe's apartment block, were less clear and slightly grainy. Their bodies were silhouetted by a light behind them; Joe's hand was pushing up Molly's top while her hand was fisted into his hair. It was clear what was going on, but their faces were obscured and they could have been any couple. Molly read about their previous relationship and how they'd reconnected resulting in Joe coming back to the club. 'A source close to Mr Bennett stated that he had bought himself out of his contract with Real Madrid in order to return to Miss Pearson, with whom he had been having a long distance relationship for the last six months'. She smiled at the untruth, but everything else about the article was true. Thankfully, Rob's illness wasn't mentioned, and he was only spoken about as her 'new husband of a few weeks'.

Once Joe had hung up, Sophie called, then Becky and then a couple of Molly's other friends, her Grandma and her Auntie Sheila – all of them offering support but, apart from Sophie and Becky, Molly could sense their surprise and disappointment. She was extremely grateful that her parents decided to stick to their agreement and not call her.

Rob's phone was also hot with calls, and he had to have a difficult half hour conversation with his Mum, confirming that he was okay, begging her not to come over from Sheffield. Molly could sense that she was being called some fairly unpleasant names on the other end of the line because Rob kept glancing at her and wincing. She totally understood why his Mum would feel the need to castigate her, so she left the room hoping it would allow Rob to feel more relaxed about letting his mother rant.

Finally, when it was almost lunch time, they got to sit down and decide what should happen next. Rob was looking at the article, the words obviously distressing him by the look of dejection on his face. He read quietly, occasionally punctuating the silence with heavy sighs.

"How could you be so stupid?" he finally asked, stabbing the picture of Joe and Molly at the training ground with his finger. "Didn't you think you might get spotted? All eyes are on *him* all the time. Christ, you should know that better than anyone, you're the Player Liaison Manager."

Molly rested her forehead on the dining room table, the cool wood soothing her pounding head for a few seconds.

"I know" she groaned. "And I know I keep saying it, but I'm sorry."

"You know if you weren't happy you should have told me." Rob pushed the iPad away and sat back in his chair.

Molly looked up at him and fixed her eyes on his, they looked so tired and he was washed out. This was exactly why she hadn't wanted him to find out while he was still ill.

"Do you feel okay?" she asked. "You look really pale, perhaps you should go and see your consultant, or at least give him a call."

He shook his head. "No, I'm fine. I didn't sleep much last night. I've got my next lot of chemo' in a few days, I'm probably just ready for it."

"I can't believe you're being so calm about all of this today." Molly put her head on one side and looked at him. He was like a different person to the one who had slapped her last night. It would have been no surprise had his anger exploded when faced with the pictorial evidence of Molly's betrayal.

"I did a lot of thinking through the night and I know I'm not going to be able to change your mind. I know you, and I can see it in your eyes that it's him you want. We're done. You're going to leave, so what will bawling and shouting change?" He shrugged and stared out of the window into the garden.

"I know, but what I've done to you is horrible. You must hate me."

Rob contemplated his answer for a few seconds. "I don't hate you Moll; I can't say I like you though. But him, I *do* fucking hate."

"It wasn't just him, it was me too and he was single, I wasn't." Molly reached over and poured them both a cup of tea. "I'm sad it's ended this way."

"Well it's not how I thought we would end up. I have to be honest, I never envisaged us breaking up, ever."

Molly gasped as the enormity of what she'd done to him hit her again, like a great hulking wrecking ball to the gut.

"I know we haven't been getting on recently, but I had hoped that once I was better then things between us would be too."

"Did you have an idea something was wrong, is that why I've been annoying you so much recently?"

Rob shook his head and picked at the hem of his t-shirt.

"No, I just couldn't find it in myself to be pleasant to you. I hate having the treatment, and I'm scared it won't work, so what is there to be nice about?"

"I can't imagine what you're going through, but it will work, I know it will."

"If you say so." Rob let a small smile touch his lips.

A deep affection for him swept over Molly, and she gently cupped his face with her palm.

"I don't expect you to forgive me, but I will always regret what I've done to you because I do love you." She knew that it wasn't strictly true, but what would be the point in hurting him anymore than he already was.

Rob nuzzled his cheek against her hand for a moment. "You just love him more."

Molly dropped her hand and turned her face away. She couldn't fathom how he could be so damn decent about it all. Last night he had been furious, and a little scary, but today he was being calm, measured and practical, even after seeing the evidence of her betrayal.

"Anyway, what now?" Rob asked, taking a drink of his tea.

"I don't know, what do you think we should do?"

"I have no idea. I assume you still want to be with him."

Molly eyed him warily, not wanting to add to his pain.

"Well, do you, or have you changed your mind?" he asked.

"I still want to be with him," she said quietly.

"Okay, well you go and I'll stay. I'm guessing lover boy won't want to live here." He swept his hand around the room. "But, in the meantime I'm going to go and see my Mum and Dad for a few days. I'm going to have to tell them about the cancer, plus I don't want to be here if the press come knocking on the door. Can you be gone by the time I got back?"

Molly flinched as darkness cloaked Rob's face, but then he smiled again and she relaxed. He was bound to go through peaks and troughs of emotion, she thought, but there had been an intensity in the look that had scared her.

"Okay, I'll go today" she replied. It wasn't what she and Joe had agreed, but she knew he wouldn't mind. "I may have to leave most of my stuff for now, is that okay?"

"Oh I'm sure lover boy will buy you everything you need."

"Rob!"

"What? Just saying what I think. Look, take what you can…in fact take whatever you want. I can't stand the thought of sitting here for hours dividing up our CD and DVD collection; it's too depressing for words. Actually, there's a chance you'll get everything anyway if I die before we get divorced."

"Don't say that." Molly could sense that his mood was changing again, quite rapidly, and she wanted to avoid another argument. "I'll take my clothes and stuff for now, and we can talk about everything else another time."

"Whatever" he sighed. "I'll speak to you when all the fuss has died down."

"Okay" Molly whispered. "And I am sorry."

"Yeah, you said."

***

With a tear stained face, Molly packed up her clothes and other essential things into a couple of suitcases. She had called Joe and told him she would be there in a couple of hours, he was surprised but told her he would be waiting. He was a modest man, not one to boast about his skills or the money that he had amassed because of them, so even though Molly could hear the joy in his voice, she wasn't surprised that he had tempered his excitement out of respect for the situation.

Panting with frustration as she tried to push her hairdryer and a large box of curlers into the suitcase, Molly wondered whether she was taking too much with her. However, Rob's comment about Joe buying her everything new had stung and as much as the thought of three cases of stuff was a little excessive for the short-term, she hated the idea even more of people thinking she was after Joe's money. Letting out a scream of defeat, she threw the hairdryer, the curlers and three pairs of shoes, onto the bed. She knew Rob had an overnight bag in his wardrobe and she was sure he wouldn't mind if she borrowed it.

Flinging open the wardrobe door, she dropped to her knees and started to feel her way to the back of the darkened cupboard, moving piles of shoes, old jumpers and ties that had fallen from the rail. Finally, she found what she was looking for, a brown checked overnight bag that had been folded into itself.

Molly set the bag on the bed and opened it up. As she put her hands inside to straighten it out, she felt a cloth bag, with something inside it, pushed into the corner. Curious, she pulled it out. It was a small, yellow cotton sack, the sort of bag that you took money to the bank in. Molly frowned and wondered why Rob had one and why he'd hidden it away. Opening it up, she peered inside and then started to pull out the contents: two watches, a wad of cash, a man's silver ring and a black velvet covered box. She lifted the lid on the box and there, nestled inside, was the heart shaped diamond pendant on a white gold chain that Joe had tried to give to her, the necklace that she had refused and that Joe had said he would keep, just in case she changed her mind.

CHAPTER 28

As Molly stared at the box in her hand, a blanket of cold sweat covered her body and she started to tremble. Her legs suddenly forgot they had bones in them and buckled beneath her. She grabbed for the edge of the bed and sat down, still clutching the box.

"Oh Rob, what the hell have you done?" she whispered. "You stupid, stupid idiot."

Putting the box to one side she looked again at the other items in the bag. She picked up one of the watches and studied it; it was a Hublot Classic and she was pretty sure that she had seen Joe wearing it. The other watch was equally as expensive and the ring, on closer inspection, she saw was platinum not silver. The expensive items, the necklace and the cash undoubtedly belonged to Joe, but what the hell was Rob doing with them? Had he been one of the burglars, or was he just hiding them for one of his dodgy friends? A hundred questions chased each other around Molly's head but whatever the answers, one thing was clear: Rob was somehow involved in the robbery.

With the realisation, Molly felt a wave of nausea wash over her. She ran to the bathroom and threw up into the toilet. After emptying her stomach, she sat back against the cool tiles and reached up for some tissue paper to wipe her mouth. Her hands were shaking and anger bubbled in her stomach as the enormity of Rob's actions hit her. She wasn't sure how involved he was, but he definitely had something to do with the robbery at Joe's apartment. Luckily Joe's injuries were only minor, but he could quite easily have been badly hurt, or killed, and that along with the fact that Rob had obviously known about their affair long before she'd told him, not only frightened Molly, but incensed her too. If he'd known, why hadn't he confronted her about it, and what sort of person was he to consider such an act? Molly knew he must have been hurting, but this was an evil way to deal with the matter.

Molly desperately tried to make sense of things, so pulling up her knees; she rested her forehead against them and closed her eyes.

***

She wasn't sure how long she had been asleep, but it must have been a while because her neck was aching and her body was shivering from the coldness of the bathroom tiles. She hauled herself up to her feet and thought about what her next move should be. She knew that she should call the police, but wanted to speak to Joe first. On unsteady legs she made her way back across to the bed, picked her mobile and tapped out Joe's number.

"Are you on your way here?" he asked excitedly.

"Not yet, there's something I need to speak to you about first." Molly's voice was barely audible.

"What's wrong, you are still coming aren't you?"

Molly let out a sigh. "God yes, but something has happened that you need to know about."

"What's happened? Are you alright?"

"I'm okay, it's just...I think I know who robbed your apartment."

"What? How the hell have you found that out?"

Molly rested her head back against the wrought iron bedstead and took a deep breath.

"I think it was Rob, I found a bag in his wardrobe and it's got all your stuff in it, except for your iPad."

Joe was silent for a few seconds.

"Rob. You're joking right?"

"No, I'm not. I'm looking at the stuff now."

"Are you sure it's my stuff?" he asked.

"I'm pretty sure, because the necklace you tried to give me is with it. Did they take a Hublot watch too?"

"Shit, yes, yes they did…oh my God. What the fuck has he done?" Joe fell silent again, obviously mulling over what Molly had told him. "I need you to get out of there as soon as you can. Where is he now? He can't find out that you know." Panic echoed in Joe's voice as he shouted instructions down the line at Molly. "Put my stuff back where you found it, get your bags and get here as soon as you can."

"Joe, calm down, he's not even here. He's gone to Sheffield to see him Mum and Dad."

Joe gave a sigh of relief. "Thank God, I couldn't stand it if you got hurt. Okay, bring it with you, but get out of there anyway. I won't feel happy until you're here and I can see that you're safe."

"Do you think we should move it though? He might deny it was ever here."

"I didn't think of that. Okay, put it back and then come here, once you get here we can call the police. Have you touched it?"

Molly dropped her head into her hand. "Oh shit, my finger prints will be all over it."

"Don't worry; his will be too…hopefully. But please, sweetheart, just get out of there."

"Okay, I'll finish my packing and then I'll be over. Should I call Sophie and ask her for some advice on what we should do?" Molly thought about Rob and how this was going to ruin his life. How could he have been so stupid and malicious?

"Yes, but don't let her call the police, we need to talk first. Do you think he knew about us all along?" Joe broke her thoughts.

Molly contemplated the question. Why else would he be involved in something so serious?

"I don't know. He's been moody and off hand with me but if he did know his reaction last night was pretty good acting. He looked totally shocked and hurt."

"Christ, I don't know what to think. The man's a bloody psychopath, I know what we've done is wrong, but this, well this is really fucked up."

"If I'm honest it's not so much of a surprise, he's not exactly Mr Clean and has some extremely dodgy friends. I'm just so angry at him Joe, you could have been killed. What the hell was he thinking? Yet again making decisions to take control of my bloody life. I'll kill him when I see him." Molly's voice cracked with emotion as anger rose in her chest. "Did he not think what losing you would have done to me?"

"Probably not, he was hurting and all he was thinking was what losing you would do to him. Okay…" Joe paused and sighed heavily. "We'll talk about it later, but for now please hurry and get here, I need to know that you're safe, but be careful, there are quite a few photographers at the gate."

"Okay, I won't be long, I promise."

***

Before leaving for Joe's apartment, Molly tried to call Sophie but there was no reply. She left a voicemail, asking Sophie to call her back, but she knew deep down what Sophie would say – ring the police straight away.

As she pulled up to the gate, Molly saw a group of photographers hanging around and as soon as they spotted Molly there was a commotion as they all jostled to take a photograph of her. As the flashes exploded in her eyes, Molly held her arm up to her face to avoid being blinded. Sounding her horn to try and move them from her path, Molly drove slowly up to the gate. Joe, who was waiting for her near the apartment's entrance, spotted her car and he ran down the drive, pointing his fob at the gate. Molly nudged her car through the crowd and up the drive and pulled up next to Joe.

He jumped inside, pulled her into a tight hug and kissed her face, her neck, her hair, not caring about the long lens cameras that flashed away behind them.

"I've been so worried about you" he sighed. "I was convinced he'd do something stupid."

Molly took his hand and kissed his palm.

"What, more stupid than being involved in a robbery? I'm fine, he wouldn't hurt me. At least I don't think he would anyway."

"Let's get you inside and settled in. I've asked Denny to park outside the gates for tonight, just to be on the safe side. Park around the back, I've propped the fire exit open."

After dragging her three cases into Joe's room, Molly flopped onto the sofa, exhausted. Joe pulled her to him and kissed her softly. It was a long, gentle kiss full of love which left Molly breathless.

"Welcome to your new home," he said, gazing at Molly adoringly.

"Thank you, I can't believe I'm here."

Joe grinned. "Excited?"

Molly nodded. "Just a little bit. What about you, how do you feel?"

Joe sat back and looked up at the ceiling. "Well, how do I feel, let's see?" He looked back at Molly and, taking her hand, kissed it. "Absolutely fantastic, I love that you're here at last."

"But…" Molly knew she had to mention what was hanging in the air between them.

"But, we have to decide what to do about Rob." His reply was almost apologetic.

Molly shook her head. "No question about what we have to do – we have to report him, but I do feel some responsibility; I drove him to it."

"We both did. I'm not condoning it, because I felt the sharp end of their fists don't forget, but knowing he was losing you must have driven him crazy, and love makes you do stupid things."

"Stupid yes, but illegal to the point of evil, no way" Molly blasted.

Joe rubbed Molly's shoulder gently, trying to calm her. "I know, but I definitely don't think Rob did the robbery."

Molly frowned. "What makes you think that?"

"They were big blokes Moll, bigger than Rob, from what I can recall. Not particularly muscular, fat really. That's how I was able to put up a fight, being fitter I managed to give them the run around, so I think that's why they ran off in the end, they couldn't hold me still long enough to get any more punches in."

"Maybe that's what they were here for, to beat you up. After all they didn't take an awful lot, did they?"

Joe thought for a few moments and then nodded. "Maybe, because once I was locked in the bathroom they could have taken some more of my gear. There was no way I was going to come out of there and try to stop them. I'm surprised neither us nor the police thought of that before."

"Well, you wouldn't would you? Anyone would think it was a robbery pure and simple."

"I guess so. Anyway, what do we do now? I'll do whatever you want, if you want to let it go we can. It's only stuff after all, and we could get it back, although if I don't follow the insurance claim through the police may want to know why. I know you care about him and if reporting it hurts you, then I'm happy to let it go."

Molly looked up at Joe. She knew that despite the hurt she'd caused Rob, the day Joe had come back to the club had been the best day of her life. Even as a young girl she'd had little confidence in own ability, her looks or her personality, yet from the minute she'd met Joe he'd done nothing but help her to have belief in herself and her own capabilities. He had made her feel beautiful, many people had told her she was, but it was Joe who had helped her to believe it, and she realised that she had to show him the same belief. She loved him immeasurably and life without him by her side was inconceivable.

"No, Joe" she said. "He's involved in a robbery that saw you beaten up in your own home, so we have to report it. I feel so sorry for what I've done to him, particularly as he's so ill, but we all have a choice in life and the choice he made was wrong. It was illegal, so we have to report it."

Joe listened carefully and smiled.

"I love you so much and the time away from you hurt more than you will ever know, and all I want to do is spend the rest of my life caring for you, loving you and protecting you. So no, I don't want to report it. If I report him the press will find out and they'll have a field day. You saw them outside, like a bunch of vultures, but it will die down and will be a non-story in a few days, but if Rob gets arrested it will all start up again and they will blame you and I don't want to put you through that." Joe's cobalt blue eyes shone as he gazed at Molly. "You loved him and neither of us wanted to hurt him, so let's leave it. We can speak to him together. I can threaten him with Denny even; to make sure he gets the message. He's ill Moll, he's got enough to worry about."

Molly leaned forward and flung her arms around Joe's neck.

"If you're sure, but I think you'd be totally justified to call the Police – I don't think I'd be so forgiving. But, it just proves that you're a wonderful man, and I love you more than anything in the world and I think you should take me to bed."

Joe reached behind and, removing Molly's hands from his neck, he pulled them both up from the sofa and then flung Molly over his shoulder. She started to giggle as Joe shifted her slightly so that she wasn't likely to fall.

"Joe, put me down, I'm too heavy."

"You're not heavy at all, I'm an athlete don't forget. I'm going to take you to bed and show you in lots and lots of ways just how much I love you, so shut up woman."

With that Joe smacked her backside and marched towards the bedroom.

CHAPTER 29

♥

"Oh don't go, stay here with me." Molly pulled at Joe's arm. "Can't you say you're injured?"

Joe smiled and bent down to kiss her, a deep, lustful kiss that left Molly panting, desperate for more.

"I know you want to come back to bed." Molly lifted back the duvet and patted Joe's side of the bed that was still warm.

Joe groaned, looking down at Molly's naked body. "Cover yourself up, you're killing me. I have to get a shower."

Molly stuck out her bottom lip and gently kicked a foot at his bare bottom. She watched him disappear into the en-suite bathroom and marvelled at his body, then remembering the previous night, a huge grin spread across her face. Covering her eyes with her hands, Molly let out a quiet scream and kicked her legs up and down. She felt like a teenager who'd just met her favourite member of her favourite boy band.

"Are you okay?" She heard Joe laughing.

She opened her eyes to see him, looking sexy, in the bathroom doorway.

"Aww, now I'm embarrassed." Molly pulled the pillow from under her head and hid her face in it.

"Don't be, I'm glad you're happy. So," Joe said, pulling her down the bed by both her legs, "why don't *you* come and have a shower with *me*?"

Molly moved the pillow away and smiled up at him, instantly ready for more of Joe Bennett's special attention.

"You might be late for training," she teased.

"I don't care. Besides, I'm not going to be with you tonight, so I need to give you some extra care this morning."

Instantly Molly's high dropped dramatically. The team were playing away at Newcastle the next day so were travelling in the evening and obviously Molly wouldn't be with them.

"I forgot you were playing away."

Joe dropped onto the bed beside her and ran his hand across her flat stomach.

"I know, I don't want to go, I'd much rather come home to you. Hey, why don't you meet up with us at the hotel?" Joe's eyes sparkled with excitement at the prospect.

"I can't do that, Mr Grahame asked me to stay at home. I definitely will get the sack if I do that. Anyway, it's only one night." Molly tried to sound as though it wasn't a big deal, but she was dreading the thought of being away from him, even for the few hours that he would be at training, never mind the whole night.

"Well if you're staying here I'm going to ask Denny to stay in the spare room."

Molly sat up and stared at Joe, her mouth agape.

"What for? I don't even know Denny. What on earth would I talk to him about all night?"

Joe started to laugh and dragged Molly back down.

"He'd make sure you're safe. Anyway, you wouldn't have to talk to him; he'd probably stay in his room. No one's expecting you to sit in the lounge and play Twister with him." Joe lay back and tucked his hands behind his head.

Molly couldn't help but smile. For a modest man he was quite happy to lie back, unashamedly naked and quite obviously aroused.

"I'll be fine, I'll lock all the doors and keep my mobile with me all the time," she said batting away his hand that had started to stroke her thigh – he was not going to distract her into agreeing to have Denny sleep over.

Unperturbed, Joe put his hand back and continued to stroke.

"You'll be the only person in this damn building. There's no way I'm letting you stay on your own."

"I'll go and stay with Sophie then." Molly knew Sophie wouldn't mind, no doubt she was dying to find out what had happened since the newspaper story had broken.

"Well that would be better than you staying here alone. Although, I'd much rather you let Denny keep an eye on you."

Molly loved that he was being protective of her, but she felt that there was no need. The burglars wouldn't be coming back, especially as their aim appeared to be to rough Joe up, and Rob was in Sheffield so he wasn't a concern. Her good mood dropped again as she thought of Rob.

Despite them both agreeing not to tell the police, Molly was still so angry with him that she wasn't sure that Joe and Denny warning him off would be enough. While Joe was sleeping, last night, she had lain awake watching him breathing contently, tracing his handsome features with her eyes and she realised that she could have lost him if Rob's plan had succeeded. What he'd done wasn't just a knee jerk reaction; it was calculated and hateful. She decided to broach the subject with Joe again.

"You don't need to worry you know, I'll be okay at Sophie's, but changing the subject, are you positive you don't want to report Rob to the police? He ought to be punished for what he's done." Molly put her head on Joe's chest. She heard his heart thumping a soft, rhythmic beat.

"Yes, I think it's the right thing to do. I know what he did was wrong, but I can't put you through any more pain, and there would be if the press found out. Don't get me wrong, I fully intend to let him know exactly what will happen if he does anything else like that." He leaned towards Molly and kissed her forehead. "Are you okay with that?"

Molly nodded. "Okay, as long as you are, don't do it just for me, I can cope with what the press have to throw at me, if I have to."

"No, it's the best thing. There's been enough trauma already and he must have been devastated to do something so stupid." Joe stood up and stretched. "Okay," he said. "Enough talk of Rob for now. I really do have to get a shower, so are you coming?"

A shiver of anticipation crept over Molly's body as she watched Joe.

"Most definitely," she said. "Multiple times if I'm lucky."

***

Driving over to Sophie's house, Molly felt a sense of peace that she hadn't experienced in days. The newspaper story had been bad enough, but having to tell Rob had been much worse. Then, discovering that Rob was somehow involved in the robbery had built an anger inside her, a level of which, she didn't think existed – she had wanted to do him damage, just as his 'friends' had done to Joe. Deep down she thought that they ought to report him, but she had to abide my Joe's decision, no matter how much she thought he should be punished. Plus, it was easy in some respects to accept Joe's wishes as it went a tiny way to repaying Rob for her betrayal.

She and Joe were finally together and she felt more loved and desired than she ever had before. This time their relationship was intense, mature; she had loved him before, but now it was deeper, as if they were two parts of the same person. She drove along in the early evening dusk, singing aloud, extremely loudly, to the songs on the radio, feeling happy and serene.

Pulling into Sophie's village, Molly decided to stop at the Off License and treat both of them to a couple of bottles of wine and some chocolate. Sophie had offered to cook, but as she wasn't particularly good at it the chocolate would be a positive bonus when they were feeling peckish later.

As she got back to the car, Molly pointed her key and pressed to unlock it. There were flashing lights but no beep, meaning that it was already unlocked. Molly frowned, certain she had locked it earlier.

Sitting back in the car, she placed the bag of goodies on the passenger seat and reached for her seatbelt. Just as she buckled it in, she felt something cold and sharp push against the back of her neck. A heavy breath blew into her ear. With her heart racing at Formula 1 speed, Molly let out a yelp and turned her head slightly.

"Sorry" Rob sneered as he grabbed the top of Molly's seatbelt and pulled it tightly across her chest, "Did I make you jump?"

She gasped, a mixture of shock at seeing Rob and the pain as the belt cut into her breast.

"What are you doing? You're hurting me."

Rob loosened his grip on the belt, but she still felt the sharpness digging into the back of her neck.

"Just shut up and drive."

CHAPTER 30

♥

Molly's only thought as she drove was Joe – she knew that he would try to call her as soon as he was settled at the team hotel, so what would he think when she didn't answer? Would he think that she was busy and then when she didn't answer every time he tried would he think that she'd left him, or would he know instinctively that there was something wrong? Her lips trembled as she realised that she might not see him again, never look into his beautiful blue eyes again, feel his body next to hers, hear his deep laugh, or his terrible singing voice in the shower.

Rob barely spoke on the journey, except to bark directions at her and the only sounds echoing in Molly's ear drums were Rob's heavy breathes alternating with the thud of her own heartbeat. Unnerved and shaking, Molly glanced at Rob in the rear view mirror and saw that his nostrils were flared and his eyes were dark and full of anger, and as his breath blew against her neck, it sent ice cold drops of fear down her spine. She was also highly aware that something sharp was being pushed against the back of her neck, and Rob didn't look as though he would care one bit about hurting her if he had to.

Finally, after about half an hour, Molly realised that Rob was taking her to Cheshire, where Joe had his restaurant. She tightened her grip on the steering wheel and tried to think how Rob knew about it. If he hadn't looked so full of hatred she might have asked him, or even played dumb and pretended that she'd never been there. But, if he knew about it then he must know that Molly did too.

"Why are we going to Joe's restaurant?" Molly's eyes locked with Rob's in the rear view mirror.

"It took you long enough to realise. Just keep driving and park as near to the entrance as possible."

"What are you planning on doing Rob? You won't be able to get in and Joe will find us there eventually."

"That's my plan. Now shut up."

Molly felt a prick in her neck, and knew instantly that whatever he was using had drawn blood. Instinctively, she moved her hand to feel the wound.

Rob grabbed the seat belt and tightened it, as he had done before, making it cut into her chest.

Molly dropped her hand back to try and loosen the belt.

"Keep your hands on the steering wheel," Rob said "otherwise it won't be just a little pin prick at the back of your neck."

Molly nodded and put both her hands back on the wheel. She turned into the street where, just ahead of them, was Bennett's Restaurant, its new brown and cream sign blowing in the wind.

"Alright" Rob said. "Now park up like I told you.

"Molly's mind whirred with thoughts on how she might be able to warn Joe. It was obvious that Rob wanted to hurt him, or maybe both of them, but she had no idea how to stop him.

Molly parked the car in a marked parking bay on the road, directly outside the restaurant. She was pleased to see it was in darkness. At least Gabi and Luna hadn't been dragged into any of this nightmare. Rob thrust his hand through the space in the seats.

"Give me the keys" he said.

Molly pulled her keys out of the ignition and passed them to him and he got out of the car without a word. She realised there was no point trying to lock herself in because all he would do is let himself in again so, defeated, Molly got out of the car and allowed Rob to grab her arm and steer her toward the restaurant door.

At the door Rob reached inside his pocket and pulled out a key, unlocking the door, all the while pressing what Molly now saw was a knife against her waist.

Once the door was open Rob pulled her inside, holding her arm tight with his fingertips digging into her. While the alarm beeped in a steady rhythm, he punched four numbers into the keypad on the wall. With one long beep, the noise stopped and Rob held Molly against the wall with his forearm against her chest, as he reached for a series of light switches. As the wall lights flickered alive, Rob pushed Molly in front of him and she stumbled into the main restaurant, falling against a decorator's pasting table that had been left there. She looked up and saw bare wires hanging down from the ceiling in readiness for the new light fittings that Joe and Gabi had decided on only three nights ago.

"How the hell did you get a key?" she asked turning to Rob.

"Let's just say your boyfriend is a little too trusting with some of the tradesmen he uses." Rob took Molly's elbow and pushed her towards a chair near the window.

"What?" Molly sat down with a thud.

"A joiner friend of mine 'just happened to be passing' when they started work on the place, so he popped in to check if there was any work he could quote for and there was. That's his handy work over there." Rob pointed with the knife at the bar with its new oak top. "He had to work late, so of course he needed a key and the alarm code to lock up."

Molly gave a frustrated moan at Joe's usual lax attitude to security. "But…"

"Be quiet, eh? We're going to be here a while so you don't want to exhaust all the conversation do you?"

Rob's jaw clenched as he glared at Molly, daring her to speak. The way his shoulders tensed and his eyes narrowed were enough for her to keep her mouth firmly shut.

As Rob stared at her, Molly looked down at his hands and she saw the knife properly, and almost laughed – it was from a set of chef's knives that she had bought him as part of his birthday present. Looking at Rob clutching the sharp, silver knife, Molly knew that she had to try and think of some way of getting the hell out of here. But if she was to do that, she needed to try and remain calm to help her brain work. Hopefully her experience of sorting out the mishaps and traumas of twenty-two men had actually prepared her for something like this – keeping cool when kidnapped and held at knife point by your husband in your lover's restaurant.

After a long silence, void of any other ideas, Molly wondered whether she could talk him into giving up.

"Rob this is ridiculous. Whatever you plan on doing you won't get away with it. In fact, do you actually know what you're going to do?"

"Of course I do, I've had it planned for weeks, I'm going to make that shit wish he'd never set foot back in this country, never mind come sniffing around you."

"I know you're angry, but you'll never get away with this. Please, just let me go before you get in too deep. What about your family...?"

Rob held up his hand to silence her. "Molly, just shut up, I don't want to hear your voice anymore."

"But..."

"Enough!" Rob glared at her, daring Molly to speak.

Molly sighed and looking away, glanced at the huge clock that hung on the wall, it was almost six o'clock. Sophie would be frantic by now and if Joe hadn't already called her, he would soon. Rob moved over to the window and pushed open a gap between two slats of the wooden blind with his fingers. As he peered out onto the empty street, Molly glanced down and quickly pushed her hand inside her leather jacket pocket feeling around for her iPhone.

"Ooh, sorry stupid me, I almost forgot to take that." Rob's hand slammed against Molly's that was in her pocket. He pushed his palm towards her. "Give it to me."

Molly blew out a heavy breath and pulled her phone slowly

from her jacket and placed it in Rob's upturned hand, looking at him warily as he flicked it to silent and dropped it into his own jacket pocket.

His eyes searching hers, Rob leaned in. He was close enough for Molly to be able to smell stale coffee on his breath, making her want to retch.

"I'm not going to hurt you," he said his dark eyes scouring Molly's face.

"But you are going to hurt Joe?"

"Oh God yes. He's taken everything from me." A pulse twitched below his eye as he continued to scour her face, their noses almost touching.

In the distance, a church clock chimed six times, sending a shiver down Molly's spine. It felt like a death knell.

"It wasn't just him Rob; I was as much to blame."

He shrugged and pulled a chair over, sitting so close to Molly that their knees touched. Molly instinctively moved her legs to put a gap between them.

"You see, if he hadn't come along, you would never have dreamed of doing that." He pointed at her knees with the knife. "He turned you against me. You're my wife, you shouldn't be shrinking away from me."

"You know as well as I do things weren't right between us. I'd been having doubts for a while, and if you're honest, you probably had too."

"No, I was happy." Rob's eyes were wild as he leaned close again. "And you would have been again, in time."

Molly thought about arguing, but she didn't want to push his mood any further over this cliff edge of madness. Plus he seemed happy to talk now, so maybe, if she was patient, she could get him to drop his guard

"So, how did you find out?" Her eyes leaving his face, Molly picked at the cuff of her jacket.

"Greg Pounder."

Molly's eyes darted back up to Rob's.

"Greg, how the…?" Molly leaned forward. "Greg?" She said

again.

Rob nodded. "He saw what went on at the hotel when I was on my course. I've been putting bets on for him for a while, it wasn't just the once I month I told you about, but I kept it quiet. Plus I had to 'gently remind' him a couple of weeks ago about his debt, so he thought letting me know might get him off another beating."

Molly gasped. "*You* beat Greg up?"

"Well not me personally, I got a couple of blokes that I know to do it for me. I think your friend Joe may have met them too." Rob winked at Molly, a thin smile at his lips.

"What exactly did he say he saw?" It didn't really matter, but Molly was curious.

"He spotted Joe sneaking off from the bar and thought he might be sniffing around you, so he followed him and saw him go into your room and then as luck would have it, Greg was going down for an early morning swim when he saw Bennett sneaking back into his own room the next morning. He called me and I came home that day and stayed at a mate's house. I suppose I could have confronted you about it, but I knew you'd choose him, so I followed you for the rest of the week while I decided what to do. In fact I can tell you every place that you've ever shagged him, including here" he paused pointing the knife around the room "and I also know that you stayed over at his apartment last week. In fact, I know everything about your fling, when it started, when you finished it and when he got his claws into you again."

"You mean you weren't in France last week?" Molly leaned back in the chair, amazed at the lengths he had gone to.

"That's right; it's not nice being deceived is it darling?" Rob leaned closer and gently tapped the knife on Molly's knee. "I *was* going to France, but before we were due to go I had a suspicion that this thing between you two had started up again, but I had to be sure. The stupid thing is, it's probably down to me that it did. Just as I thought I'd got you back to myself."

Molly knew he meant the robbery. He'd organised it and she had gone falling back into Joe's arms because of it.

"I know all about the robbery" Molly replied, glaring at him, all thoughts of talking him around forgotten. "I found your little stash in the wardrobe."

Rob shrugged. "Oh well it doesn't matter now, but just so you know, it wasn't about robbing him."

Molly let out a hollow laugh. "Hah, I gathered that, I'm not stupid, Rob. You obviously just wanted to hurt him."

"Actually, they were supposed to end his career, but he managed to get away and lock himself in the bathroom. He surprised them by coming home so soon after leaving, so they took the stuff to make it look more like a robbery."

"But you obviously knew that I'd finished it with him once you got ill, so why try and hurt him?" Molly stifled a gasp with her hand, thinking about what could have happened to Joe that night.

"Don't know. I just hated him and if I'm honest I knew that it was only a matter of time before you left me for him, so I had to make sure he had nothing to offer you. Actually, I followed you that night too, to the hospital and the hotel, and the next morning when you went to pick him up – it killed me knowing what you were doing in there." Rob's tone was calm but his staring eyes were full of fury.

Molly ran a hand through her hair, and opened her mouth to protest that even if Joe didn't have anything, she would still love him, but the look in Rob's eyes told her that now wasn't the time. She watched as Rob picked at the heel of his shoe with the knife, and suddenly the realisation hit Molly with a thud between the eyes.

"They were supposed to do more than hurt him, weren't they? You fucking mad man." She flew at Rob, her hands flailing trying to make contact with his face.

Rob quickly got to his feet and held up his arm to keep her at distance but Molly was wild, slapping and scratching. He kicked out at her, and as his foot met her stomach, Molly fell backwards landing hard on the floor, her head bouncing off the leather seat of the chair that she'd been sitting on. She clutched at her stomach and panted heavily, trying to alleviate the pain that ripped through her body and her head.

"What are you doing?" Rob cried. "I didn't want to hurt you, but you made me."

Molly didn't look at him. She sat on the floor with her hair hanging over her face, rubbing the back of her head. After a few minutes she pushed back and looked up at him with shimmering eyes.

"What the hell have you turned into? It isn't love that's made you do all this. I think it's that bloody chemotherapy that's turned you crazy." She carefully pulled herself up and sat back on the chair.

Rob also sat down and sighed. "About that by the way."

"What?" Molly asked, rubbing her stomach.

"I don't actually have cancer."

That was it: a quick, no nonsense admission, as though he were telling her that he'd lost a five pound note.

Molly felt her heart drop like a stone to her gut. "Say that again" she said.

"I don't have cancer. I lied. I rigged up the letter. I'd been tested because I found a lump under my arm, but it was just a cyst."

Tears weighed heavily in Molly's eyes, she wanted to run at him again and punch his stupid face, but had no energy or fight left.

"You put me through all that worry for nothing? Now I understand why you didn't want me involved, you lying bastard. I ended things with Joe because I thought you needed me, I *married* you because I thought you needed me." Her voice was calm and low.

"Hey come on Moll, I was only paying you back for screwing someone behind my back. I did what I had to do, I knew that you'd feel guilty enough to stay with me, but to be honest I was a little shocked how easy it was to persuade you to bring the wedding forward. I thought I'd have to work harder on that one."

Molly was silent, rubbing her hands up her face and resting them on top of her head. She didn't know this man, or rather she knew that when he was younger he had hugged the line of illegality without actually passing over it, but it was all petty stuff. But she should have known, the signs were there. The man in the nightclub that he'd punched repeatedly for touching her, the illegal betting, and now the beating up of Greg and Joe. Stupidly she'd turned a blind eye to the way he ran the betting shop, thinking that if he was doing something wrong his bosses would find out and put a stop to it. But now he'd reached another level, graduating from a few dodgy deals to kidnapping and god knows what else was to come, via attempted murder and lying about having cancer.

Suddenly she had a thought. "Did you tip the press off about us?" she asked.

"God no, what would be the benefit of that? It forced you to confess and to tell me that you were leaving."

"But that night I told you, you were so hurt and angry. It was as if you had no idea."

"I *was* hurt and angry. Hurt and angry that the press had found out and spoiled everything and that you were going to leave, even though at that point you still thought I was ill. That's when I decided to put this part of the plan into action. I'd already sorted it all, just in case you ever did leave, but was hoping I wouldn't have to go ahead with it." Rob smiled and leaned back, tilting his chair onto its two back legs.

"You're crazy" Molly said, shaking her head. "You know Joe's gone to an away game and won't be back until tomorrow, don't you? We can't stay here for the next 24 hours; people are still working on it. They'll all turn up tomorrow and find us here."

"I don't think we'll have to wait that long."

"What do you mean, are you taking me somewhere else?"

"No, Joe will be here soon. I'm pretty sure he'll figure out where we are."

Molly looked up to the ceiling and gave a cry of frustration.

"Did you not hear what I said? He's in Newcastle at the team hotel. Okay, he might start to worry when he can't get hold of me but he won't be here anytime soon."

"Oh didn't he let you know, he's not keeping secrets already is he?"

"What the hell are you talking about?"

"He was injured this morning. He didn't go with the rest of the squad."

Molly's breath caught in her throat and her stomach flip flopped as she realised that he could soon be walking into danger.

"How do you know?" she whispered.

"I wasn't going to go ahead with this today, with him being away, but when he got injured Greg thought it might be a nice gesture to let me know. You see I'd told him that I was going to have it out with Joe, warn him off and then try and get you back. So, he thought that maybe today was a good opportunity."

Molly sighed and shook her head. "Bloody Greg Pounder. Does he know what you've been planning, is he in on it?"

"No, he's a stupid, big mouthed footballer with a weakness for betting on anything including snail racing, so there's no way I'd let him on it. So we just have to wait for lover boy to figure out where we are and then the fun begins.

CHAPTER 31

As the minutes bled into each other, Molly's earlier thoughts of keeping calm began to crumble. She'd tried to talk him out of his plan, but hadn't been able to keep cool and had blown it by attacking him and now she had no idea whatsoever of how to end this. Rob also seemed to be growing more and more anxious as time went on. He had started to pace up and down in front of her, occasionally moving over to peer through the window into the growing darkness.

Molly glanced at the clock. It was almost seven and she knew that both Joe and Sophie would be panicking by now. She wondered if they'd contacted the police, she guessed they would have – Sophie was a stickler for the law. She also knew that they would have desperately been trying to contact her, but how many times that they had tried to call her she had no idea, as Rob had turned her phone to silent.

As if reading her mind, Rob reached inside his pocket and pulled out Molly's phone. "You never go anywhere without this bloody thing, do you, in case one of your precious boys needs you?" He cocked an eyebrow and then sighed as he jabbed at the screen with his finger. "You really should think of using a different PIN for everything. Blimey, twenty missed calls, all from your sister and lover boy, they have been worried. I suppose we'd better put them out of their misery."

"What are you going to tell him? Let me speak to him, please Rob," she begged.

Rob frowned and shook his head. "I'm not stupid, so unless you want me to do something I'll regret, keep your mouth shut."

Rob placed the knife tip at her temple, giving Molly a glimpse of the cold steel in the corner of her eye. With the other hand he pressed out a number with his thumb and waited for a few seconds. Then obviously someone answered.

"Ah that's nice, although I don't really feel that we're well enough acquainted for you to call me baby, do you?" Rob pressed a button and suddenly Molly could hear Joe's voice, full of fear and anxiety.

"What the fuck have you done with her, you bastard? I'm telling you now, if you've hurt her I'll kill you," Joe shouted down the line. "Where is she?"

"She's safe for now, but if you want to be sure then you'd better get yourself over here." Rob paused and looked sideways at Molly. "I'll give you until ten tonight, and if you haven't found her by then well, I'm guessing you're quite happy for me to keep her."

"Where are you? It's obviously me you want to hurt, so just tell me and I'll be there and we can settle this between ourselves." Joe's voice quaked. "Please, tell me."

"I'm not making it easy for you, lover boy. If you really love her, you'll find her."

"Please, Rob," he pleaded. "Just give me a clue."

Molly's heart constricted as she heard Joe's words. She let out a quiet whimper as tears rolled down her cheeks.

"Ah, I'm gutted for you mate. Well, now you know how it feels. I'm sure you and Sophie can figure it out."

"How did you know I was with Sophie?"

"Lucky guess. She can't help but stick her nose in where it's not wanted, always has done."

"What did he say about me?" Sophie shouted in the background. "What the hell has he done with my sister?"

"Oh tell her to relax," Rob laughed. "She'll end up having a heart attack. Anyway, time is pressing on Superstar, so you'd better get your thinking caps on…oh and no police. Come alone or, despite the fact that I love her, I will kill you both if I have to. I hope you haven't already called them."

"No we haven't, we were just about to."

"Well don't."

Rob finished the call, put the phone back into his pocket, and tapped it gently. "Nice and safe" he muttered, smiling at Molly.

Molly dropped her head into her hands, afraid for Joe and what he was going to walk into, if he ever worked out where they were.

"When he finds me, he'll beat the crap out of you for this," she said.

"He's got to find you first," Rob said, sitting back down and staring at Molly. "And don't forget I'm not actually ill. I can give as good as I get. Besides, I have a little surprise in store for him."

Uncomfortable under Rob's gaze, Molly turned away and stared at the wall. As unease snaked through her body, she grew more anxious and she felt as though her lungs were about to burst. This was how it must feel when you're drowning, she thought, not able to take in air or think, just panic flooding your brain and your body. Wondering what trap Rob had set for Joe, she started to hyperventilate, short panting breaths escaping from her lips as she rocked gently and tears rolled slowly down her cheeks. Rob stared at her emotionless.

"Please don't hurt him," she gasped. "I'll come with you, wherever you want to go. I'll never see him again, but please don't hurt him."

Rob shook his head and sighed. "That's never going to happen is it? You wouldn't stick to your word."

"I would, I promise, I would." She screwed her hands together and leaned forward to plead with Rob.

"No you wouldn't Molly, and anyway too much has happened, I can't ever forgive you. You've spoiled everything."

Rob's eyes were black and hard and Molly knew there would be no budging him. He was stubborn at the best of times, but now, with a grudge to bear, he was as solid and unmoveable as a boulder.

Molly blew gentle breaths and rubbed her hands up and down her thighs, trying to calm herself. After a few minutes her breathing was easier and her heart slowly stopped racing.

"If he doesn't find us what will you do?" she asked in a whisper.

"If he's not here by midnight we'll be going on a trip somewhere. A mate of mine is going to meet us, it's all sorted."

"What's all sorted and what's the surprise you have for him?"

"Just something. Now stop pestering me and just concentrate on praying lover boy finds you."

Molly couldn't stand to think of where he was planning on taking her, because she knew if they left the country she would never see Joe again. She looked at Rob steadily and saw that there was perspiration on his top lip and his foot was tapping rapidly on the floor. He was desperate for Joe to find them and she knew at that moment if he didn't work out by himself where Rob had taken her, then Rob would undoubtedly let him know – after all he wanted his revenge.

As Molly watched the hour hand of the clock snail around, her feeling of dread grew heavier. She sighed, and shifted uncomfortably in her seat. Her neck, legs and arms ached because she'd been holding herself so stiffly; not wanting to move hoping Rob would forget she was there. Looking at him now, she felt nothing but contempt, and wondered how she could possibly have loved him without realising that someone so evil and malicious was harboured inside.

"I wonder if Superstar has figured out where you are yet?" Rob glanced at his watch. "It's almost an hour since I spoke to him, a little early to give him a clue just yet."

"So you do want him to find us then? What about your plan to magic me away?" Molly looked at him warily. If he was so adamant about 'keeping her' then why offer Joe a clue to their whereabouts? Then she knew she had been right, he wasn't going anywhere until Joe found them, even if it was midnight tomorrow, because all he cared about was pay back and hurting Joe.

"You're not planning on taking me anywhere, are you?" Molly asked.

Rob stared at her, his face emotionless, empty. He leaned forward and taking a strand of her hair between his fingers, he wound it around the knife. Molly stiffened and held her breathe as Rob's face came closer and he placed his free hand on her knee. She pulled her head back and Rob tightened his grip on both her hair and her knee. Molly winced and eyed him warily, aware of the silver flash in the corner of her eye.

"What happened to you?" she whispered. "When did you become so twisted?"

"The day that you broke my heart by sleeping with him. Do you know how that made me feel, when you picked him over me? He'd broken your heart once before and yet you still chose him. But then he's the one with money and fame, how could I compete with that? "

Molly shook her head. "I've already told you, it wasn't like that. I've explained it to you."

Rob laughed. "Oh yeah, sorry I forgot, you love him. Well you used to love me."

"I did, but things had already changed before Joe came back." Molly gently pushed his hand from her knee. She didn't feel confident pushing the knife away in case he thought she was trying to grab it, forcing him to do something stupid.

"Oh things changed alright, you lost your sense of humour and stopped trying for me. When we first met you were sexy and funny. You'd always wear short skirts and sexy underwear, but then you stopped. "

Molly let out a small gasp. "I don't *ever* remember wearing short skirts, nothing any shorter than those I wear now, and as for losing my sense of humour, *your* digs about my clothes and my figure weren't funny and were pretty boring after hearing them for the hundredth time."

"I was just helping you, telling you what suited you and what didn't. A lot of women would love a partner who would do that. I wanted you to make the best of yourself, that's all."

"You wanted to control me, more like." Anger making her feel braver, Molly pulled at the strand of hair still wrapped around the knife. "And get that knife away from my hair."

"What's wrong? Does Superstar like to run his hand through it when you're telling him how great he is?" Rob unwound the hair from around the knife and laughed. "Anyway, I've never tried to control you, you're the one who is always pushing me to change my job because the one I have isn't good enough for you."

Molly edged her legs away from Rob, eager to put a space between them.

"I don't think that there's anything wrong with your job, it's the petty criminals that you mix with that bothered me, and this stunt has proved me right. But you, you've always tried to control me – you knew that if you proposed in front of everyone I wouldn't say no, you were adamant that we should get married this year and then it was you who insisted we bring the wedding forward when you were supposedly ill."

Rob leaned back in his chair and casually draped his arm across its back. "I never had any chance of making you happy did I, not while Superstar was around?"

Molly sighed. "I am sorry I hurt you, honestly I am, but I can't help that I love him." She looked at Rob with tears nudging at her eyelashes. "Please Rob, can't you just stop this now, before someone gets hurt. We won't report you to the Police, not about this or the burglary, I promise."

Rob let out a hollow laugh. "You promised to love and honour me until death us do part only a couple of weeks ago, so your promises don't really cut it with me to be honest"

Molly decided to try and talk him around again. She was getting desperate and time was passing.

"What about your family? Your mum and dad will be horrified; it will be awful for them when this hits the papers, because it will get into the papers if you insist on following your plan through. Do you really want that sort of heartache for them?" Molly leaned forward and took Rob's hand.

He immediately snatched it away. "Don't try and get around me like that," he spat moving his chair back. "It won't make any difference to them; they've always thought I was a disappointment. I was just the inconvenience that played up at school, smoked dope and mixed with the wrong crowd. Gary was always their favourite. They couldn't wait to move to Sheffield to move away from me once I'd left home."

"That's not true, both your Mum and Dad love you." Molly had no idea that Rob felt this way "They moved to be near their grandchildren, not to be further away from you."

"You don't know, you weren't even around then. I know exactly what they think of me."

Rob produced a packet of chewing gum from his pocket and pulled a piece out with his teeth before offering it to Molly. She took the packet and smiled, hoping a charm offensive might help. If she could keep him talking, she might buy herself some time.

"Thanks" she said handing it back. "Did you actually go and see them after you left the house?"

"Yes, I did, for a few hours."

"Were they okay?" Molly edged her chair forward slightly.

Rob shrugged and arched his brows. "Mum was upset obviously. Let's just say you won't be getting a Christmas card off her anytime soon, and Dad, well he was just Dad. He didn't say much, just looked at me with his usual look of "something else you've cocked up I see". He made some comment that you wouldn't have strayed if you'd been happy."

"I wasn't totally *unhappy*, Rob. I just knew things weren't how they should have been. You know, we probably would have split anyway, even if Joe hadn't come back, because be honest, I was getting on your nerves wasn't I?"

Rob didn't answer, but smiled and nodded. "Yeah, you were a bit."

"So you see, this isn't worth all the trouble it could get you into, is it?" She leaned forward and took hold of his hand, stroking the back of it with her thumb. "Why don't you put the knife down and let me go?"

Rob looked into her eyes for a moment and Molly thought she saw a flicker of doubt in them. He dropped his head and puffed out his cheeks, his grip on the knife relaxing slightly. Molly took her chance. She grabbed at the knife but even though he was off guard, Rob's reflexes were still quick. He snatched his hand with the knife away and in the same movement, twisted around Molly's hand that was holding his own. Crying out in pain, Molly tried to pull herself free, but before she had chance she saw a flash of silver and felt he sharp edge slicing into her skin. She screamed as she felt a searing, red hot pain in the palm of her hand. Rob released her and she fell back into her chair, clutching her hand to her chest, hot, sticky blood pouring from the wound and soaking her blouse. .

"You bitch, how stupid do you think I am?" Rob raised his hand and swung it at Molly's face.

The force pushed her off the chair and into the side of the bar. Her cheek slammed into the wood and sent a jolt of pain through her eye and into her ear. She fell to the floor, dazed and barely conscious but aware of Rob's sneering face swimming in front of her eyes. She felt another, sudden jolt of pain and the world, and everything in it, disappeared.

CHAPTER 32

♥

Molly didn't know how long she'd been unconscious, but when she came round she was propped up against the side of the bar. A pain sliced through her cheek, her hand throbbed and her wrists were burning. She looked down to see that they had been bound together with what looked like silver electrical tape and it had been wound it so tightly so that it cut into her skin. She lifted her arms and gently touched the back of her hand to her face and could tell immediately that her cheek and top lip were swollen. Her mouth was filled with the metallic tang of blood. She raised her head slowly and let a quiet moan of pain escape through her lips, a moan which she barely managed to stop becoming a cry of panic when she saw Rob standing over her, a dark grin on his face. It was a face she no longer recognised. Gone was the Rob who could be as charming and witty as the best of them, and instead all she could see were his two eyes, now filled with pure hate. He still had the knife in his hand, and swung it loosely between his thumb and forefinger.

"You asked for that," he said. "Trying to trick me. You thought you'd be nice and I'd hand over the knife, well I'm not that much of an idiot."

Molly opened her mouth to speak, but was silenced by the pain in her face. As she looked up at Rob she realised that she couldn't see out of her left eye and she knew that it was completely shut.

"Please, Rob" she managed to moan, pain throbbing through every part of her head. "Help me."

Rob crouched down and looked at her.

"Oh dear," he said. "Not so sure Superstar will fancy you after this."

"He'll kill you for this" she groaned, before letting out a ragged, pained sob. "Well, he'll have to find us first. Now, get up." Rob stood up and pulled Molly with him.

As the pain in her cheek and wrists tore through her once more, Molly let out a howl like an injured animal. She had wanted to try and remain calm and brave, but the agony had broken her, and as Rob pushed her back onto the chair, her chest heaved with sobs.

"Please don't hurt me anymore." Her head hung like a drooping flower with her hair curtaining her face. Huge tears dropped onto her knee.

"I wasn't going to hurt you at all, but you're just as bad as him. You never loved me; all I was to you was a distraction until he came back."

Molly shook her head and whimpered. Rob pushed his face closer.

"You know what?" he said, tilting his head to the side. "Maybe kicking the shit out of him won't be enough. Maybe I need him to lose you so he knows how I feel."

"I'm not going anywhere with you, you'll have to kill me first." Molly turned her face away, sickened by the sight of the man she thought she once loved. "I didn't say anything about taking you with me." Rob lifted the knife and held it beneath Molly's chin, forcing her to look into his face again. Then he slowly teased its point down to her throat and then further. She felt the cold metal as it slid toward her breasts.

Despite her best attempts to show defiance, when she felt the blade, as cold as a shard of ice, pressed against her chest, she let out a gasp of fear.

"Please Rob."

Rob looked at her with narrowed eyes and bit at his bottom lip, before moving his mouth to Molly's ear.

"I may just have some fun with you first," he whispered.

He pulled Molly up from the chair and then pushed down onto her shoulders, forcing her onto the floor.

"Lie down," he ordered.

"Don't do this." Molly shook her head, pleading with Rob.

Rob, ignoring her, forced Molly onto the floor and straddled her, his weight pushing down on her stomach. Then, placing the knife point at her throat, he started to unbutton her blood soaked blouse with his other hand. Molly started to bring her hands up to stop him but he shifted up her body and pinned her arms to her side, digging his knees heavily into them and rendering her helpless.

"You owe me this, so don't even think about stopping me."

"I hate you" Molly whispered, closing her remaining good eye as tears slid down her cheeks.

"Ooh that hurts."

As her blouse fell open, Rob grabbed her bra strap and pulled it down roughly.

Molly choked back a sob, as she felt his lips on the fullness of her breast, and then it was his teeth biting at her. She let out a sob and screamed.

"No Rob, please, no!"

Then suddenly, she felt Rob's weight being lifted off her. She opened her eye and saw him being dragged away from her by a pair of strong hands that she recognised instantly.

"Joe" she cried, trying to pull herself up into a sitting position.

"You fucking bastard, what the hell have you done to her?"

Joe punched Rob hard in the face. Rob's nose split and sent blood spattering through the air. Rob rocked on his feet for a second, shook his head and then lunged at Joe with the knife. Molly shuffled back towards the chair, if she could just get to it she would be able to pull herself up and maybe help Joe. She knew that if Rob killed Joe, then she would be next, once he'd finished what he'd just started. While Rob and Joe carried on fighting, she watched as Rob jabbed the knife towards Joe, and Joe jumped back. Rob lifted his knee and brought it into Joe's stomach, making him double over in pain. As Joe gasped for breath, Rob grabbed his hair. Desperate to help, Molly tried to prise her wrists apart, thankfully the blood from her hand had soaked the tape and as she pulled it was helping to loosen it. She had almost stretched it enough when she thought her heart had stopped beating. Rob pulled Joe towards by his hair with one hand, while the one holding the knife was pulled back ready to stab him. Adrenalin took over and with one last pull Molly was able to free one of her hands of the tape. Without hesitation, she lifted up the chair. She staggered towards Rob and with an animalistic scream, and with all her strength, brought it down against his back. She didn't have the strength to knock him out, but it was enough to distract him and make him drop the knife by Molly's feet.

Rob's eyes widened when he saw Molly bending down to pick up the knife. With his hands tight around Joe's hair, he kicked out at Molly, his foot landed against her side, sending her flying across the room.

"You bastard" Joe roared, his eyes black and menacing.

He swung his fist up into Rob's jaw, pitching him across the room. He hit his head against the bar and slid to the floor next to a terrified Molly.

Joe ran over to her, and lifting her gently from the floor carried her across to a chair.

"Sit down Sweetheart, I just need to make sure he doesn't try anything else, okay?" He stroked a hand down the side of her head, his eyes searching hers for confirmation that she was okay.

Molly nodded, her bottom lip quivering.

Joe ran behind the bar and after a quick look around pulled out a reel of cable that had been left by the electrician. He then searched around the floor, and spotting the knife where Rob had dropped it, picked it up and cut the cable into strips. Joe then kicked Rob onto his stomach and tied his legs together and his hands behind his back. Finally, with Rob completely bound, Joe gave him a quick kick in the stomach with his famous left foot.

Joe then moved over to Molly and took her in his arms, taking care not to touch her face.

"Oh God, I thought I'd lost you" he cried. He kissed Molly's hands, which were still covered in blood. "Are you hurt anywhere else?"

Molly shook her head as she sobbed, "My face Joe; it hurts."

"Okay, don't worry. I'm going to ring for an ambulance." He reached into his jeans pocket and pulled out his phone and pressed the screen. "Ambulance and Police please."

***

Almost two hours later, Molly was tucked up in a hospital bed, with Joe clinging to her hand.

Rob had still been out cold when the police arrived at the restaurant and only came round when the Paramedics held some smelling salts under his nose. As they took him away, he spat at Molly and cursed Joe, wishing that he would rot in hell.

The doctors said that Molly had been very lucky and they didn't think her cheek was fractured. However, they couldn't x-ray it while it was still swollen, so because of that and the fact that she had passed out when she hit the bar, they insisted that she stay in overnight. Joe had in turn insisted that she be admitted to the private section of the hospital and that Denny kept guard outside her room.

After the nurse had checked Molly's blood pressure and left the room, she snuggled down in the bed and turned onto her 'good cheek' to face Joe.

"How did you find me?" she asked, her voice slurred.

"Would you believe, Tino?" Joe brushed his hand gently over her head, and tucked her hair behind her ear.

"Tino?"

Joe nodded. "Yeah, who'd have thought it? He told me about that app you have on your iPhone; the one that can find another iPhone from the same address. Sophie and I made a list of all the places we thought he may take you to, but the restaurant wasn't one of them, so thank God for Tino."

"Rob's not ill you know. He lied about having cancer."

Molly's eyes started to shine with tears again.

Joe shook his head. "I'd like to think you were joking but you're not are you? He's a lunatic. Anyway, I don't want to talk about this anymore tonight, I just want to look at you." Joe pulled Molly's hand to his mouth, and kissed her fingertips. "Christ, I thought I'd never see you again. I don't know what I'd have done if he'd taken you away for good."

Molly didn't answer, but simply cupped Joe's face with her bandaged hand.

"I wanted to kill him you know, in the restaurant. I wanted to pick that knife up and stab him for what he'd done to you,

"It's over now" Molly said.

Joe leaned in and gently kissed her.

"Get some sleep now beautiful" he whispered, and pulled the duvet up around Molly's neck.

She looked up at him with fear in her eyes. "Stay with me."

"I'm not going anywhere. I'm staying right here in this chair."

"No, I need you to hold me." Molly tugged at Joe's hand.

Joe smiled and, kicking off his shoes, got up on the bed. Molly lifted up to let Joe place his arm under her head and along the pillow, and then snuggled up to him, breathing in his scent as she bunched his t-shirt into her hand. Joe pulled her close.

"I love you" he whispered, kissing her forehead.

"I love you too."

Gradually their breathing slowed and by the time the nurse popped her head in half an hour later, they were both sound asleep, clinging to each other as they always had and always would.

EPILOGUE

♥

"Hi, I'm home" Molly called, hanging her coat on the coat stand. As she moved across the vast hall, the door to the lounge opened.

"Hi beautiful, did you buy anything nice?" Joe pulled Molly to him and kissed her passionately. He never tired of feeling her lips on his, and never wanted to be without Molly, ever again.

"Hmm, that's a nice welcome home, have you missed me?" Molly asked, planting a kiss on Joe's nose.

"Of course, don't I always? I've got something for you actually, but you may want to sit down." Joe gently took Molly's hand in his and pulled her through to the lounge.

As Molly sat down, Joe handed her a letter.

"From your solicitor" he explained.

With shaking hands, Molly opened up the letter and then read it, in silence, with Joe watching her intently.

"Well?" Joe bit at the side of his mouth, as Molly put the letter back in the envelope.

"It's done, Rob's *finally* agreed and signed the divorce papers."

"Okay, and how do you feel?" Joe moved next to Molly and took her hand in his.

She sighed and then smiled weakly. "Okay. Sad that it ended like it did, but glad it's over now. After everything he did, it seems hard to believe that I did love him once." She looked at Joe earnestly.

"I know."

Molly touched Joe's cheek and smiled. "I never loved him in the way I love you though."

"Well, maybe now we can relax a little." Joe gave a huge sigh.

"Yes and maybe now you can stop getting Denny to follow me everywhere. Rob's not coming out for a long time, and the two thugs he snitched on for beating you up are far more likely to want him than us, when they get out of prison."

Molly thought back to how scared they had both been after Rob had been arrested. Joe was constantly checking up on Molly at first, scared beyond belief that somehow Rob would get out of prison, and take Molly again. He regularly rang or texted, just to check how she was, and would meet her out of work whenever he could, and if he couldn't he would send Denny, his security guard, to pick her up. It took almost six months for him to relax, and realise that Molly was perfectly safe.

"We'll see, but I think Denny quite likes going shoe shopping with you." Joe winked and gave a wry smile. "Anyway, let's not talk about it anymore. What time are Sophie, Tino, Beccy and Pete coming around tonight?"

Molly couldn't help but laugh at the mention of Sophie and Tino in the same breath. They'd been enjoying a hugely sexual, fun romance for almost six months, since they'd met up again at a house warming party at Joe and Molly's new house. Their relationship had surprised an awful lot of people, as they were mutually exclusive, with Tino not even glancing at another woman – in fact, they were both totally besotted.

"I told them about eight, Pete said they'd pick up a takeaway on the way over."

"Okay, great. Well we'll have something to celebrate now."

"Hmm we certainly will. So, I spoke to Marcus today, he seems to be doing really well at my old job."

"Yeah, he's doing okay, although the lads still miss you." Joe cupped Molly's face and kissed her gently on the lips.

"I don't know why, they see me all the time now after games and at parties."

"Yes, but they all found the strict, bossy Molly very sexy – Marcus just doesn't quite have the same thrill for them."

"Hah, yes well it's just you I have to get bossy with now. Seriously Joe, being your PA is no easy task, especially now there's two branches of Bennett's. Which reminds me, have you found those petrol receipts? No I didn't think so." Molly shook her head as Joe grimaced.

"I've had other things on my mind."

"Like what?" Molly scoffed.

"Whether Rob would sign the divorce papers. But, now he has, does it mean we can start to fill some of these rooms now?"

As soon as they'd bought the house, they'd both wanted to start a family, but had reluctantly agreed to wait until Molly was divorced.

Molly giggled and ran her finger along Joe's jaw line. "Great change of subject, but I suppose it does Mr Bennett."

"Excellent, but before we do there is something else we need to sort out." Joe detached himself from Molly and dropped to one knee in front of her.

"Joe what are you doing?" Molly asked, pulling herself to edge of the sofa.

Joe swallowed as he looked up at Molly, a half-smile at his lips.

"I wanted to make some huge gesture when I did this, sweep you off to some exotic island and have a romantic dinner on the beach, but I can't wait any longer, and that's not what this is about. This is about you and me, about us being together, just like we always should have been, because I've loved you from the moment I set eyes on you down at the training ground all those years ago. I can't imagine my life without you in it; I don't *want* a life without you in it. You're everything I want and need. So..." he exhaled slowly, "please my beautiful, kind, sexy Molly, will you marry me?" From his jeans pocket, Joe pulled out a small, duck egg blue box with Tiffany & Co written on it, and with shaking hands passed it to her.

Molly gasped as Joe opened it up. Nestled inside was the most beautiful cushion cut diamond she had ever seen, and all around it and along the platinum band were smaller diamonds, all creating a myriad of light as they glistened brightly.

"Well, is it a yes?" Joe asked as he wiped a stray tear that was falling down Molly's cheek. "Or have I just made an absolute idiot of myself?"

Molly nodded and held out her hand for Joe to slip the ring on her finger. "Of course it's a yes. It's beautiful," she whispered, her voice full of emotion. "When did you get it?"

"When we went to New York on the pre-season tour. I was going to use the one I bought all those years ago, but thought it was probably cursed. Plus it wasn't half as beautiful as this one. I've been carrying it around in my pocket for months, just waiting for the right moment." He reached up and kissed Molly gently on the cheek.

"If you kept the other one, you shouldn't have bought this one." Molly scolded him light-heartedly. "But I'm glad you did, it's stunning." She held out her hand, moving it backwards and forwards watching it sparkle on her finger. "You went to New York six months ago though, I can't believe you've kept it a secret all that time?" She stroked his hair away from his face, giving herself a better view of his beautiful blue eyes.

"It took me nearly seven years to get you back, so a few more months weren't a problem. I promise you that nothing will come between us ever again, I won't let it."

"I know you won't, and neither will I. I love you, and I can't wait to be Mrs Bennett and start a family with you."

Joe kissed Molly's lips tenderly as he cupped her face, "That's what I want too. So, this family we want, how do you fancy starting now?" He murmured into her ear, as he started to slowly unbutton her blouse.

"I think that's a great idea," she whispered breathlessly. As usual, her body immediately responded to his touch, and she pulled Joe's t-shirt over his head. "In fact I think I've read somewhere it takes the average couple over six months to get pregnant."

"Really" Joe gasped as Molly started to un-button his jeans.

"Well, it looks as though we might have a really busy few months then."

"Hmm, although there's nothing average about you Mr Bennett" Molly whispered into Joe's ear as she put her hand inside his boxer shorts.

"Christ Moll," Joe groaned. "For once I just hope I don't score first time!"

"Don't you worry about that, we can play as much extra time as you like, now get your kit off."

IF YOU WANT TO FIND OUT HOW JOE FELT WHEN MOLLY WENT MISSING, THEN READ THIS BONUS CHAPTER

Joe winced as Ken the physio dug his thumbs into the top of his thigh.

"Christ Ken, do you have to do it so hard?"

"Yes if you want to be fit for the midweek game. Did you feel it before training?" Putting oil onto his hands, Ken started to rub them up and down the offending thigh.

Joe had pulled up with a strain during the morning training session, and so now wasn't travelling with the team to Newcastle, but being subjected to an intense physiotherapy session instead, and while it was extremely painful the plus side meant he got to go home to Molly.

"Does it feel as though it could be serious?" Joe asked pulling his head up so that he could see Ken's face when he answered.

Ken shook his head. "No, nothing too bad. You've probably played too many games without much of a rest."

Joe nodded. "Hmm, maybe. I've played every game this season both here and in Spain, and had a couple of games for England, so you could be right.

Ken continued with his work as Joe lay back down with a smile on his face. Not only had he played lots of games but he and Molly had enjoyed some pretty active sex last night, and this morning before he'd left for training, so it was little wonder his body had finally given up. It was possibly seen as irresponsible just before a game, but there was no way he could resist her, or that little noise she made just as she was about to orgasm.

***

An hour later, driving off from the training ground, Joe felt a buzz of anticipation grow in the pit of his stomach. With each junction of the motorway that he passed, the closer he was to surprising Molly. He gave a deep sigh of contentment as he thought about her. Joe knew that many of his teammates lusted after her, because before their relationship had become common knowledge, he would hear lots of lewd comments about her bandied around the dressing room, and he hated it, tightening his fists so tightly that his nails would make four lines in his palms.

It was little wonder though that she was the object of so many desires, she was beautiful – it was only Molly who didn't realise it. Many women would kill for her olive skin, dark chocolate eyes and luxurious long brown hair. That along with her hot body, sexiness, humour and kindness just made her the perfect package as far as Joe was concerned. She made him feel complete, and there was nothing else he wanted or needed anymore – he didn't think that anything he achieved in the future would ever give him as much of a thrill as the one he got waking up next to her this morning.

As he approached the apartment block, he noted, with satisfaction, that the group of photographers had thinned out slightly. Tony had released a statement earlier saying that Joe and Molly were now living together and while they were both very happy it was still a difficult time for other people involved, so they would be grateful for some space and wouldn't be making any further comment. Molly had tried to call Rob and run it past him first, but couldn't get a reply – which worried Joe immensely, but Molly was sure he was just ignoring her, so she left a voice message instead. Obviously the statement had done the trick, and Joe had been correct, it wasn't much of a scandal anymore. Although, Joe wondered how Rob would see it, and would he try and cash in by selling his side of the story? He hoped that they would get to speak to Rob soon about the robbery, then at least they would have something to bargain with if he did threaten to go to the papers.

Sounding his horn, the photographers moved aside letting Joe through in his metallic blue Mercedes SL. As he parked up disappointment thudded in his chest as he realised that Molly's car was missing, then he remembered that she had gone over to Sophie's for the evening. He didn't want to appear controlling or possessive, so although he was desperate to see her, decided not to call her yet. He would make himself some dinner, watch the Italian football that he had recorded, and then let her know that he was home. It would be Molly's choice if she came back to the apartment, but he hoped that she would be just as anxious to see him as he was her.

By the time Joe had finished his dinner, it was still not quite six o'clock, and he had no desire to watch the football as planned. All he wanted was for Molly to come home, so despite his earlier resolve, he picked up his mobile and pressed out her number. By five rings her voicemail kicked in.

"Hi it's me, I hope you're having a nice time with Soph', but I wanted to let you know I'm home. I picked up an injury in training. Nothing serious, but enough to rule me out for tomorrow. Anyway, give me a call when you get chance. Love you."

Joe sighed and threw his mobile onto the empty seat next to him, he was bored and void of any ideas of how to fill his time. In fact, how had he filled his time before Molly had moved in? He let out a laugh, she had only been there one night and he was lost without her already – God he had it bad, but he knew that anyway.

Over the next hour, he tried Molly's mobile four times, and with each voice message that he left his anxiety heightened. A knot the size of a fist was being tied in his stomach, and a cold sense of fear inexplicably shivered over his body. Picking his phone up once more, Joe didn't care whether he came across as controlling, or possessive, he was going to call Sophie. He didn't have her number, but he knew Tino took it on Molly's hen night.

"Tino, sorry to bother you, but do you still have Sophie's number, you know Molly's sister?"

"Joe my friend, it is no bother. I am resting in my room. Hey, because you are not here Charlie he has gone into room with Jimmy. He say I snore like pig, he is…"

"Tino mate, look I hate to rush you, but do you have it?" Joe paced a furrow in the carpet that a prize ploughman would have been proud of.

"She very beautiful and funny, does the Pope shit in woods? Yes I have it."

Joe took a breath, desperately trying to hide his frustration and impatience.

"Okay, great. Can you send it to me please?"

"Yes, but why Joe? You have not lost love for Molly have you?"

"No Tino, no chance. I need to speak to Sophie about something."

"Phew that is good. I like Molly, but I also like her sister, she very sexy" Tino replied huskily.

Joe could almost see the mental images in Tino's mind.

"Tino, can you just send me the number and stop undressing Sophie in your head?"

Tino started to laugh. "You know me well, my friend."

"Tino!"

"*Okay* I send it now."

Joe waited for a couple of minutes, staring at his phone, willing for the number to come through. It felt like hours, but eventually it arrived, followed by a smiley face and two kisses. Joe couldn't help but smile, Tino was really something very special indeed.

He pressed the number within the text message, thrusting his other hand deep into his pocket as it formed into a tight fist.

"Hello," Sophie answered sounding somewhat wary.

"Sophie, its Joe. Can I speak to Molly, her phone must be off."

"She's not here Joe, I've been trying her since six and just keep getting her voicemail." Sophie was no longer wary but anxious. "I was just about to start calling the hotels in Newcastle to try and find you. I've tried all the local hospitals, and she's not there and I rang a Policeman friend of mine in traffic and thankfully there have been no accidents."

Joe exhaled. "Thank God for that at least. When was the last time you spoke to her?" He ran into the hall and picked his car keys up from the console table.

"About five, she was just leaving. It should take fifteen minutes at the most from your place, so when she didn't arrive by six I started to worry. I'm sorry I should have called you before now, but I didn't want to worry you until I'd tried everyone else I could think of."

Joe ran out into the hall and pushed the lift button.

"Don't worry, its fine. Come on," he muttered watching the neon numbers go from one to three. "Text me your postcode, I'm coming over?" As soon as the lift arrived he jumped inside and punched the button for the ground floor.

***

A little over ten minutes later, Joe was pulling up outside Sophie's pretty mews cottage. She was waiting on the doorstep, the lamp on the hall table throwing an amber glow around her as she hugged herself against the cool wind that was starting to blow.

"Come in." She beckoned Joe inside.

He followed her into the warm, cosy lounge with its beech wood floors and cream furniture.

"You still haven't heard anything have you?" Joe asked, rubbing his temple furiously.

Sophie shook her head, her eyes looking at him warily.

"Have you tried Rob?" she asked.

"I don't have his number; why, do you think he might have done something to her? If he's fucking hurt her I'll kill him." Both of Joe's hands flexed as he imagined them around Rob's throat.

Sophie pulled at his arm.

"I don't mean that" she sighed and looked away.

"What, what do you mean?" Joe moved to stand in front of Sophie, forcing her to look at him.

"You don't think she's gone back to him do you?"

Joe's shoulders slumped. He hadn't even thought of that, but that was because he knew beyond doubt she wouldn't – she hadn't, not after what they had found out.

"No, she won't have." Joe scratched his head, messing his hair boyishly, and wondered whether he should tell Sophie the truth. If it meant finding Molly, then he had to. "She wouldn't because…well because we found out that Rob was involved in the robbery at my apartment."

Sophie thrust her hands to her hips.

"Sorry, say that again."

Joe repeated his statement, telling Sophie what Molly had found, also adding that they had decided not to tell the police.

"You are joking, right?"

Joe shook his head and looked down at the floor. He felt as though he was nine years old again being chastised for writing on his bedroom wall.

"We thought we'd put him through enough, so I was just going to warn him off."

"Oh, so the thugs that knocked you about, what reason have you got for letting them get away with it too? Are your brains in your sodding football boots, just because you 'warn him off' it doesn't mean it will apply to them. And now Molly has gone missing. You fucking idiot!" Sophie pushed Joe in the chest with a flat palm. "If anything happens to my sister I will sue your fucking arse for every penny you've ever earned through poncing about on a football pitch."

Joe took a step back to steady himself. "It was Molly's idea too. We both agreed."

Sophie shook her head and put a hand to her mouth. Joe could see her eyes were bright with unshed tears.

"I'm sorry Sophie; please don't be mad, because if he or anyone else has hurt her, then I'll need you on my side, defending me in court." He gently rubbed his hand up and down Sophie's arm.

Sophie's face softened as she looked at Joe.

"I'll be next to you in the dock," she replied. "So we'll have to get some other hotshot barrister."

Joe dropped his hand blew out a long breath.

"I think we should call the police" he said.

"No shit Sherlock. I'll call my friend Polly in CID, she's on duty tonight." Sophie moved towards the fireplace and picked her mobile up from the mantelpiece.

"Thanks Sophie."

"You do know that you're going to have to tell them about the robbery don't you?"

Joe nodded and flopped down onto an armchair.

"Yes, I know. I just wish we'd done it before."

"Well" Sophie sighed as she started to dial a number. "Hindsight is a bloody wonderful thing."

Suddenly Joe's mobile burst into life.

"Molly!" he cried, pulling Sophie's arm, stopping her from continuing to dial. "Baby, where are you?"

"Ah that's nice, although I don't really feel that we're well enough acquainted for you to call me baby, do you?" It was Rob's voice on the other end of the line.

""What the fuck have you done with her, you bastard? I'm telling you now, if you've hurt her I'll kill you" Joe shouted down the line. "Where is she?"

Joe asked, ignoring Sophie's pleading eyes. He clenched his hand into a tight fist as he paced up and down.

"What is he saying?" Sophie put her hands on Joe's shoulders, forcing him to stand still.

"She's safe for now, but if you want to be sure then you'd better get yourself over here. I'll give you until ten tonight, and if you haven't found her by then well, I'm guessing you're quite happy for me to keep her."

"Where are you? It's obviously me you want to hurt, so just tell me and I'll be there and we can settle this between ourselves." Joe's hand fisted in his hair, his desperation showing in his wild eyes, as his voice quaked. "Please, tell me."

"I'm not making it easy for you, lover boy. If you really love her, you'll find her."

Before his legs could give way, Joe flopped down onto the chair. "Please, Rob," he pleaded. "Just give me a clue."

"Ah, I'm gutted for you mate. Well, now you know how it feels. I'm sure you and Sophie can figure it out."

"How did you know I was with Sophie?" Joe's chest heaved as his breath became shallow.

"Lucky guess. She can't help but stick her nose in where it's not wanted, always has done."

"What did he say about me?" Sophie kneeled in front of Joe. "What the hell has he done with my sister?"

"Oh tell her to relax," Rob laughed. "She'll end up having a heart attack. Anyway, time is pressing on Superstar, so you'd better get your thinking caps on...oh and no police. Come alone or, despite the fact that I love her, I will kill you both if I have to. I hope you haven't already called them."

"No, we haven't; we were just about to."

"Well don't."

Joe thought his heart had now stopped. Surely he was dead and this was some sort of hell that he'd been sent to.

"Rob, Rob" he shouted into his mobile. "Shit he's gone. Fuck Sophie, he wouldn't tell me where he was, and if I don't find them by ten he's going to take her away." Joe grabbed hold of Sophie's arms, digging his fingers into her skin. "I can't fucking lose her Soph, I have to find her."

"What did he say, tell me word for word?" Sophie placed her hands either side of Joe's face, forcing him to look at her. "Look at me Joe, what did he say?"

Joe repeated everything to Sophie, and as he finished realised that she was crying. He had to pull himself together. He dragged her into a hug.

"Come on we can do this, we can find them."

"I'll ring Polly." Sophie pulled her phone from her pocket, only for Joe to knock it from her hand.

"No! He said no police."

"Oh and like that's worked well so far. You have to tell them."

"No, I can't risk him doing anything to hurt her." Joe started to pace the room again, desperately trying to think of where he may have taken Molly.

"It must be somewhere I know" he said, almost to himself. "Otherwise he would give me some sort of clue, surely."

"Unless he doesn't want you to find them." Sophie's eyes were shining with pools of tears.

Joe shook his head. "No way, he wants me to find them, he wants to settle things with me, and he wants to finish what those thugs didn't."

"Joe, you need to call the police, please." Sophie rested her head against the edge of the mantelpiece.

"No." Joe exhaled a long breath, using his sporting experience to try and slow down his heart rate. He focused his mind on Rob's words, sifting through them for a clue. It was seven-thirty, he had two and a half hours to find them.

"Joe."

Sophie's soft voice interrupted his thoughts, and he turned to face her.

"How did Rob know that you hadn't gone with the team?"

The blood rushed from Joe's face and his heart started to hammer rapidly once more. "Either he's been watching me, or someone at the club is giving him information." Joe desperately felt like vomiting, but looking at Sophie's scared eyes and shaking hands, he knew he had to try and keep it together for her, and for Molly.

"Come on Sophie" he tried to be upbeat. "Let's think hard about where he could be. We need to make a list and then plan a route, we need to be organised because we've only got a short amount of time."

Sophie smiled weakly and wiped her eyes. "I'll get a pad and pen."

After ten minutes they had made a list of around five or six places that Rob may have taken Molly, with a rough route mapped out.

"I can't believe he just expects you to find them without any clue or anything" Sophie sighed pinching the bridge of her nose. "This is impossible Joe, you'll never find them. He's playing you; he has no intention of letting her go."

"Hmm, but he's not given me long which means she can't be too far away." Joe was busy studying the list, wondering if there was anywhere else he should add to the list before leaving. He was so engrossed he didn't hear his phone ringing.

"Joe, your phone," Sophie cried shaking his arm.

"God, sorry."

He snatched it from his pocket, and without looking pressed the answer button.

"Rob?"

"No Joe, it is me Tino."

Joe scrubbed his hand across his face and sighed.

"Tino I'm sorry but I really can't talk to you now."

"Okay Joe I wonder if you see Molly's sexy sister yet. I hope you put in good word for me."

"Look Tino, I don't have time for this," Joe cried, wondering whether to explain the gravity of the situation to Tino. "We can't find Molly and we need to keep the lines free in case she calls, so I'm going to cut you off, okay?"

"Molly she is missing, she has left you?"

"No Tino, I'll explain to you tomorrow." Joe pushed the end call button and put his phone of the arm of the chair. He leaned forward, with his elbows on his knees and dropped his head into his hands.

Noticing that Joe was struggling to keep his emotions in check, Sophie moved across to sit on the arm of his chair, and put an arm around his shoulder.

"I'm sorry to be so negative. You'll find her, I know you will. Just stick to the route and keep calm, and when you do find them be careful and let me know where you are as soon as you can."

Joe stood up, still looking at his list. "I will, I'm not sure how but as soon as I can I'll let you know." He shifted his eyes to the floor, having no intention of letting Sophie know where they were until he'd got Molly out of there safely.

Suddenly his mobile burst back into life – it was Tino again. Joe hit the end call again without even picking up the phone. Within seconds it shrilled out again, and again Joe dropped the call. By the time Joe had reached the hall he had repeated the same process three more times, on the fourth time he decided to answer.

"What?" he shouted, causing Sophie to recoil.

"Do not end me again, I can help find Molly," Tino shouted, equally as loud.

"Please Tino, I don't have time for this, I need to keep the line clear."

"Molly she find me when I have my wheels stolen. She use her phone to find my phone, Jimmy please you tell Joe, I cannot explain." There was murmuring and the noise of a chair being moved in the background.

Then Jimmy Cavanagh's voice came on the line.

"Joe, it's me. Tino said Molly is missing, is that right?"

Joe sighed. "Jim, please just explain to him that I need to keep the line clear in case she tries to call me."

"Yeah, I know that mate, but listen believe it or not he's got a good idea. You know how shit we are with our phones, always losing them, well Molly has this app thing on her iPad that can trace another iPhone or iPad from the same address, well we're all on the club's account, and so is Molly, so if you download the app' onto your phone you might be able to find her."

Joe couldn't take in what Jimmy was saying at first, it was so simple, why had it taken Tino to think of it?

"Joe, are you still there?"

"Yes, sorry Jim. He's a bloody genius."

"Hmm not sure about that, but at least we know he's got a brain in there," Jimmy replied.

"Whatever, just give him a kiss from me."

"Hey steady on, I'll tell him you owe him a beer instead."

Joe managed a smile. "Okay, thanks Jim. Don't let anyone know about this, just keep it between you and Tino for now."

"Sure, no problem. I just hope she's okay whatever has happened."

Joe ended the call and quickly started pushing buttons on his phone, looking for the App that Tino was talking about.

"What's going on?" Sophie followed Joe as he stormed back into the lounge.

"Well if Tino is right we may be able to find Molly's phone, and if we find her phone, then hopefully we'll find Molly" he whispered as he looked up at Sophie.

After a few minutes, a smile of satisfaction spread across his face, then as his mobile phone screen changed a look of desolation spread across his features. "Shit, shit, shit?"

"What, where are they?" Sophie poked her head over Joe's arm to look at his phone screen.

"He's taken her to Cheshire, to my restaurant." A cold shiver ran through Joe as he realised that Rob must have been following him, or both of them, to know about the restaurant – he hadn't even told his teammates about it.

"Let me ring Polly, my CID friend, please Joe." Sophie was only half a step away when Joe pulled at her arm.

"No" he hissed. "If we tell them they'll send police cars in there with lights flashing and sirens squealing and it might scare him into doing something stupid, I'm going on my own, just like he asked."

Sophie shook her head and tried to pull away from him grasp.

"The more I think about that, the more dangerous I think it will be. It's obviously some sort of trap."

"Well I can handle him, apart from anything I'm a professional sportsman and he's got cancer, so at the risk of sounding crass, I reckon I can have him."

"Who the hell do you think you are, Jack Reacher?" She poked Joe in his shoulder. "What happened last time you didn't tell the police, oh yes my sister got kidnapped by her jilted husband, so no, not a good plan Joe."

"Look, I hear what you're saying, but I'm doing this. I can't risk him doing anything to hurt Molly." Joe glanced in the direction of the hall, desperate to be on his way, but aware that Sophie still hadn't agreed not to call the police.

"This isn't some sort of T.V. drama, this is real you idiot. You have no idea what's waiting for you, you need to let the professionals deal with this, and I will not lose my sister because you think you'll look good with your underpants over the top of your jeans."

Joe grabbed hold of Sophie's hand. "Please Sophie, he doesn't want to hurt Molly, I'm the one he had beaten up, it's my restaurant he's taken her to."

"Well when I spoke to her this morning, she told me that he slapped her the other night, so who says he doesn't want to hurt her?"

Joe's eyes narrowed and his jaw clenched as a pulse throbbed in his cheek.

"Why didn't she tell me, I'll fucking kill him when I get there" he hissed between thin lips.

"For precisely that reason probably, so you going there might just tip him over the edge, please Joe, I'm begging you let the police deal with it."

Joe lowered his eyes and thought for a few seconds, and then shook his head.

"No, she's my life Soph and if anything happens to her because I didn't do as he asked, then I'll never forgive myself. I have to make her safe. I can't function without her."

Sophie sighed and nodded, her bottom lip trembling.

"Okay, I'll make a deal with you. I'll give you exactly an hour from when you leave here, and then I'm calling the police."

"Two hours, that gives me an hour and a half at least to talk him around."

Sophie eyed him warily. "Okay, but if anything happens to you or my sister I will fucking kill you."

Joe nodded and rushed out of the house, hoping that Sophie stuck to her word.

Printed in Great Britain
by Amazon